White Jade

By

Alex Lukeman

© Copyright 2011 by Alex Lukeman

http://www.alexlukeman.com

The Project Series

White Jade
The Lance
The Seventh Pillar
Black Harvest
The Tesla Secret
The Nostradamus File
The Ajax Protocol
The Eye of Shiva
Black Rose
The Solomon Scroll
The Russian Deception
The Atlantis Stone

Chapter One

The dream splintered into shards of red and black, a kaleidoscope gone wrong. William Connor sat up gasping for air and waited for his heart to stop pounding. The green numerals on the clock by his bedside read two-thirty in the morning.

Something wasn't right.

Had he set the alarms?

After a moment he got out of bed and shrugged on a robe. He moved to the stairs of his San Francisco home. Below, a pool of yellow light from a single desk lamp spilled across the polished wooden floor. The rest of the room was in darkness.

His old body protested as he descended the stairs. He started toward the alarm box. A large man stepped from the shadows and blocked his way. Connor's heart skipped a beat and settled to erratic thumping.

"You! What are you doing here?"

Strong arms grabbed Connor from behind and wrestled him to the chair by his desk. Someone wrapped tape around him. The robe fell open, exposing his pale genitals. He was helpless.

"Is it money? I have money. Tell me what you want."

The large man loomed over Connor. He smelled unpleasant, a greasy smell of testosterone and stale sweat.

"Yes, money. And I want the book."

"What book?"

The large man slapped Connor across the face, a casual blow.

"The book. The one from Bhutan."

Connor tasted blood. "It's not here!"

"Then you will tell me where it is. First, the money. I want the account numbers and access codes."

William Connor was a rich man. Access to those accounts gave control over hundreds of millions of dollars.

"Who are you?"

"I am your worst nightmare. Tell me what I want or I will hurt you."

Almost as an afterthought, the man picked up and examined a delicate, antique porcelain vase covered with an exquisite design of flowers and birds. The soft glaze glowed in the dim light. He smiled.

There were only two things William Connor truly loved. One was his niece, Selena. The other was the joy of things old and beautiful.

"Please be careful with that," he said. "It's very old."

The man looked at the fragile vase and smiled again. He held it in front of Connor in his huge hand and squeezed. It shattered into dust. Connor felt his chest tighten.

"If I ask a question and you do not answer, I will hurt you. Do you understand?"

"Yes."

"The numbers."

"I don't have them here. All that is in my office."

The man sighed. He went into the kitchen. Connor could hear him rummaging through the kitchen drawers. He came back with a small red-handled pair of pruning shears Connor used on the rose bushes in the garden.

He grabbed the old man's left hand and pinched the blades together and cut off the little finger.

Connor screamed.

The man dug the point of the shears into the bone below Connor's eye. Connor screamed again from the pain. Blood ran down his cheek.

"The fog is thick, outside. The house is solid. No one will hear you scream. Your right eye is next."

The old man's bladder emptied, soaking his robe and the chair. Someone laughed, behind him.

"I'll tell you! I'll tell you! Don't hurt me again!" He began babbling the numbers, blurting them out. Sudden pain started and spread to Connor's left arm, sharp and immediate, a burning, blossoming bolt of fire. He stopped speaking and tried to catch his breath.

"Where is the book?" The man was shouting.

Pain exploded in Connor's chest. As vision faded, his last sight was the terrifying, angry face of his executioner.

Chapter Two

Nicholas Carter wasn't thinking about the grenade. He was thinking about the temperature gauge on his rental Ford, pegged in the red. He pulled into the parking lot at the Project and stepped out into the heat. Steam boiled under the hood. A green pool spread out under the car. His head felt like it was wrapped in iron. He wished he was back at his cabin in California, not standing in Virginia with his shoes sticking to the asphalt.

Carter scanned the surrounding area. He noted the parked cars, all empty. He crossed the lot to the building housing the Project, like hundreds of others in the Metro area. The only difference to a casual observer was the array of antennas bristling on the roof.

Carter went through security and walked past the elevator to the stairs. He climbed past the second floor housing the computers and backup generators and communications. He passed the third floor where the analysts lived. He exited the stairs on the fourth floor, the top floor, where Director Harker's office was. He placed his hand on the biometric scanner outside the door of her office and went in.

Elizabeth Harker looked up from behind her desk. She was small, with milk-white skin, small, pointed ears and raven black hair. Her eyes were like a cat's, wide and green. She looked like an elf dressed in black and white, but a kind of elf you wouldn't want to mess with.

On her desk was a file with his name on it, a silver pen that had belonged to FDR and a picture of the Twin Towers burning on 9/11. She kept the picture to remind herself of why she was there.

"Have a seat." Harker opened the file.

He sat and waited.

"The shrink says you're fit to go back in the field. Are you?"

"I'm fine."

"No more flashbacks?"

"No."

Not for three months. He'd thrown out the pills the doctor had given him. They'd flattened everything into a narrow monotone that made him feel like he was living in a fading black and white picture. He didn't think Harker needed to know about the dreams.

Harker nodded. She made a note in the file and placed it in a drawer.

A large, flat monitor was mounted on one wall of the office. Harker did something at her desk and the display came to life with a picture of an elderly man. His eyes were blue. He looked like the sort of man you'd like for a Grandfather.

She said, "This is William Connor. He was a very rich man. He was also a personal friend of the President."

"Was?"

"Someone tortured him until he died of a heart attack. They cut off one of his fingers with pruning shears. Then they transferred money from his accounts and tore his home apart."

An electric tension settled across his shoulders. Cutting off the finger of an old man made things personal, something he could grab on to. It was better when it was personal. He needed personal. It helped motivate him. Going forth for God and Country didn't work too well for him anymore, not since Afghanistan. Not since South America.

"That's cold. How much money?"

"Around four hundred million."

"Why are we getting involved with this? This looks like FBI or Treasury territory."

"We intercepted an encrypted satellite transmission last week from the Chinese consulate in San Francisco. There's a Colonel from Chinese Military Intelligence in the consulate named Wu. He pretends he's a trade official. He called his boss, General Yang. Yang is chief of their MI. Wu told him about an old book Connor found in Bhutan and Yang ordered him to get the book and Connor's money. The money went to accounts in Macau controlled by Yang."

"Chinese MI? Why would they do something as stupid as that? It doesn't make sense. What's in the book?"

"We don't know. Connor had a niece who might know. I want to ask her about it. Doctor Connor is coming here today."

"Doctor?"

"PhDs in oriental and ancient languages. She's one of the top experts in the country."

Carter pictured an expert PhD niece. Someone academic looking. Maybe in an earth tone baggy suit, with large glasses and gray hair, around fifty.

Harker said, "The FBI had Wu under routine surveillance. I requested a photo and they sent one over but my gut says they're holding something back."

Nick didn't respond.

"Zeke Jordan is the liaison. You know him. Talk with him and see what you can find out."

A voice came from the intercom on Harker's desk.

"Director, Doctor Connor is here."

"Escort her up."

While they waited, Carter thought about his car and decided to call Triple A and ride back with the tow.

Chapter Three

Selena Connor didn't look like a fiftyish, gray-haired professor. It wasn't the way she looked that got Carter's attention, though that would have been enough. It was the way she came into the room, all contained, taut energy, with the rippling grace of an athlete. She was in her thirties. Her hair was short and reddish blond. Her face was tan from the outdoors. She had high cheekbones and violet eyes. There was a small mole above her lip.

She wasn't wearing a baggy suit or big glasses. She had on a smooth silk jacket and slacks and a pale blouse that picked up the violet color. In her left hand she carried a black leather computer case.

Carter stood and Harker introduced him. They all sat down.

Harker said, "What have you got there?"

"My uncle's laptop. He'd never left it with me before. I haven't looked at it, but I thought you might want to." Her voice was controlled. There were lines of tension in her face.

Got the lid on, Nick thought.

"Doctor Connor," Elizabeth said.

"Please call me Selena."

"Selena. The people who killed your uncle were after a book he acquired in Bhutan. We need to know what's in it."

Selena gave Harker an odd look. How did she know about the book?

"It's gone. I don't know where it is. I haven't read all of it, but it's a copy of an ancient text about immortality, mostly written in Sanskrit. Books like that are rare, but this one is unique. What's in it is impossible."

"Impossible?" Harker tapped her pen against her lip.

"Part of it is written in Linear A. If I hadn't seen it with my own eyes I'd never believe it. Linear A is one of two written languages from the Minoan Empire, before 1600 BCE. There are no books written in Linear A. There shouldn't be anything Minoan in the Himalayan region at all."

"You're sure the book is gone?"

"My uncle kept it on his desk, but it's not there now. He was going to scan it onto his computer."

"So it might be on that laptop you brought."

"It could be."

Harker began tapping on her desk. "The money from your uncle's accounts went to China."

"China? Part of the book is about the first Chinese emperor, Qin Huang."

"Emperor Huang?" Carter said. "The one with the soldiers and horses?"

"Yes. Huang placed an army of terracotta soldiers and horses outside his tomb. Chinese farmers found it in '74. It's a big tourist attraction."

Selena brushed a wisp of hair away from her forehead.

"The book described Huang's search for immortality. He was obsessed with it. It also repeated old stories of treasure in his tomb. Everyone knows where it is but it's never been excavated."

Harker told Selena about the intercept.

"Then you know who did this! Can't you arrest him, this…Colonel, or whatever he is?"

"We don't have hard evidence. Besides, he has diplomatic immunity."

Nick's ear began itching. Since he was a kid it had itched when things were about to get complicated, a personal early warning system. Then again, sometimes it was just an itch. He scratched it.

Harker set down her pen. "Maybe there's something on that laptop. Let's take a look."

Selena handed her the case. Harker took the computer out and plugged it into a port on her desk. The display booted up on the wall monitor. The screen filled with folder icons.

"Lots of files." She clicked on one labeled Beijing. The file was a list of bank account numbers in the Chinese capitol.

"That might help track the money. I don't see anything about a book."

Selena said, "It looks like financial files labeled by location, like the Bahamas or Caymans, or by industry and city. There's one labeled Li Shan. That's where the emperor is buried. Open that one."

The file was a draft proposal to excavate the tomb of the First Emperor, complete with time lines and cost breakdowns. There was nothing about the book in the file.

"There's a file with my name," Selena said.

"Let's see it."

It was a letter from William Connor to his niece, dated a week before his death.

My Dearest Selena,

You know how I hate clichés. Please forgive me for the one I use now. Quite simply, if you are reading this letter then something has happened to me. I do not contemplate this with equanimity, my dear, but life sometimes forces unpleasant possibilities upon us. I am leaving this note and my computer with you in hopes you never read it.

I think I am being watched by agents of the Chinese government and that it has something to do with the book I acquired in Bhutan. My translation is incomplete, but it seems there are historical inaccuracies regarding the death and burial of the First Emperor, and that these relate to a supposed elixir of eternal life.

I have prepared a proposal regarding possible excavation of the First Emperor's tomb at Li Shan. A week ago I met with a Chinese consular official named Wu Chen to discuss obtaining permission to fund and participate in such an important project. Wu offered to put me in touch with the correct people in Beijing.

In the course of our meeting I talked about the book. Not long after that I noticed a large and rather menacing Chinese man observing me at a restaurant I frequent. Then I noticed that same man in other places, at other times. It may have nothing to do with Wu, but it seems too coincidental to me.

I feel threatened. So I write this letter to you, although it may be just the foolish act of an old man.

I have placed the book in a safe place. If it does hold a clue to the secret of immortality or a key to the emperor's treasures, it is a dangerous thing to have in one's possession.

Do you remember, when we used to have our summer time together at the old mine, when you were a child, the special place you found to secret away your most precious things? That is where you will find the book.

My dear Selena, if you are indeed reading this, please know that you have always been a source of joy and delight for this old uncle of yours.

With all my love, Uncle William

They read the letter again. Selena sat rigidly in her chair. Carter watched her. It was an old habit, watching. It told him things. Right now it told him Selena was wound up tight. Close to her uncle, he thought, but she wasn't going to let anyone see it. How she really felt.

He knew what that was like.

Harker said, "Do you know what he was talking about? The place he hid the book?"

Selena's voice was controlled, neutral. "My family found gold in California in 1850. There's a house at the old mine property. In the front yard there's an ore cart full of rocks from the mine. When I was a child I hid things under the rocks. That must be where he put it. I'm surprised he didn't put it in one of his safe deposit boxes."

"No safe deposit box keys have turned up." Harker twirled her pen.

"He had at least three."

"The FBI searched his office and home. We'll check with them."

"If they have the keys, they know what's in the boxes." Nick looked at Harker. "I'll ask Jordan when I talk with him."

"Do that. Then I want you to go to California with Doctor Connor and retrieve that book. Does that work for you, Selena?"

"Anything that helps."

"Why do you want me along?" Carter said.

"They didn't get the book. If they think Selena has it they might go after her. I want you to keep an eye out." She looked at her watch and turned to Selena. "It's too late to get a flight today. We'll book one for tomorrow. What airport, Selena?"

"Sacramento. The mine is only an hour away."

"We'll arrange a car."

Carter said, "We can use mine. It's already there." He'd flown out of Sacramento. His truck was in the long term lot at the airport.

"Good. Hook up with Jordan before you go. Call me after you find the book. We'll search the rest of these files and follow up."

"What do I tell Jordan?"

Harker tapped her pen on the desk. "Tell him about the financial accounts. We'll keep the book to ourselves for now. There's no need for the Bureau to know about it."

Chapter Four

Earlier that same day, Colonel Wu Chen was sitting in a secluded red leather booth at the Happy Family restaurant in San Francisco.

Muted sounds drifted up from the street below. The only other customer was an old man across the room reading his newspaper. The smell of rice, pork and noodles mingled with the murmured conversation of waiters huddled in a corner. Wu sipped his tea. He took a bright red carnation from the vase on the table and twirled it in his hands. He thought about his conversation with the General.

"Tell me about this book."

Yang's wet voice had echoed through the satellite link.

"The American obtained it in Bhutan. The book concerns the First Emperor. It is a medical text with a formula for a draught of immortality. That is why I contacted you."

The General was always interested in anything to do with the First Emperor and his quest for immortality. Wu needed to keep General Yang happy.

"What is the name of this book?"

"The American said it translates as 'The Golden Garuda'."

Wu heard a sharp intake of breath. When Yang spoke again, his voice was controlled. Wu sensed his excitement.

"I have an assignment for you."

"Sir."

"I require the book. Obtain it and deliver it to me." There was a pause. Wu waited. "The American is rich?"

"Yes, sir. He has great wealth."

"Access his financial accounts. Transfer the funds to the account numbers I send after this conversation."

"Yes, sir. Are there any restrictions?"

"Use any means necessary. Make sure there are no complications after."

"Yes, sir."

"Inform me when you have succeeded."

Wu toyed with the flower and sipped his tea. The book hadn't been in Connor's home. The niece must know where it was. His agents would bring her to him for questioning.

Wu thought about interrogating her. He felt the beginning of an erection. He would strip her naked and bind her. That always unnerved prisoners, especially the women. Choy could question her, but sometimes his sergeant got carried away and damaged the subject beyond repair before Wu learned what he needed. No, he'd do it himself.

The water technique was effective, but time consuming if the subject was stubborn. Wu preferred the blowtorch and pliers. Or knives, the kind you'd find in any kitchen. Simple tools were always best.

He reached for his tea and glanced down. The shredded petals of the flower made a delicate pattern against the scarred table top. He brushed them aside with his hand. They fell to the floor in a shower of red, like drops of blood.

Tinkling green jade prosperity symbols over the restaurant doorway announced the arrival of his Sergeant.

Choy Gang's skin was the color of the Mongolian desert on a winter evening, betraying his mixed heritage. He was tall and weighed over two hundred and fifty pounds. His head was large and sat like a cantaloupe with crumpled ears on his massive shoulders. His hands were broad clubs, the knuckles scarred and bulbous.

Choy's fleshy face was marred with acne scars. His eyes were small and close set, almond-shaped, an odd golden color. A shiny blue shirt stretched taut across his massive chest and arms under a loose fitting brown jacket.

In the People's Liberation Army, Choy had found a home. In Colonel Wu, he had found a Master.

Choy cast a contemptuous glance at the elderly customer across the room. He squeezed into the booth. One of the waiters poured more tea. Wu ordered food in a rapid burst of Mandarin.

When the waiter was gone Wu said, "You had no trouble obtaining the information for Connor's accounts?"

"No, sir. He resisted at first, but it didn't take much to convince him to give me the numbers." Choy thought about how the old man had screamed when his finger had been snipped off. He smiled, showing the gaps between his yellowed teeth.

"You are sure the book was not in Connor's home?"

"Yes, sir. I am positive it was not there. His heart gave out too soon, before he revealed its location."

"That was unfortunate. But you did well. Now I have another task for you."

Wu watched Choy perk up. He's like a good dog, Wu thought. Give him something new and interesting to do and he's happy.

"The American owned a house three or four hours from here. Take some men tomorrow and search for the book. Use a vehicle from the black pool."

The black pool was a small fleet of cars untraceable to the Chinese Consulate.

Wu took an envelope from his jacket and slid it across the table to Choy. "Money and a driver's license. The directions to the place are also there."

Choy put the envelope in his jacket pocket as the waiter returned with steaming plates of food.

"Sergeant," Wu said, "enjoy this delicious dim sum. It's as good as we get at home."

Across the room, the elderly Chinese man took a last sip of his cold tea. He folded his newspaper and rose. He shuffled by the cash register to pay and carefully made his way down the steep stairs. His superiors would be pleased when they learned of the meeting he had just overheard.

Chapter Five

Nicholas Carter and Selena Connor stood in the heat of the parking lot. All the parked cars were still empty. Carter put his phone away. Two and a half hours before Triple A could get him out of here.

"Can you give me a ride into town? My rental's no good." He gestured at the mess under his car.

"Of course. I'm parked just over there."

A new Mercedes CL600 gleamed in the late afternoon light. Twelve cylinders and over five hundred horsepower. A fast, luxury car. A driver's car. A money car. Not many women drove cars with that kind of power. It said something about her. Nick got his bag from the rental and climbed in.

"Nice car."

"I just got it a few weeks ago."

She started up, drove out of the lot.

"Where are you staying?" he asked.

"The Mayflower Renaissance. I stay there when I'm in Washington and leave the car there when I'm out of town."

"That's not far from my place. Where do you live when you're not in D.C.?"

"San Francisco. I've got a loft in North Beach."

They pulled onto the Interstate. The interior was quiet except for the whisper of the air conditioner. Carter relaxed into the leather.

They were doing a little over seventy. Selena glanced in the rear view mirror and switched lanes. A BMW 740 with blacked out windows passed her and cut sharply in front.

"Jerk," she muttered under her breath. In the side mirror Nick saw a black Suburban pull in behind, riding their tail. His ear began itching.

They entered a construction zone. The right lane of the highway was bordered by heavy cement barriers laid end to end. Orange signs warned of doubled fines and men at work.

The Suburban rammed into them and drove the Mercedes into the cement. The car rebounded from the barrier in a shower of sparks and fishtailed back onto the roadway. In front, the BMW blocked them. Selena fought for control. The Suburban came alongside on the left and broadsided her back into the barrier.

The front right fender and hood buckled. Something flew over the roof. Sparks streamed by Nick's window. The Mercedes slid along the cement in a din of screeching steel.

Drivers swerved around them, horns blaring.

Carter pulled out his .45. Selena's eyes narrowed.

"Hang on," she said.

She hit the brakes and the big discs on the Mercedes grabbed the wheels. Carter wasn't ready. The seat belt stopped his head inches from the dash. The Suburban surged past on the left, scraping strips from the car, taking the mirror with it. Selena shifted down. She floored the accelerator and the five hundred horses came to life. She cut across panicked traffic into the outer lane.

They shot past the SUV and the BMW. The car filled with the smooth growl of the engine and the sound of pavement under the tires.

The speedometer climbed past ninety. Selena wove in and out of the traffic and clipped a red Honda. It skewed across the highway and flipped over onto the grass median. In the side mirror, Carter saw a gray sedan slam into an old pickup filled with furniture. Chests and chairs spilled across the roadway.

A quarter mile ahead a blinking yellow arrow on the back of a truck and a string of orange and white barrels funneled three lanes into two. They were about to run out of room. The cement streamed by on the right, a blurring, silent ripple of gray outside his window.

Shit, he thought. He calmed himself, lowered his heart rate, getting ready for whatever was coming. The gun rested on his thigh. He was out of control, but the car was so comfortable. Carter glanced at Selena. She gripped the wheel, her face set, absorbed in the traffic and the road. The speedometer hung at a hundred.

A long, wide gap in the cement barrier opened along the right onto an excavated parking area with neat rows of equipment and stacks of supplies. Selena slowed, shifted down, stood on the emergency brake and wrenched the wheel over. The rear end slid smoking to the left in a howl of burning rubber. In one fluid motion she released the brake and whipped the wheel back to center. The Mercedes shot through the gap and went airborne over the edge of the road and down hard onto gravel.

The front tires blew out. The car corkscrewed and slewed sideways and sprayed gravel and dirt in a wide arc. They fishtailed across the lot. The car slammed to a jarring halt against a pile of rebar and steel. Steam erupted under the buckled hood.

The BMW and Suburban caught up and stopped on the highway. Two men jumped from the car, guns in their hands. Two more piled out of the Suburban.

Carter pushed Selena down into her seat and fired twice at the windshield. The shots deafened him inside the car. The glass spider-webbed. He fired again. A large piece of the windshield blew out. He fired at the first man out of the BMW and missed. He fired again and the man spun backwards, arms splayed wide.

Carter shot the second man in the chest, then turned toward the others. He ducked. The two from the Suburban opened up with their pistols. The car windows disappeared in a shower of flying glass. Bullets thumped into the sides of the car.

Something clipped his ear. Selena was bent low behind the wheel with her hands covering her ears. He let off three more rounds over her head. A third man doubled over and fell face down on the pavement. The fourth ran back behind the Suburban. Carter made out a driver hunched down behind the wheel and shot him.

The BMW drove away, fast. The last man pulled the body of the driver from behind the wheel of the SUV. He climbed in and took off on smoking tires. Carter fired after him until the slide locked back on his pistol.

For one or two seconds the Suburban kept going straight. Then it heeled right in a tilting, impossible turn and flipped over onto the driver's side. It slid along the pavement showering sparks and shedding pieces of metal, glass and chrome until it came to rest. With a loud thump, it burst into flame.

The BMW was gone, out of sight.

"Are you all right?" His words sounded flat and far away. His ears rang from the pistol shots.

"What? Yes, I'm okay, I think." She sat up, brushed glass from her hair, and looked at him. "You're bleeding."

The Suburban burned with fierce, red beauty. A black column of smoke rose into a sky scattered with clouds turning pink and gold from the lowering sun. He felt blood dripping on the side of his neck.

He wanted to look in the rearview mirror but it was gone.

On the highway, people were getting out of their cars. Holding the .45 high, Carter ejected the empty magazine and inserted a fresh one. He racked the slide.

His door was blocked shut.

"Can you open your door?"

She pushed hard. It groaned open with a sound of bent metal. Selena got out. He slid across the seat and stood beside her.

"Stay here." Smoke from the flaming Suburban swirled around him. It smelled of burning rubber and roasting flesh. Nick felt his mind try to pull him back to Afghanistan. He pushed the memory away.

He walked toward the motionless figures on the ground, toe to heel, bent low, holding the .45 straight out in front with both hands. He nudged the first body with his foot. A pistol lay on the ground, a Beretta by the looks of it. He kicked it away.

The thick steel and leather of the Mercedes and bad shooting had kept the nine millimeter rounds from penetrating far into the body of the car. Something with more punch, he thought, he'd be dead. Selena would be dead.

Sightless Asian eyes stared up at him. Carter checked the others, one by one. His .45 hollow points had done a lot of damage. None of them were breathing. They all looked Asian. He figured the driver cooking in the SUV would turn out to be the same.

He put the pistol in his shoulder holster and went back to where Selena stood by the car.

"What did they want?" She was pale under her tan.

"You. I don't think they expected trouble."

She clasped her arms around herself. He wondered if she was about to faint. Then her face got tight and angry.

"Goddamn it, this is America, not fucking Afghanistan! This isn't supposed to happen here. That was a new car. Look at it!"

She surprised him, the language. He hadn't figured her for someone who would swear like that. He looked at the car.

Her hundred and fifty thousand dollar Mercedes was totaled. The front end was buckled and listing to the right. The tires were spider webs of shredded metal and rubber. There was a long dented scrape along the driver's side. All the windows were gone. The ground around the car was littered with tiny fragments of broken glass. The beautiful paint job was pocked with bullet holes. Antifreeze and oil made a widening pool on the dirt.

"Maybe the insurance will cover it," he said. "I'm going to make a call."

She looked at him like he was crazy. She shook her head.

A news helicopter circled overhead, getting pictures to feed the greed for violence on the evening news. Sirens wailed in the distance. Carter took out his phone and called the Director. She'd get them out of the clutches of the law a lot faster than explanations would.

At least his headache was gone.

Chapter Six

Word came down. Two hours later the cops let them go. The Director sent a car. They rode in silence over to the Mayflower.

"I need a drink," she said. "Let's get one here at the hotel."

Carter's jacket and shirt were streaked with blood. His ear was bandaged where a round had taken off most of the lobe. He gestured at the ruined jacket.

"You think they'll let me in? Might scare the customers."

"They'll let you in. You're with me." She was wired.

They went inside. People turned to look and then quickly away again. They strode through the lobby and into the bar and took a table in back.

The waiter came over. He seemed not to see Nick's bloody appearance.

"Good evening, Art."

"Good evening, Doctor Connor."

"I'll have a Long Island iced tea, with the premium."

"And you, sir?"

"A double Jameson's, straight up, soda back."

He wrote it down and left. They waited for the drinks. The waiter returned.

Selena downed a third of her drink and set her glass on the table.

Carter said, "I was going to offer you dinner somewhere. Maybe another time."

"People just tried to kill us and you're thinking about dinner?"

He shrugged. "Still have to eat. You all right?"

She took another hit from her glass. "Better."

"Want another?"

"Yes."

Carter signaled the waiter.

When he came over she said, "Art, can you bring us some calamari and a cheese plate, maybe some bread and oil on the side, with some of those little sausages? And another round?"

Nick reached for his wallet. "I'll get it."

She touched his hand. "Please. Let me. If you hadn't been with me I wouldn't be sitting here right now."

True. He put his wallet away.

"Where did you learn to drive like that?" he said.

"I took a course in case I ever needed it. My uncle was wealthy, it made me a potential target. I thought I might have to get away fast some day."

"You were right. Why didn't the airbags deploy?"

"I turned them off. There's a switch on the dash." She emptied her glass. "I never thought anyone would shoot at me."

"They missed, that's what counts. Harker's putting a guard outside your room tonight."

Selena fiddled with her straw. "You always carry that gun?"

"Yes. You shoot?"

"I've got a Ladysmith, but I don't carry it. I never felt I needed to, but I will now. I'm a good shot."

She took the straw from her glass, looked down at it and twisted it in her hands.

"I can't get over how fast it was. I don't know what to think. People died out there."

"Better them than you."

"Maybe they just wanted money. I could have given them that."

"I don't think so. I think someone wants that book. It would have been bad if they'd grabbed you."

"You think they know about the house? Where we're going?"

"Probably not. They don't know the book is in California and they think you're here in D.C. It should be okay."

Carter wasn't sure it would be okay, but there wasn't anything to do about it. Keep his eyes open.

Art brought the food and another round.

"How did you get involved with Harker?" she asked.

"She recruited me when I came back from Afghanistan. A friend introduced us."

"What was it like, over there?"

The memories started. He didn't want them. "It was insane." He picked up his glass and changed the subject. "Harker said you're a language expert?"

"Dialects and ancient languages. I give lectures and I consult with NSA. I come to Washington a lot." She sipped her drink. "Your Director seems pretty sharp."

"Not much gets by her."

"What branch of the service were you in?"

"Marine Recon, thirteen years."

There was an awkward pause. Carter picked up a piece of bread. She said, "You have any family around here?"

"No. My mother's in California. She's got Alzheimer's. My sister is two years older than me. We don't see eye to eye on things. My father's dead."

Something about Selena made it easy to talk.

"My father was a drunk. He used to beat the hell out of my mother and me. He was one of the reasons I went into the Marines, to do something about people like him. People who use fear to get what they want. I figured the Corps would give me a shot at making a difference. It didn't work out like I thought."

Nick looked at the gleaming bottles behind the bar, thinking about his father.

"How about you?" he said.

Something flickered across her face, a moment's darkness. "My parents and brother died when I was ten. Uncle William brought me up. There's no one else now."

She set a half eaten snack down on her plate. "How are we going to stop these people who came after us?"

"With Harker on it we'll get them. It might take some time."

"I want to help."

"We need to know what's in the book and why they want it. Maybe you could translate it."

"The Sanskrit's no problem. Everyone guesses at Linear A."

Nick looked at his watch. "I have to make a call. Thanks for the drinks."

"My pleasure."

"Here comes your bodyguard." He gestured at a tall man coming into the bar. "Harker will send a car in the morning. You want me to walk you to your room?"

"No, I'll be fine."

He got a cab outside the hotel and thought about her standing on a highway littered with spent shells and bodies. Standing in an instant war zone. She could have gotten hysterical. Instead, she'd been pissed about her car.

He liked her for that.

Chapter Seven

General Yang Siyu peered out at the barren wasteland of China's Lop Nur nuclear testing range. The desert rippled under the furnace glare of the Mongolian sun. Yang stood with his feet planted apart, hands clasped behind his back. The hardened concrete building smelled of stale stress and the dry odor of electricity. Racks of instruments lined the long room. Rows of fluorescent lights reflected from banks of electronic equipment, cold counterpoint to the searing sunlight outside.

A thin, dry, angry looking man stood next to Yang's squat form. The creases on his immaculate uniform were as sharp as the harsh contours of his face. Lieutenant General Lu Cheng commanded the missile base at Luoyang, where China's long range ICBMs were targeted on the West. Lu looked at the clock on the wall.

"Two minutes. This warhead will increase our strike range and destructive yield at the same time. We must have these."

"If the test goes well." Yang's voice was wet, throaty.

"Deng has assured me it will go well."

Deng Bingwen was chief research scientist in China's nuclear weapons program. A graduate of America's MIT, he was considered a treasure among the scientific elite of the People's Republic, if always suspect because of his American education.

The treasure himself came over to the two generals. Deng was a mouse of a man, small, his sparse hair slicked back from his domed forehead. Large glasses with thick plastic frames set crookedly over his nose. He wore a white laboratory coat two sizes too large on his stooped frame, making him seem even smaller. He nodded his head nervously at Yang, almost a bow, smiling to hide his feelings of unease.

He looks like one of those little dogs, Yang thought, a Pekinese under a white tent.

"Thirty seconds, General. I think you will be pleased with the result."

The men watched as the countdown reached zero. In the distance three columns of white smoke rose skyward, marking the underground shaft where the warhead would detonate. A deep rumble under the ground vibrated through the thick concrete beneath their feet. The earth erupted in a black, towering geyser rising hundreds of feet into the air. The blast expanded outward in a wide ring, a boiling cloud of churning sand and dust racing across the desert floor.

Lu Cheng smiled.

Deng glanced at the instruments recording every detail of the blast.

"Even better than we hoped. Eight point two megatons. Over fifty percent increase in output."

Deng looked again at the readings.

"A bit dirty. We'll hear from the IAEA about this."

"Let them wag their fingers and cluck like chickens," Lu said. "There's nothing they can do about it. How soon can we go into production?"

"There is the question of resources," Deng said. "If we had a high grade source of ore and more centrifuges we could produce fifty of these warheads a year, even a hundred. As it is, perhaps eight or ten."

China's entire strategic arsenal consisted of only three hundred missiles of varying capabilities, and none carried a payload bigger than five megatons. Lu's smile widened at the thought of a hundred powerful new missiles each year.

Yang spoke. "Begin production immediately. You will formulate two plans, one based on our current resources and one based on having what is needed for high production. The hundred or so you mentioned."

"But we have no resources for so many," Deng protested.

"That is not your concern. Prepare the plan anyway. Or you may find yourself working on a different kind of project. Understood?"

Yang's eyes were hooded and bulging under the red star on his green, high-peaked military hat. Deng looked at Yang's, coarse, toad-like face. The General was not a man to be denied.

This new nuclear demon was smaller, lighter, more destructive. The expression on the faces of Yang and Lu said they wanted more of these things, many more. There was only one reason for that. Only aggression required high numbers of missiles.

Deng thought about his days of freedom as a student in America, before this insanity of nuclear weapons had trapped him. In China careers were dictated for men like him. Deng had rationalized his feelings about building weapons meant to kill millions by telling himself that China's nuclear forces were defensive in nature.

Looking at Yang and Lu, he had a chilling intimation of the future. Deng's face gave nothing away of his thoughts, but he suspected more about Yang's plans than the General imagined. Deng was not without his sources of information. It was necessary for personal survival in a position as sensitive as his.

"UNDERSTOOD?"

Yang shouted in his face, sending flecks of spittle onto Deng's glasses. Deng was shocked. He kowtowed, twice, nervously.

"Yes, of course, General, two plans, as you suggest."

Yang grunted. "Keep me informed." He turned to Lu. "I have to get back to Beijing. Ride with me."

Lu nodded and the generals rudely turned their backs and walked outside without a further glance at Deng. He stared after them and felt a hot flush of shame. Everyone in the room was suddenly absorbed in their instruments and charts. No one was looking at him but they had all witnessed his humiliation. He had lost face.

Yang acts like he thinks he can find resources to up production, Deng thought. Then what? More orders, more bombs, more threats. They have no respect. They have no honor. I might as well be dog shit under their boots.

He marched into his private office and shut the door, his rage building. Enough was enough. He sat down at his computer, furious. He opened his email and sent a brief, innocuous, message to an address he'd never thought he would use.

On the road leading away from the facility, Yang and Lu sat in the back seat of their vehicle. The salt flats of the old lake bed of Lop Nur slipped by in a blur, billows of brown dust trailing far behind the speeding car.

Lu drummed his fingers on the armrest. "We must have more warheads."

"We will," Yang said. "Once I give the order, we will have the centrifuges in six months. All that remains is to locate the ore."

"You are sure the deposit exists?"

"Reasonably sure, yes. The location is being sought as we speak. We'll have it soon. Meanwhile our plans go forward."

"I worry about Chen. We need the railroads."

"Let me worry about Chen. So far, he has done all that we asked. Of course, he may not get what he wants afterwards."

"What does he want?"

"To be President."

Lu laughed. There was no mirth in the sound.

"President! He deludes himself, as usual." Lu paused, sneezed from the dust. "What do you think about Deng?"

"He bears watching, but I already have full surveillance on him. Meanwhile, he continues to produce. For such a small man he builds big bombs, and they are getting better."

"Yes. One day we may see how well they work."

"The West is weak, they have no political will. When we have control, they will be afraid to do anything. Just the threat will be sufficient. Then China will step into her rightful place."

Lu nodded agreement. The two men sat lost in their thoughts as the car barreled along the gravel road, each in his own way contemplating a new China, dominant over the world.

Chapter Eight

The security guard stared as Nick came through the door.

"You okay, Mister Carter?"

"I'm fine, Bob. Just an accident."

Nick walked ten flights up to his floor. He didn't like elevators much, not since Kabul. He went into his apartment and into the bathroom and looked in the mirror. The bullet had taken away the left earlobe. It wouldn't do much for his looks when the bandage came off. A woman had told him once that he had rugged good looks. He got the rugged part, but he wasn't too sure about the rest. He didn't much care.

He poured a whiskey, tossed his jacket on the couch and took off the shoulder rig. He needed to call Jordan. He thought about the FBI and the way the Bureau kept things close. He probably wasn't going to get much help there, but Jordan was a pretty good guy.

"Jordan."

"Zeke, it's Nick Carter."

"Nick. I saw you on the evening news. What happened out there?"

Jordan's voice was deep and vibrant. A big man, stone coal black, he was an anomaly for an agent, unafraid to speak his mind. Nick wondered how he'd lasted as long as he had in the rigid culture of the FBI. He'd made it all the way to the WFO in Washington in spite of everything.

"I was catching a ride with William Connor's niece. Two vehicles full of Chinese goons tried to grab her."

"You must have been a big surprise." There was a pause. "What can I do for you?"

"You're the liaison for the Bureau on Conner's murder. Did you turn up anything we haven't heard about yet?"

"Funny, I was going to ask you the same thing."

"You know it was Wu who set up Connor?"

"Yes."

"We have a computer belonging to Connor. We hoped it would give us leads. All we got were business reports, financial info and a draft proposal for work in China."

"What kind of work in China?"

"An archeological dig. Connor wanted to fund it and get permission to dig in return."

"Can you get that financial info to me?"

"First thing tomorrow. I wanted to ask if you found anything in Connor's office."

"Not much. Just the kind of things you'd expect. Lots of financial records."

"Any keys? Safe deposit keys?"

"We did find some keys."

"And?"

"We got warrants to open the boxes, but there wasn't anything helpful. Some antique jewelry, diamonds, sapphires, gold coins, bearer bonds, that sort of thing. Just your average billionaire's little treasures."

"Do I detect a note of judgmental envy?"

"Nah, everyone should have something set aside for a rainy day."

Nick said, "Zeke. If there's something going on we don't know about it might help if you guys came clean. About Wu."

Silence. Then, "Off the record?"

"Yes."

"When Harker asked about Wu it dovetailed with an ongoing investigation. You know about the Chinese criminal underworld here in the States? The Triads? Also known as the Black Societies?"

"I know the Mafia are newcomers compared to them."

"Yeah. The Triad oaths make the Mafia Code of Silence look like a radio talk show. They're planning something and Wu is mixed up in it.

"Wu met with them at least three times. He's up to his eyeballs in the murder of Connor and you say Chinese thugs tried to grab his niece. Seems like more than a coincidence."

"We didn't know about the Triads." Carter paused. "We might have a lead. I'm going to follow up on it."

"There's always a lead, sooner or later. Can you let me know what you find out?"

"Subject to Harker's wishes, yes. Maybe off the record."

"Okay. Let's stay in touch. Nice talking with you."

"Likewise." Carter broke the connection.

He went over the conversation in his mind. The Bureau had told Harker nothing when she requested their files on Wu. Now he knew there was a connection between the Triads and Colonel Wu, and by extension General Yang.

If the book was at Connor's country place tomorrow, some questions might get answered. He hit the rack and fell asleep.

He had the dream.

They come in low and fast over the ridge, the relentless hard drumbeats of the rotors echoing from the valley walls.

The village is a miserable, dust-blown cluster of low, flat-roofed buildings, baking in a bleak hollow of sharp, brown hills. A wide, dirt street runs down the middle. They drop from the chopper and hit the street running. On the right, low flat roofed houses. On the left, more houses and the market, a patchwork of ramshackle bins and hanging cloth walls. Clouds of flies swarm around things hanging in the open air of the butcher's stall.

He leads his team past the market. Close enough to the buildings to be able to duck into a doorway. Far enough away so a round fired won't burrow down a wall and right into him.

He hears a baby cry. The street is deserted. Where is everyone?

A dozen bearded figures rise up on the rooftops and begin firing AKs. The market stalls disintegrate around him in a firestorm of splinters and plaster and rock exploding from the sides of the buildings.

He dives for cover. A child runs toward him, screaming about Allah. Nick watches and hesitates, a second too long. The boy cocks his arm back and throws a grenade as Nick shoots him. The M4 kicks back, one, two, three.

The first round strikes the boy's chest, the second his throat, the third his face. The child's head balloons into a red fountain of blood and bone. The grenade drifts through the air in slow motion...everything goes white...

He woke shouting, twisted in sweat-soaked sheets.

He got up, made coffee, poured in a double Jameson's. When he had the dream there was no point in going back to bed.

When he joined the Marines he'd been gung-ho. Naive. Ready to change the world. But all the nameless and meaningless landscapes of loss and death had changed him. The world stayed the same.

That kid in Afghanistan couldn't have been more than eleven or twelve. Old enough to throw a ball, or a grenade, a pretty good distance. Young enough to believe the bullshit he'd been fed about what God wanted him to do and put himself right where Carter would have to kill him.

The child and the grenade always waited in the back of his mind. Carter knew there wasn't anything else he could have done, but it didn't help. It was one more death in a chaotic war that couldn't be won, in a corrupt and brutal land.

Working for Harker gave him a way to bring some kind of meaning to it. It was personal. A way to stop the kind of people who'd sent that child against him. People who thought it was a really good idea to put grenades in the hands of children. People who thought that whatever they wanted was the only right way for everyone. That killing anyone who didn't agree with them was righteous. People who thought God was pleased by that. Carter was damn sure God hadn't told that kid what to do.

He waited for sunrise.

Chapter Nine

Sunlight shone on streets wet with early morning rain. Water on the pavement mirrored a clear, bright sky of light blue with scattered white clouds. The heat wave had broken. The smog had blown away in the night. The city smelled fresh and clean.

A black Ford Crown Vic with plain wheels and government plates pulled up where Carter waited outside his building. A man sat in the front passenger seat wearing a gaudy red Hawaiian shirt covered with white flowers. A loose, cream colored linen jacket bulged over his holstered Glock. He was wearing wraparound shades and a pork pie hat. He looked like he'd just stepped off the set of CSI Miami.

Ronnie Peete was a full blooded Navajo, born on the Reservation. His skin was a light, reddish brown. He had broad shoulders and narrow hips and sleepy brown eyes that could spot a hawk or a sniper at a thousand yards. Ronnie had been a Gunnery Sergeant in Nick's Recon unit. Carter considered him the best combat Marine he'd ever known. He was also a friend.

"How's the ear?" Ronnie asked through the open window.

"Itches like hell."

Nick climbed in back. They pulled away. Ronnie looked back over the front seat.

"They had some great shots on the news last night. Bodies and wrecks on the highway, you covered with blood. How come you have all the fun?"

"Lucky, I guess. Harker find anything out yet?"

"Nope. No ID on any of them. The attackers were probably Chinese. Harker filled me in. Maybe it's about that book. It's too much of a coincidence."

"That's what I think."

"She asked me to ride along to the airport, just in case."

They pulled up at the Mayflower. Selena waited outside with her bodyguard, dressed in jeans and Nikes, a light jacket over a gray silk blouse. She got in the back with Nick. She looked tired, stressed out.

"Morning," he said. "Sleep well?"

"Good morning. Not very. I kept thinking about yesterday."

"This is Ronnie. You'll see a lot of him."

"Morning."

The driver picked his way through traffic. Selena was quiet, lost in thought. They got to the airport without incident.

Ronnie left them at the counter. Carter looked at his ticket. Booked in First Class.

"How did we luck out with this? I usually end up next to the baggage."

"I called in and got us upgraded. I didn't see any point in getting squeezed into coach. It's a long flight."

"Maybe they'll have some real food for a change."

"I wouldn't count on it. I bring my own. The hotel made up a package for me. Do you like roast beef?"

"Any horseradish with it?"

"I haven't looked, but they seem to think of everything."

Carter took Selena through private security. There was a discussion about his gun. A look at his ID with the Presidential seal on it and they let him keep it. They settled into the comfort of First Class.

The attendant brought mimosas.

Selena said, "I was thinking about immortality. If you're immortal, what happens to your friends and lovers? Are they immortal? Do you think someone could stay married for, say, a thousand years?"

"No one could stay married that long."

"Have you ever been married?"

His whole body went tense.

"No. I was engaged, once."

He remembered.

Megan was laughing, her fine, brown hair blowing in the wind coming off the Pacific. They'd gone up the coast to Trinidad for the weekend and found a Victorian bed and breakfast, on the cliffs looking out over the water.

From the deck outside the room they'd watched the seals sunning themselves on the black rocks out in the ocean.

They were getting ready to leave. Megan was beautiful, that day, her green eyes sparkling in the morning sun, excited about going to her new job down in San Diego. Nick had held her close.

"I love you," he'd said. "I'll always love you."

"Nick. You've got to come back to me, come back safe."

"We'll get married when I get back. My tour is up in six months. I'll be a civilian and we can have a real life together."

"And a very, very fine house?" She'd smiled and punched him lightly in the chest with both hands while he held her.

"And two cats in the yard, just like the song." He'd kissed her.

"Why didn't you get married?" Selena asked.

He took a breath. "She died."

"I'm sorry."

"It's all right. Anyway, I haven't been involved with anyone since then."

The plane lifted into the air.

They'd gotten to the airport in plenty of time. They were both flying out, Megan to San Diego, Nick back to the East Coast.

They'd killed time in one of the airport cafes until she had to go. Nick had watched her enter the gangway to board her plane. She'd turned and smiled, waved at him, and disappeared in the stream of passengers.

He'd stood by one of the big windows looking out over the runways, waiting to see her plane take off.

In a few minutes he'd seen it. The plane picked up speed down the runway, lifted into the air, the wheels coming up. He was about to turn away when the aircraft made a strange motion, the wings dipping unevenly right and then left, the nose angling downward.

Fingers of ice wrapped around his chest.

Then the right wing turned straight down. The plane arced into the ground and exploded in a billowing fireball. The shock wave slammed against the window and shook the terminal. At the end of the runway a dense column of orange flame and black smoke boiled up into an indifferent sky.

Megan.

He shoved the memories back into their dark box.

"Have you ever been married?" he said.

"No. I was close, once. I thought I was in love. We'd had dinner and a few drinks and then we got into a big fight. I forget what it was about, some stupid thing. He hit me. It made me mad. I broke his nose, kicked him where it hurts and walked out."

"You broke his nose?"

"He asked for it. I'm good at martial arts."

She shrugged, as if to say what else could she have done?

"Since then I haven't met anyone I wanted to know better. Men are attracted by the way I look. When they find out who I am and don't get what they want, they back off. I guess I scare them away."

"Too much competition for the male ego?"

"If it is, that's not my problem."

She shifted gears. "How would those men yesterday know where I was?"

"It's not hard. You're high profile."

"Do you think they'll try again?"

"They might. Until this gets resolved you should always have people around you. Right now all you've got is me."

"That was good enough yesterday."

She looked out the window, pulled a box from under the seat. "Hungry?"

After lunch and the mimosas, he was slowing down. He fell asleep. One thing he'd learned in the Corps was how to fall asleep anywhere. Asleep, he wasn't remembering anything, unless he was dreaming.

Chapter Ten

Selena looked over at the man sleeping next to her.

Who is he, she wondered. They let him take his gun right on the plane. He's some kind of spy or something. He lost half an ear and killed five people and never blinked an eye. All I know about him is he's got a mother and a sister, had a jerk for a father and he probably saved my life yesterday.

His fiancé died. He didn't say how. Maybe that explains the wariness I feel in him. Like he's waiting for something bad to happen. Like he thinks something is going to jump out at him.

She watched Nick twitch in his sleep.

Black hair, strong jaw, he's already got a trace of shadow. He's not handsome, but he's not bad either. Black eyebrows. And he's got those odd eyes. I've never seen eyes like that, like some kind of animal, a big cat or a wolf. He's built, but not like one of those body freaks in the gyms. I wonder how he is in bed?

Sudden heat and moisture between her legs took her by surprise. She couldn't remember the last time she'd had that thought about someone.

She shook her head. No way was she getting in bed with him. She felt too vulnerable to deal with the intimacy sex would bring up. Besides, this man was dangerous.

Selena looked out the window at a layer of white cloud passing below. She thought about her uncle and her parents.

She could remember her parents, but she couldn't quite remember their voices. The day everything changed, she'd been playing by the window at home. She wasn't supposed to. She was sick and supposed to stay in bed while her brother and her mother and father headed down Highway One toward Big Sur.

When her Uncle came into the room she'd known something bad had happened. He'd started to tell her but she wouldn't listen, drowning his words with a song she'd learned in school the week before.

The engines droned outside her window. I should have been with them in the car, she thought. If I'd been there it would have been all right. We would have stopped somewhere, to get something to eat or so I could go to the bathroom or something. Then they wouldn't have been there when the truck came around that curve.

Her fault.

She'd buried the guilt and armored herself against the world. She knew she'd done it, she wasn't unaware. Be the best in everything. Sports, dangerous hobbies, martial arts, academics. All that success, all her training, hadn't prepared her for this. She wasn't in control anymore. She couldn't make things work the way she wanted.

It scared her, and that was something new. She didn't like it.

She took a few deep breaths and glanced again at Nick. This man doesn't scare, she thought. Maybe he'll make it right, if anyone can.

Chapter Eleven

Carter watched the crowd as they walked through the airport terminal. Nothing seemed out of place. Nobody paying any attention. The shuttle dropped them in the lot and they walked over to his Silverado. A light coating of dust lay on the windshield.

He opened the door for her. "Climb in. Not like your Merc, but it's pretty comfortable."

He took them out of the airport onto I-5, then moved onto 99 North and headed for the Sierra foothills. It was a classic June California afternoon, clear and in the eighties.

"Tell me about where we're going."

"Connorsville," she said. "In Gold Rush days it had saloons, hotels, fifty bordellos and five thousand miners and Chinese living in shacks and tents."

"The Chinese again."

"They did the heavy work. There are stories that they dug secret tunnels leading away from Connorsville and the mine. They did that in Marysville and Sacramento. We never found any, though. My uncle always warned me not to go into the mine. It's not safe."

She looked out the window. "My uncle had a metal detector. We'd walk around where the town used to be and find all sorts of things. It was fun."

"Did you find gold?"

"A coin and a couple of nuggets. One was almost as big as my hand."

At Marysville they picked up Highway 20 and turned east, past flat, green rice fields and wide pastures spotted with cattle. A flight of white herons exploded into the air from one of the ponds alongside the road.

After a while, they crossed the Yuba River. A few minutes later Selena pointed ahead.

"The turnoff is up there on the left. The bridge looks bad, but it's safe to drive over. Just go slow."

He turned onto a short stretch of rough pavement and across the bridge. It looked like it was ready to collapse. Signs warned off trucks and trespassers. They bumped across and followed a gravel road in. On the right a tall, brick chimney rose from the weeds and brush, a ghost from California's golden past.

"Is that what's left of the town?"

"That was the Wells Fargo building. Follow the road down, over there."

The ground sloped away through a field of tall grass dotted with blue oaks. In the spring it would be green as Ireland, ablaze with orange poppies and wildflowers in white and yellow and purple. Now, as the heat of summer built, the flowers were gone. The grass was turning golden brown and dry.

The road curved and dropped down. The house came into sight between two large outcroppings of rock rising out of the grass. The river was a hundred yards beyond.

The building was single story with a green metal roof, stained log siding and a pillared porch in the old country style. A broad swath of gravel lined with white rock spread out in front. Tall camellia bushes bursting with red blossoms lined and crowded the porch. In the yard he saw the ore cart.

"Where's the mine?"

Selena pointed through the windshield. "Down there on the left toward the river, on the other side of the hill."

He parked on the gravel in front of the house. When he shut down, the only sounds were the river going past below and a dog barking in the distance.

Selena walked onto the porch, took out her keys and opened the door. She disappeared inside for a moment and reappeared.

"I thought I might as well turn everything on. We've got lights and power. Nothing in the fridge, but there's canned food and spaghetti, and wine if we get thirsty. The well's good, so we've got water too."

She came off the porch and stood by the corner of the cart. She rested her hand on the rusty edge.

"I used to put things right here, under the rocks. In a metal lunch box. It might even still be here."

The cart was deep. Carter took off his jacket. He started lifting out rocks and stacking them on the ground. He got to the bottom without finding anything.

"Nothing here."

"Try another corner."

He dug out some more rocks. Nothing. He started emptying the cart in earnest. A glint of plastic caught the afternoon light. He pulled out two more rocks and a rectangular package and held it up in the air.

"No lunch box. I think we just found what we came for."

"Let's go inside."

Carter put his jacket back on and they went into the house. On her way in, Selena plucked a blood red flower from the bushes. She set it on the table in a bowl of water.

Chapter Twelve

Choy was in a bad mood. The Mercedes was old, the motor pool mechanic slow. When the car was ready, one of his men rushed to the toilet complaining about food from the night before. The passenger seat would not move all the way back. Choy crammed in as best he could, knees up against the dash, his head touching the roof of the car.

The men in the car sensed his mood and kept quiet. The driver was named Li. Everyone called him "noodles" because of his long, thin looks. He clenched the wheel, trying to make sense of the unfamiliar exit signs and heavy freeway traffic. Twice he made a wrong turn and had to backtrack for miles before they could continue.

The second man, Chung, squirmed in the back seat, trying to control his uncooperative intestines. They stopped twice more so he could relieve himself, using up more time. But for the last two hours there had been no more delays. Now they were past Marysville, heading for the house marked on Choy's directions. Li kept to the speed limit, watching for the Highway Patrol.

Choy hoped they would find the book quickly so he could get back to the Consulate. There was a woman who worked there, cleaning halls and meeting areas. He would make her pay another visit to his bed. She had been satisfying, if uncooperative at first. He was sure she secretly wanted what he had done to her. When they got back he would bring her to his room. Choy settled into the uncomfortable seat, his mood improving as he thought about her.

They swept across a long, curving bridge over a river. The highway narrowed and began to wind about.

Choy peered out the window. "Slow down, we should be getting close."

"There's a truck behind me."

"Never mind him. The place should be up here somewhere on the left."

Li looked in his rear view mirror and began to slow. Choy wasn't sure where they had to turn.

"Look for a bridge," he said. "There should be a bridge on the left."

"There it is!" said Chung. Just then the truck following behind blasted his horn and the Mercedes shot forward as Li floored the gas pedal. They missed the turn.

"Fool! That was it."

"Yes, Sergeant."

"Keep going until we get rid of this dung behind us and turn around."

Soon they saw a marker pointing to the town of Smartsville.

"Take that road."

They pulled off the highway toward the town. As the truck roared by the driver stuck his arm out the window and lifted his finger in salute.

Choy controlled his rage. "Fucking Americans," he said. "Turn around."

Back on the highway, Li drove slowly until they came to the turnoff. He pulled in and stopped.

"Why are you stopping?"

"The bridge, Sergeant. It doesn't look safe."

"Just drive over it. It has to be strong enough. There's a house back there."

The car crept over the bridge and onto the road. They crested the rise and saw the house below. Parked in front was a silver pickup.

"Pull over behind those rocks," Choy said.

"Do you think they saw us?"

"I don't know. Maybe the woman is there. That would be good. Out here no one will notice if we have to question her."

The thought of questioning Connor's niece excited him. Choy licked his lips. They got out of the car.

Each man checked his pistol. All three carried Chinese copies of the Beretta 9mm. From the trunk, Li took out three micro-Uzis, lethal at close range, although not very accurate. Choy reached into a box and took out two type 82-1 grenades, stuffing them into his jacket pockets.

"Do you think we'll need those?"

"Do you want to find out we do if we don't have them?"

"It's just a woman."

"We don't know that. Now shut up and let's get going. Remember your training. Noodles, you go that way. Stay low and work around to the back of the house. Chung, you come with me. We'll circle to the right and approach the front from the side. If it's the woman, we go in and take her. If there's anyone else, take them too. Remember, any trouble, don't kill the woman."

The three men moved toward the house.

Chapter Thirteen

Carter and Selena had been inside the house for half an hour. The windows were open. A light breeze pushed the stale air away.

A large, oriental rug covered the wooden floor in the main room with an intricate pattern of blues and reds. A long brown leather sectional couch and two chairs were grouped in front of a fireplace built from rounded river stones.

The living area and kitchen were separated by a wide granite countertop with a swirling pattern of light and dark colors. A ceiling fan turned above an antique French country kitchen table. The back door opened out by the refrigerator. A hall ran to the right of the living area to a bath and bedrooms.

He sat down at the table with the package. Selena opened a bottle of wine and took two glasses from a cabinet over the counter. She took a seat across from him and poured.

"This is a nice wine, Silver Oak. You like Cab?"

"Yes. Ready to take a look at this?"

"Let's do it."

Carter sipped the wine. He took out his knife and cut away the wrappings of the package. A dark, wooden box appeared.

"That's the box for the book. It was on my uncle's desk."

He opened the box. The book was about eighteen inches long and ten inches wide. The covers were cracked, stained wood, with the remains of red-colored cords that had once bound the flat pieces together. He lifted away the wooden cover. The writing on the page was meaningless to him.

"That's Sanskrit," she said. "This page is in Devanagari. The calligraphy and style suggest it was written around 1200 CE. The rest of the Sanskrit part is in Rgvedic. That's a much older form. This page was added at a later date."

"You can read it?"

"Yes. The language is one I studied for years."

"What does it say?" He tugged at his bandaged ear.

"It's a prayer to the Compassionate Buddha, sort of an introduction. That's typical for a Buddhist text. But this isn't a Buddhist work. The scribe says it should be studied for its medical knowledge but not taken at face value. The text of the book predates Buddhism."

Nick turned the page over with the blade of his knife. Selena moved her finger across the writing.

"Now we're looking at the older script. This word here means treasure. This one means journey, or trip. This one means map. And this one is 'endless life'. These words here translate as 'Golden Garuda'. So the book is called 'The Golden Garuda' and contains directions for finding the treasure of endless life."

"What's a garuda?"

"It's a big, mythical bird, like an eagle on steroids, sometimes half man, half bird. It first shows up in the Vedas. Those are the earliest recorded Indian religious teachings, around 1700 BCE."

The next page was an elaborate anatomical diagram of a naked man squatting down and looking over his shoulder at a stylized sun. It was recognizable, but in a style far from modern drawings.

"That's a diagram of the circulation of the blood, drawn centuries before Harvey discovered it in the West."

He took another sip of wine. She bent over and pointed at the next page.

"This page is a warning. This word means danger or calamity. There's a sentence about guarding or hiding something. I can't quite make it out, there's damage, but it refers to a great king or emperor."

"The Chinese emperor?"

"Maybe. From what I can see, the whole passage says danger awaits anyone who pursues the information in this book."

There was the sound of a car outside.

Nick looked at Selena. "You expecting anyone?"

"No."

"I heard a car."

"I did, too."

He moved over by the window, but couldn't see anyone. The rocks hid whoever was there. A car motor stopped. Doors closed softly.

He pulled the .45 from his holster. "We've got company. Get the book."

Selena put the book in its box and the box in a bag she pulled from under the sink.

"What's out the back door?"

She brushed a hair away. "There's a path down to the river. It goes by the entrance to the mine."

Carter remembered houses in Afghanistan and Iraq, full of death waiting in every room.

"I don't like being inside the house. There's no place to go. Whoever it is can't be here for a good reason, or they'd just drive to the front. They would have seen my truck, so they know someone's here. I think they're after that book."

"How would they know we were here or where the book was?"

"I don't know. But I don't want to stick around and ask them. You game for a run?"

"To the river?"

"Right. That way they have to come at us through the grass and I can see them. They can see us too, but that's better than being trapped in here. I'll cover us."

He opened the back door. A brown, grassy slope led down to the river.

"You go first, you know the way. I'll be right behind you. Let's make it to the other side of the hill and take it from there. Ready?"

She nodded.

"Go!"

She took off. Nick followed. Selena was fast and he was glad he'd kept in shape. He looked back and saw a man raising a weapon.

He dove and pushed Selena sprawling into the dirt just as the intruder fired a long burst. Uzi, he thought. He aimed for a body hit and squeezed off two shots. The shooter stood for a second and then crumpled into the grass.

As he pulled Selena to her feet, a big man stepped around the corner on the front porch. Nick fired and the man ducked back out of sight. They began running again. The chattering sound of an Uzi came from the house. A man with a pistol ran from behind the house and fired three quick shots that streaked by in a whisper of heated air. Carter went into shooter's stance, two hands, aim, take a breath, squeeze, fire. Two rounds, the .45 bucking back in his hands. The man went down screaming.

They ran. Another burst of automatic fire kicked up dirt behind them. Seconds later he heard three pistol shots and sensed the rounds pass by. They reached the hillside. He saw the opening to the mine, crossed off with old boards. Past the hill were open fields and the flatness of the river bed. There was no cover.

"Head for the mine," he yelled.

Selena turned, arms pumping. They reached the entrance and he kicked in the boards. They entered the mine.

It was cool in the tunnel after the hot June sun outside. Fallen rocks from the ceiling littered the floor. Selena put her hands on her knees and bent to catch her breath. The plastic bag with the book in it was clutched in her hand.

"What do we do now?"

"We're too close to the entrance," he said. "We'll move back. Anyone comes to the front, I shoot him."

They went deeper into the tunnel until the light began to give out. A large, empty ore cart sat rusting on tracks vanishing into the blackness of the mine. In the dim light they couldn't be seen from the entrance.

"How many are there?" said Selena.

"At least three. Two of them are down. Maybe just one more."

Carter thought about their situation. Tactical assessment. An old habit.

"We're outgunned," he said. "They've got automatic weapons. How about you get inside the cart. That way you've got good protection."

"What about you?"

"I'll get behind the cart. That will give me a shield and I can move around if I need to."

"How do we get out of here?"

"We wait until dark. That's a couple of hours from now. Then we sneak out. Best I can think of at the moment."

Selena climbed into the cart and peered over the edge. Carter watched the tunnel entrance and thought. He'd fired twice at the first man, once at the big man on the porch and twice at the second man. Five rounds. His H-K held fifteen plus one, so that meant he still had eleven in his pistol. He had a spare magazine, so another fifteen. Not a lot, but so far it had been enough. It would have to do.

Chapter Fourteen

The sound of Li's Uzi behind the house and two loud reports from a large pistol had sent Choy to the end of the porch. He'd started past the corner when another shot threw flying splinters by his face.

"Chung, go around the other side and see if you can spot the shooter. I'll keep him busy." Chung took off running.

Choy stuck the Uzi around the corner and let off a burst in the general direction of the shots he'd heard. There was no return fire. The crisp, sharp sound of Chung's Beretta came from behind the house. It was followed by two more loud shots and a scream. Choy looked around the corner and saw a man and a woman forty or fifty yards away, running toward the river. Chung and Li were nowhere in sight. He let off another burst, but the Uzi was no good at distances like that. He switched to his pistol and fired three rounds. The running pair disappeared behind a hill.

Choy ran to the back of the house and saw Chung lying in the grass, hands clasped across his bloody abdomen.

"Chung. How bad?"

Chung gasped. "Bad. In the gut. Two of them. The man has the gun."

"Where's Li?"

"Don't know."

"Hold on. I'll be back."

Choy ran across the field, trying for cover from the hill. There was no sign of the man or the woman. He passed Li's body lying face down in the weeds and reached the hill. He inserted a fresh magazine into the Uzi, crouched low and moved through the dry grass until he saw where the running couple had gone.

A tunnel opened into the side of the hill, broken boards scattered on the ground in front of it. They must have gone inside. If he went up to the tunnel mouth he'd be silhouetted against the light.

Choy had had enough for one day. He reached into his pocket and took out a grenade. He pulled the pin and with an easy throw lobbed it into the tunnel opening.

The explosion buried the entrance in an avalanche of red dirt and flying rock. Choy hadn't expected that, but it served his purpose. There'd be no more trouble from the two inside.

He walked back to where Noodles was lying. Li was dead. He went to where Chung lay in the grass clutching his abdomen. Dark blood soaked his shirt and seeped through his fingers. Choy knelt beside him.

"All right, Chung. We'll get you fixed up."

That bastard American, Choy thought. Now we've got problems. And Chung didn't look too good.

"Water," Chung said.

"No water. I'm going to get you to the car. It will hurt."

He bent down and lifted and Chung cried out in pain. Choy straightened and carried the moaning man to the Mercedes. He laid him down on the ground.

Choy walked to where Li's body lay in the grass. He picked up Li's weapon and dragged the body back to the car, then placed the dead man and the Uzi in the trunk. He glanced at Chung. There wasn't much he could do for a wound like that. Chung's only hope was a hospital. Choy couldn't risk it. He'd have to go back to the Consulate, but he didn't think Chung would last that long. It was either that, or end it now and put him with Li. For a moment he considered that option. He decided to think about it.

He went back to where Chung had been hit, retrieved his weapons and took them to the car, placing them with Li's body in the trunk. Then he walked to the house and into the living room. An open wine bottle sat on the kitchen table.

Choy picked up the bottle and took a long swallow. Too bitter compared to the sweet plum wine he liked, but better than nothing. He wiped his lips and looked at scraps of tape and plastic piled on the table.

Something had been unwrapped. Choy had a bad feeling. If the wrappings had protected the book he was sent to find and it was now buried with the Americans, the Colonel would be angry.

Thinking back, Choy realized the woman had been carrying a white plastic bag. The more he thought about it, the more he was convinced the book was in that tunnel, with two dead Americans. The whole mission had turned into a disaster. He took another pull from the bottle.

There had been a lot of noise. The house was in the country, and everyone knew Americans were always shooting at things in the country. Probably no one would think much about it. But the grenade had been loud.

Time to leave.

Choy made a cursory search of the house so he could tell Colonel Wu he'd looked for the book. He found a purse on the couch, opened it and scattered the contents. He took the wallet and looked at the driver's license. The Connor woman. Who was the man?

Choy took the money and license from the wallet and tossed it onto the couch. He took a last drink from the bottle, walked onto the porch and over to the truck parked in front of the building. He opened the glove box and rummaged through it. He found an insurance slip with a name and a California address. Choy pocketed the paper.

He walked back to the Mercedes and looked at Chung. What if he was stopped along the way? How would he explain the wounded man?

"Water," Chung said.

"You will have as much water as you need, my friend, very soon," Choy said, softly. He patted him on the arm. Then he took out his pistol and shot Chung in the head. He opened the trunk and lifted the body in with Li. There was just enough room for the two of them. He closed the trunk and got in the car, adjusted the seat and started the engine.

He'd be back at the Consulate in a few hours. That would give him time to compose his story for the Colonel. At least the American man and woman were finished. That thought brought a smile of satisfaction. Choy began humming tunelessly as he pulled onto the highway and headed back to San Francisco.

It was dark by the time he reached the city. Another twenty minutes, he thought. Then the flashing lights of a patrol car lit up the night behind him.

Choy signaled and pulled to the side of the road, leaving the engine running. The patrol car sat behind him as a few vehicles passed by. Choy was nervous. Why had he been pulled over? He wasn't speeding. He tried to think what it might be. Finally the patrolman emerged from his cruiser. He approached the car and tapped on the glass, hand resting on his holstered gun, signaling Choy to lower his window.

"Yes, Officer. Is there a problem?"

Choy spoke passable English. Colonel Wu had made sure of that.

"Sir, did you know that one of your taillights is out? May I see your license, proof of insurance and registration please?"

"Yes, sir. The papers are in the glove box." Choy reached over and opened the compartment, fumbled with a map and took out the registration and insurance. It was good Chung wasn't lying on the back seat. The patrolman shone his flashlight on the papers.

"License, please."

Choy handed it over.

"Wait here," the cop said, and went back to his cruiser.

The highway patrolman sat in his car and wrote something. Then he returned.

He handed the papers and license to Choy.

"I'm giving you a safety warning," he said. "You need to get that fixed and return this form to the address on the back. You have five days to get it done."

"Yes, officer. Thank you for your help." Inside, Choy was seething. Would anything go right today? At least the cop was going to let him go.

"Say, there's something leaking back here, under the trunk."

Choy watched the cop's face harden and his hand move toward his gun as he realized the fluid leaking out was blood. Choy didn't hesitate. He fired three shots through the open window. The cop stumbled and fell sprawling on the pavement. Choy floored the gas and pulled out onto the freeway.

Half an hour later he entered the consulate compound and pulled into the garage. He turned off the ignition. The engine rattled on for a moment and died with an erratic cough.

Choy sat in the silence of the parking garage, thinking about the way this day had gotten screwed up beyond anything he could imagine. It was too bad about Li and Chung, but that was the least of his worries. What was he going to tell Colonel Wu? The only person Choy feared in this world was Wu. Wu could make life miserable.

Choy was sweating in the cool darkness, a cold, greasy sweat that formed dark circles under his armpits. He smelled his own body odor. He hated it when that happened. In basic training people had made fun of him, calling him a pig and worse when he smelled like this. That stopped after he had a chance to get them alone. Soon no one commented on how he smelled.

Choy wiped his face with the sleeve of his jacket. If he told Wu what had really happened he'd be lucky if he was guarding camels in the Gobi desert for his next assignment. At least he had the name of the man who'd fouled everything up, but the troublemaker was already out of the picture, dead in that mine cave-in.

He got out of the car. A faint, sewer smell emanated from the trunk. It wasn't Choy's fault Li and Chung had gotten themselves killed. Who would have thought there'd be someone at that house who could shoot like that while his men were firing at him? He must have been someone well-trained, a professional. Choy had to admit to a grudging admiration.

The thought of the shooter dead in the mine made him feel better. He'd report in, give as few details as possible and hope for the best. Choy began humming to himself. Everything would be fine.

Chapter Fifteen

Colonel Wu smoked and thought about the failed attempt to secure the Connor woman. Now he had five dead agents to explain. There was a knock on his door.

"Yes."

"Choy, Sir."

Wu stubbed out his cigarette and opened the door. One look told him he was not going to like what he heard. He gestured and Choy entered the room. Wu closed the door.

"Report, Sergeant."

"Sir. We ran into trouble. The woman, Connor, was at the house when we arrived but there was a man with her. He was armed and we got into a firefight. Li and Chung are dead. I chased the woman and her companion into an abandoned mine. The entrance collapsed and they were buried inside. They must be dead. I searched the house and the book was not there. I did get the name of the man who was there and confirmed the identity of the woman."

Choy handed Selena's license and the slip from the car to Wu. He had decided to omit the reason the mine collapsed and his thought the book was buried with the Americans. Better to let Wu think it was still out there somewhere.

"What did you do with Li and Chung?"

"Sir, there's more. I put them in the trunk of the car. On the way here I was stopped by a policeman. It was some sort of safety check. He was going to let me go when he saw blood leaking from the trunk. He reached for his gun and I shot him. That was about a half hour ago."

"You shot an American police officer." Wu's voice was flat.

"Yes, sir. I had no choice."

"Where is the car?"

"In the garage below."

"Give me your pistol."

Choy handed over the gun.

"Choy, you have disappointed me. I expected more discretion from you. You are certain the book was not in the house? Did the woman have it with her when she fled?"

"The book was not in the house, sir. If the woman had it with her, I did not see it."

It was true, he hadn't actually seen a book in the woman's hand.

"You are leaving tonight for home, Sergeant. I will arrange passage on one of our freighters. Go to your room and wait there. You will be escorted to your ship. As soon as you arrive in Beijing, report to me."

He gave Choy a hard look.

"Dismissed."

"Sir!" Choy snapped to attention, turned and left the room. The door closed behind him.

Wu picked up his phone and began making arrangements to clean up the mess Choy had created. He was angry. The book was not found. If it was in that mine, how would he retrieve it? Wu would wait to inform the General. Yang was not a man who tolerated failure. He'd sleep on it and decide what to do tomorrow.

Chapter Sixteen

Carter saw a dark object thrown into the tunnel and heard it clink against the rock floor and knew what it was. He jumped into the cart right on top of Selena, knocking her to the rusty floor, pressing her body under him.

The explosion blotted out thought. Shrapnel ricocheted off the sides of the cart. The entrance to the mine collapsed with a thunderous roar, shutting off the light.

Rumblings and falls deep within the mine faded away.

Total blackness.

Carter lay rigid, waiting for the ringing in his ears to stop.

She coughed. "You mind getting off me?"

He was pressing her down under him, the .45 still in his hand. He holstered it, climbed out of the cart in the dark.

"I can't see a damn thing." Selena coughed again.

"I can fix that."

Nick reached into his jacket pocket for the mini flash he always carried. He clicked it on.

Something crawled across the back of his hand.

A large, black spider.

He slapped it away, almost losing the flash. Something crunched under his foot.

He helped Selena out of the cart and tried not to think about spiders. She was covered with dirt and had scrapes on her face. Her silk designer blouse was ripped and stained with red dirt and rust, exposing most of her breast.

The entrance to the mine was blocked by tons of rock reaching to the ceiling. Thin streams of dirt trickled from the roof of the tunnel.

"We're not getting out that way," he said.

"The whole side of the hill must have come down."

He took out his phone. No signal.

"Is there another entrance?" He flicked the thin beam of the flash around the tunnel. Something moved at the edge of the light.

"I think so, but I don't know where it is. I saw a map of the mine once. There are three levels, with branches off the main tunnel and shafts hundreds of feet deep. Some parts are flooded, but I don't know where. A lot of tunnels were closed off when the mine began shutting down."

"We don't have much choice. You up for exploring?"

"You lead," she said.

The flash wasn't much. They followed the narrow beam along the rusted tracks, deeper into the mine, picking their way around rocks that had fallen from the roof. Nick lost sense of whether the tunnel was going straight or curving about. The air was stifling and hot and smelled of ancient water and older rock. The adrenaline rush was gone. He was tired and sore.

Thick wooden posts supported cracked beams holding up the roof of the tunnel. They looked weak and unstable. Webs hung from the corners where the beams and posts came together. Everywhere, spiders retreated from the light. There were pools of water on the floor and wet, dark stains on the walls, drips of water from the ceiling. The air was hot and still. Nick felt the tunnel walls closing in. He told himself it would be all right. All right. One thing at a time. He was sweating.

The tunnel split, one branch going right, the other straight ahead.

"Which way should we go?"

"Your guess is as good as mine. I never thought I'd need to know," said Selena.

"You think right, or straight ahead?"

"If the tunnel hasn't turned, the river must be somewhere to the right. I think the miners followed a vein toward the river. If they did, maybe it came out somewhere on the bank."

"Let's go right. If it did come out, it shouldn't be far."

They entered the right hand shaft. The tunnel supports were rotting and puddles of water lay everywhere. Something scurried away ahead.

"What was that?"

"I don't know. I didn't see anything."

"What's that squeaking sound?"

The passage curved and they came around the corner. Fifty feet ahead the tunnel ended in a fall of rock and a churning nest of swarming and squeaking rats. Hundreds of red eyes gleamed in the narrow light.

Carter froze. Selena gripped his arm, hard. The rats squirmed and wriggled, darting towards them and back again into the mass.

Neither said a word as they backed away. He felt Selena shudder. Back in the main shaft they passed a boarded passage on the left, then another on the right. They began to see more closed off entrances. A rat ran by his foot.

They came to the remains of a stable cut into the side of the tunnel, stalls still standing. A rope halter hung on a rusty nail.

"Why would they have a stable down here?"

It was the first thing Nick had said since the rats.

"For the mules. Mules hauled the carts."

Fifty feet past the stable the tunnel branched off in three directions. The tracks ended here in a decaying wooden triangle. The rusty head of a miner's pick lay in the dirt. Nick picked it up and put it in his jacket pocket.

"I don't like this," Selena said.

"Me neither." He shone the flashlight at the shaft on the right, then the others. There wasn't much difference between them. They all looked like highways to hell. He wet a finger and felt for a breath of air.

Nothing. Just a wet finger.

The flashlight beam was turning yellow. If they ran out of light they might never leave. He didn't like the idea of being in the dark with rats and spiders, but the batteries were fading.

"I'm going to turn off the light."

The blackness closed in. Nick remembered a cave in Afghanistan where he was almost buried alive, remembered his drunken father locking him in a dark closet, remembered a cellar in Colombia filled with the sewer odors of pain and death. He pushed the thoughts away, wished he had a drink or a cigarette or both.

Selena clenched his hand. In the black silence she heard sounds. Too many sounds. Water dripped somewhere. There was a soft, constant noise of dribbles of earth falling from the roof. The tunnels creaked and she heard wood groaning. Something scuttled close by.

Talking was strange. The relentless dark sucked words away like velvet as soon as they were spoken.

"I don't think we should go further in. Those tunnels go deeper, and they're lower. We'd have to crawl. The tracks end here and that's not good. If these passages went through, the miners would have run the tracks all the way to get the ore."

"Nick, I'm scared. What if we can't get out?"

"We can't think like that."

"Yes, but what if we can't?"

"We'll get out."

"Maybe one of the side entrances we passed back there can take us out."

"Yeah, but which one?"

"If we open them up, something could give us a clue. Those boards they used, they don't look strong. We can break them down to get in."

"That's good thinking." He smelled her fear, a faint, sour, coppery smell. Or maybe it was him.

He turned on the light. It was weaker.

Back up the tunnel they came to a side shaft and Selena held the light while Nick pulled boards away. He tossed a rock through the opening waiting for the sound. There was a pause, then a splash, a long way below.

"You heard that?"

"Yes."

"I'm not up for a swim. Let's keep going."

The next two were the same, vertical death traps dropping hundreds of feet into the flooded lower levels of the mine. They came to the next entrance. Carter played the light around it.

"There's something written there," Selena said.

Chinese characters were scribed into the rock over the entrance.

"Can you read it?"

"Yes. It says, 'Dreams'."

"Dreams?"

"That's what it says."

"Why would someone write 'dreams' on a mine shaft wall?"

"How would I know?"

He kicked in the boards. They stepped through into a low tunnel and followed it bent over. The light dimmed. After what seemed a long time the passage opened into a large chamber. The air was better, the ceiling high enough to stand upright.

The room was about twenty feet square. Against one wall, three low rectangles of wood bore old mattresses, straw spilling out where the rats had gnawed on the rotted fabric. Across the room a broken stool lay on its side by a rough wooden table. On the table was the stub of a candle in a holder. Selena walked over and picked it up, just as the light died.

Nick felt the old fear, the childhood demons of nameless, hideous monsters lurking in places without light. He took a deep breath, calmed himself. They weren't dead yet.

"Now all we need is a light," said Selena.

"You have a match?"

"I don't smoke."

"Neither do I."

"Smoking can kill you."

They started laughing hysterically.

When they had calmed down he said, "Stay where you are."

He crossed the room with hands stretched out until he banged up against one of the beds. From the tattered mattress he gathered straw and fabric and fumbled his way back to Selena. On the floor he felt around until he found a rock.

He made a little pile of bedding, took his knife and struck it against the rock. After a few tries he got a spark. He chipped at the rock, showering sparks down on the straw. It caught into bright flame.

She handed him the candle and he lit it. The room came back into view, the smoke from the fire rising upward.

"Look." Selena pointed upward.

The smoke disappeared into a hole in the ceiling.

"That's where the air is coming from."

"At least we won't suffocate. Be nice if it were bigger."

Carter looked around. "What is this place?"

"I think it was an opium den. No one except Chinese would have come in here. The miners couldn't have read the sign over the entrance and wouldn't have cared anyway."

"That makes sense. That's why the beds. And the sign makes sense, too. There might be a way out. I don't think there'd only be one exit to a place like this."

He walked slowly around the room. On the back wall was the outline of another entrance, walled up with stone, the mortar crumbling and old. Nick took the pick head he'd found and began chipping away. Soon there was a pile of dust on the floor. A rock came free, then another. He stuck his hand through the opening and touched empty space.

He kept chipping and pulling out rocks until the entrance was big enough to climb through. They looked at each other.

"It's another tunnel," he said.

"What if it's a dead end?"

"We don't have a choice. Only one way to find out."

This tunnel was narrow but it was in good shape. At one point it dipped through water that came to their knees. Nick wondered if he was about to step into a deep, deep hole, but the floor rose again and they were back on dry ground. The candle was almost gone when they came to another blocked entrance, this one walled up with brick.

"That's a change."

"The mortar looks old. Maybe I can kick it down." He handed her the candle.

He gave it a good kick. Another.

"Now I know how Bruce Lee must have felt," he said.

"Let me try," Selena said. "Better get out of the way."

Nick stood to the side. Selena closed her eyes, took a deep breath and became very still. She opened her eyes and backed away, then let out a wild yell and launched herself flying, feet first. The whole wall blew out into the room on the other side.

Squinting against light, he stepped through into someone's basement. Selena was getting to her feet. He reached down to help her up.

"How the hell did you do that?"

"Nick." She gestured with her head.

A burly man with a gray beard stood openmouthed across the room in pajamas, eyes wide, pointing a twelve gauge shotgun at them.

Carter raised his hands. "How's it going?" he said.

Chapter Seventeen

"What are you doing here?" Shotgun Man was around sixty. He looked scared. The twelve gauge shook in his hands. A large dog of indeterminate breed stood next to him, bristling and growling.

"Take it easy. I'll pay for the damage to your wall."

"You mind telling me where the hell you came from?"

"You mind putting that down, sir? I can explain. It's a long story. My name's Nick, this is Selena."

"You look like something my dog rolled in. You say you'll pay?"

"Absolutely. We'll make it new. Where are we, anyway?"

Suspicious, but he lowered the gun a few inches. Nick breathed easier.

"You're in Smartsville, California. How did you get here?"

The truth wouldn't be a good idea, considering the events of the day. He began improvising.

"Selena here owns the old Connor mine up the road. You know the place?"

"Connorsville? The Number One Mine? Sure, everyone knows about it. That's your place?"

Carter was about to say something, but she beat him to it.

"Yes." She smiled at him. "I'm really sorry we made so much trouble for you. I was showing Nick around and we went inside the mine. I tripped and grabbed a post holding up the roof. The whole thing came down and the roof collapsed. We were almost buried alive."

Carter picked up the story. "So we couldn't get out the way we got in. We wandered around in there for hours until we found the tunnel that brought us here. We broke down your wall because there wasn't anything else to do. Like I said, I'll pay for the damage."

"Well, I'll be damned." The gun dropped another few inches. "I always heard the Chinese dug secret tunnels during the gold rush."

"Why would they dig one here?"

"This was a whorehouse in the old days. It's good a reason as any, I guess. You two were damn lucky to find it, after being dumb enough to go into that old mine."

"I guess it wasn't very smart," Selena said, looking contrite. Carter caught her glancing at him from the corner of her eye. She was enjoying it, playing the dumb blonde.

"I guess you'd like a glass of something," Shotgun Man said. He lowered the shotgun all the way. The dog stopped growling and began to look interested instead of threatening. "Come on upstairs. This will be a hell of a story to tell down at the It'll Do."

Shotgun Man's name was Ed. He offered a shot of Crown Royal and a lift back to the house. Nick figured that whoever threw the grenade would be long gone and would have cleaned up the carnage. He wasn't worried about stumbling over a couple of dead bodies.

They climbed into Ed's pickup. Ten minutes later they stood on the front porch of the house. There was no sign of the shooters. Nick's watch showed midnight.

Ed drove off with a promise from Selena that he could come back with his metal detector and search the town site. They watched his taillights disappear. High overhead in the warm, June night, an airplane left a long, silver trail across the star-filled sky. A soft breeze carried the sound of crickets singing to each other.

"Feels good to have all that space above you, doesn't it?"

"I didn't think we were going to get out of there," she said.

"The spiders got to me."

"And the rats. Don't forget the rats."

She turned to him and wrapped her arms around him. He held her for a long moment, felt the warmth of her body in the cool night air.

"Let's go inside."

Selena turned on the lights. The contents of her purse were scattered on the floor and the couch. The back door was open where they'd run for it.

Selena gathered her things back together. Nick called Harker. It was three in the morning on the East Coast. The day's events were enough reason to wake her up.

Harker picked up her phone. Her voice was thick with sleep.

"It better be good, Nick." She coughed.

"You might say that. We have the book."

He filled her in on what had happened. There was a long pause.

"I'll get a cleanup team out there to process the place. No sign of the shooters?"

"It's dark out, so I can't look for bodies, but no, no sign. My guess is whoever threw the grenade took the others with him. He was in the house and got into Selena's purse, so he knows who she is and where she lives. But after that cave in, they have to think we're both dead."

"This local man, you think he suspects any of this?"

"No. He just thinks we're dumb, exploring old mines. I told him we'd reimburse him for damages, he's fine with it. I don't see any problems. Maybe another contribution to local bar lore."

"Grenades and Uzis mean serious backing. Did you get a good look at any of them?"

"I'm pretty sure they were Chinese. The big one is ugly as hell. I'd recognize him if I saw him again."

"Maybe the Bureau can help."

"If Ugly has anything to do with Wu, they might have a shot of him."

"I'll see what they've got. There have to be more photos than the ones they gave us. What's your plan now?"

"I haven't thought about it. Get some sleep, I guess."

"How's Selena?"

"She's fine."

"Tell her she is now under Federal protection and direction regarding her activities."

"Yes, Director."

"And Nick…I'm glad you both made it out safe."

She hung up.

Carter turned to where Selena was sitting on the couch, exhausted, beat up, filthy with mine dirt. She looked a little rough around the edges. He wanted to hold her. He wanted to do more than that. It had been a long time since he'd wanted to hold any woman.

"The Director said you're now under Federal protection. It means the government will be controlling your life for a while, what you can and can't do. It's the trade off."

Selena nodded, a gesture of resignation.

"Harker's sending a team to check this place out," he said. "What do you want to do?"

"I want to get cleaned up and sleep. But I don't want to stay here."

"I've got a place not far away. Why don't we go there? I can sleep on the couch."

She considered a moment, gave him a thoughtful look.

"Sounds better than a motel. You have a shower or a bathtub?"

"I do."

"Let's go."

She got up, took the book and her purse, turned everything off and locked up. Carter opened the passenger door for her. The glove box was open and he hadn't left it that way. The insurance slip was gone. He closed the glove compartment without mentioning his thoughts to Selena. The address on the slip was a P.O. Box, so they didn't have a physical location yet. They were safe for the moment.

In less than an hour they pulled up at the cabin.

While Selena cleaned up he got the book and placed it in a gun safe at the back of the bedroom closet. He sat down and leaned back on the couch, waiting for her to finish, and closed his eyes. What a day, he thought. Why were these people so anxious to get the book? He fell asleep.

He dreamed.

He was running in a twilight land, with something close behind. He ran through a bleak landscape with high mountains and large black animals in a rocky field. The sky was sickly yellow and there was a bad smell in the air.

He heard a helicopter. He was looking for Selena, but couldn't find her. He saw a cave in the side of a mountain and then he was inside. A dark figure dressed in a long robe stood in the shadows and watched him. The figure held something white in his right hand. There was a flash of light and rocks began falling. He was going to be buried alive.

Then he was standing in a crowd of people with Megan. He was naked, exposed. He was looking for his clothes.

"I don't know where my socks are."

"It's all right, Nick. But you need your parachute."

Then he was dressed and they were standing on a beach, looking out at the Golden Gate Bridge.

"I love you," he said.

"I love you, too, but I have to go. Aren't the mountains beautiful?"

Towering, snow-capped mountains were right up against the bay behind the bridge. Somehow it made sense in the dream.

Then the sky turned dark and a cold wind began whipping up whitecaps on the bay. Megan was gone.

He woke stretched out on the couch under a blanket. Everything ached. The dream stuck in his mind. At least it wasn't the Afghan village again. At least it wasn't that kid again.

Carter's Irish Grandmother sometimes dreamed of things to come. He'd inherited the ability from her, a psychic quirk that opened doors he wished would stay closed. The dreams always foreshadowed something that hadn't happened yet. It was never anything pleasant. She'd called it a gift. He thought it a curse.

This dream was one of those, but he couldn't figure out what it meant. Those black animals weren't cows, or anything like that. If it was like the other dreams he wouldn't know what it meant until he ran into it headfirst.

Chapter Eighteen

Selena had dressed in black running shorts with yellow stripes down the sides, a yellow sport bra with a black Nike swoosh on it and running shoes. A bright yellow headband kept the hair off her forehead. The only signs of yesterday were the shadows under her eyes and the scratches on her face.

The outfit showed off her trim body. "Good morning," she said. "How are you feeling? Want some coffee?"

"Morning. Yeah, coffee's good. I feel like I went ten rounds with the wrong guy."

She brought him a cup. Black and hot.

"I thought I'd go for a run and work out some of that mine."

"If you wait twenty minutes, I'll get cleaned up and go with you. There's a good trail nearby."

"You like to run?"

"It's just something I do to stay in shape."

Nick felt his brain begin to function again. He was still wearing his holster and ruined jacket. He took them off, laid the rig on the coffee table. He took the H-K from the holster, pulled the slide partway back, still a round in the chamber. He dropped the magazine and inserted a fresh one, set it back on the table.

He went into the other room. She'd made the bed. He stripped and went into the bathroom. The hot water soothed the aches and bruises and he started feeling human again. He thought about Selena. She looked good in that outfit. He felt the beginning of an erection, turned the water to cold.

He toweled off, wiped the steam off the mirror and shaved. He went back into the bedroom and pulled on shorts and a tee, put on his running shoes.

He thought about yesterday. It seemed there was always someone with a gun waiting for him, somewhere. He thought about people who would cut the finger off an old man. Someone had to do something about people like that. It was what kept him going.

He got a Colt .380 auto from the safe and tucked it out of sight under the tee. It was a lot lighter and smaller than the .45. Good for a run. After yesterday he wasn't going anywhere without something to make holes.

He came out of the bedroom.

"What happened to your leg?" she asked.

His leg looked like someone had run a cheese grater on steroids over the thigh and then taken a few digs at the calf for good measure. The scars were colorful, red, white and blue, very patriotic. Under his clothes there were puckered ridges of scar tissue on the side of his hip and ribcage.

"Afghanistan happened. A little kid threw a grenade at me. I shot him."

She looked at him. He thought he saw unspoken accusation.

"I didn't have a choice. The fragments missed the knee and the groin. Still a couple in the leg. It bothers me sometimes, but not bad. One reason I run is it keeps the leg strong."

"Let's run, then."

They headed out the door and up the hill. The morning was cool, perfect for a run before the heat built up. The trail was shady and soft underfoot. Birds darted in and out of the branches and leaves. A doe bounded across the trail in front of them. In the cool elevation and shade of the foothills, purple and yellow wildflowers still bloomed along the edge of the trail.

Carter's breathing settled into an easy rhythm, the sounds of the run and the feel of the path under his feet filling his thoughts. He felt yesterday begin to slip away. Then he remembered the man shooting at him and screaming as he went down.

The man he'd shot had tried to kill them. He'd failed, and Nick had survived. Maybe there was meaning in it, maybe not. That was a question for people who found value in probing theological and metaphysical mysteries. He wasn't one of them.

He didn't look for meaning anymore. When it came right down to it, it was all about survival. The way he dealt with it was one day at a time. It had been one day at a time for the last fifteen years. It didn't do any good to think about it. It was what he did, a job. Someone had to do it.

About two miles from the cabin they paused for a breather.

"You were right, this is a great trail." Selena looked out over a wide valley.

"I make this run every morning when I'm here."

They were soaked in sweat. Selena rested her hand on his arm, catching her breath.

"Nick...," she began. She looked at him, thoughtful. "Oh, never mind. Let's talk when we get back."

"After you." He gestured at the trail.

Back at the cabin Nick stood by the sink with a glass of water looking out the window. He felt her hand on his shoulder.

"Nick," she said.

He turned and she reached behind his head and pulled him to her. He set the water down and put his arms around her. She radiated heat. He tasted the salt of her sweat, pulled her close, probed her mouth with his tongue. Her hands moved on his back, his shoulders.

He broke the kiss. He didn't think about it.

"Maybe we should go in the bedroom."

"Maybe we should."

He kissed her again, on the mole on her lip. They moved together to the bed.

There was a kind of desperation about their lovemaking, as though life was slipping away and there was little time left to hold on to it. When they were done, he waited for his breathing to settle down to normal.

"Whew," he said.

Selena brushed hair back from her forehead, looked away. He felt her withdraw. She got up and turned her back toward him.

"I'm going to take a shower."

He lay on the bed, feeling awkward.

She went into the bathroom, closed the door. He heard the shower running. Nick remembered how it used to be with Megan.

"Do you think we'll still be lovers when we're old and gray?"

He'd stroked her hair, kissed her, run his hands over her body. They were tangled around each other in her big king sized bed, where they'd been all afternoon. Half-packed boxes were scattered around the room.

He'd kissed her breast.

"We'll never get old and gray."

"Not if you keep doing that."

"Like this?"

She'd gasped, reached for him.

"Yes, Nick, yes."

Megan, he thought. I couldn't stop it from happening. I couldn't will that plane back into the air. His thoughts turned bleak.

One day at a time.

When Selena came out, she dressed quickly. She went into the kitchen.

He pulled on Levis and a light shirt. They made breakfast in silence. They sat down at the table with fresh coffee.

She was pensive. "That mine was no fun."

He picked up his cup. "Hell of a way to get to know each other."

"You know something," she said.

"What?"

"I've heard that people who go through serious stress together jump into each other's arms." She paused. "I never felt so mortal before. Nothing's the same. The moment seems more important now, everything seems more intense."

"I know. More alive."

"Even the colors are brighter. I'm glad I'm alive." She looked out the window, then over at him. "I'm glad I'm here with you."

She drank coffee. He didn't know what to say. She was an unknown force he hadn't expected. He couldn't think of something to say that wouldn't sound stupid.

Time to call in and see what was on Harker's mind. Maybe they'd found something at the house.

Chapter Nineteen

"No bodies. Lots of forensics." Harker said. "We've got casings, blood trails, tire impressions, prints and DNA from a wine bottle."

"Selena's and my prints are on that bottle."

"We know that. There are others. Where's the book?"

"In a safe here at my cabin."

"I want you two back here now. I've sent a plane to pick you up at Beale Air Force Base. You know where it is?"

"Yes. It's about an hour from here. When do we leave?"

"1800 hours. An escort will pick you up at your cabin at 1600 and take you to the base. Ronnie will meet you when you get in. It will be late. I want you to stay at the apartment here. We'll meet tomorrow at 0700."

The apartment at the Project building was for keeping out of sight. Carter had never had to use it.

"Anything more from the FBI?"

"Jordan sent over more photos. You can look at them when you get here. Wait for your transport. I'll see you in the morning."

She clicked off.

Selena gestured at the porch, past the screen door. "You have a cat?"

Pawing at the door and looking in through the screen was an enormous, beat-up orange tomcat.

"That's Burps. It's more like he has me. He's a different sort of cat. A neighbor feeds him when I'm away, which is most of the time."

The cat was part Maine Coon, part whatever. He weighed forty pounds at least and had a pair of cojones that would make many a larger animal proud. His ears were notched and scarred, pink scars marred his orange fur and his tail was half as long as it should be. He had one long, sharp front tooth. The other one was missing.

"Big, isn't he?"

"He's a regular tiger. Let's sit outside."

Carter opened two cans of cat food, put it in a dish and took it outside. Burps began chomping it down. They took a seat on the porch. The cat paused mid-chomp and gave out a loud belch.

"UUUURRRPP."

"Did he just do what I think he did?"

"That's why I call him Burps."

"He always does that?"

"All the time."

"I've never heard a cat burp. He's loud."

"Prime TV material. I'm thinking I'll get him on American Idol."

Burps belched again, finished his meal and wandered over to them. He began rubbing his head against Selena's leg and purring. It reminded Carter of a chain saw.

Selena stroked him behind the ears and Burps held up his paw and closed his eyes, arched his neck, purred louder and drooled through his tooth onto the deck.

"He's cute."

Cute wasn't how Carter would describe him, but who was he to argue? He told Selena what the Director had said.

"What did you do to that guy's wall?" he asked.

"Kuk Sool Won. It's a Korean martial art. I've been doing it since the tenth grade."

"What's your rank?"

"Seventh degree black."

"Remind me not to mess with you."

"I think you already did." She scratched Burps on top of his head. He jumped up in her lap and she grunted. He began kneading her leg. She grimaced.

"I've been thinking about the book. The language is archaic but the calligraphy is elegant and I can read it. Whoever copied it took his time, so that's not a problem. The problem is the section in Linear A. I need to compare what's in the book to other examples and to Linear B. We can read some of that variant."

"The Project has some big Cray computers. Steph can help you there."

"Steph?"

"Stephanie Willits. She's Harker's deputy and a genius with computers. We can scan the book into the system."

"That solves some problems. Once it's in the computers, we won't need to lug it around with us. We'd have access anywhere."

She took a sip from a glass of water.

"Tell me about Director Harker."

"She was part of the post nine eleven task force at Justice. She pissed off a lot of big shots by insisting it wouldn't have happened if the right hand had known what the left was doing. No one wanted to hear that, back then. It stalled her career. When Rice got elected he tapped her to head up the Project."

"What is the Project? You've got Crays, then you have resources. What do you do there?"

"It's the President's brainchild, a counterweight to the big intelligence agencies. Project is an acronym. Presidential Official Joint Exercise for Counter Terrorism. The joint part doesn't work too well, though, except for NSA. Harker's job is to cut through the smoke and mirrors tossed out by the big agencies and tell the President what's really going on. She's not afraid to speak her mind and she's a brilliant analyst. The three letter agencies don't like her. She answers only to the President, so they can't control her or tell her what to do. That doesn't stop them from trying."

"You're not an analyst."

"No. Ronnie and I get sent into the field to find things out. Sometimes to clean up messes that wouldn't have happened if CIA and the others had been doing their job."

"That's why you carry the gun?"

He looked out at the coastal range in the distance. The mountains formed blue ridges in the haze.

"Sometimes people shoot at us."

Selena put Burps down and stood up. He meowed loudly, gave her an insulted look and stalked off under the deck.

"Let's look at the book," she said.

They went inside and he got the book from the safe. At the kitchen table Selena began reading.

He got a kit out and began cleaning his pistol. He watched her turn the ancient pages. She was concentrating, the tip of her tongue exposed between her lips.

When Megan died he'd shut down any thoughts of letting someone get close again. Selena brought up old feelings, feelings he'd thought were dead and buried. He wasn't sure it was a good idea to bring those kinds of feelings back to life. He wasn't sure he wanted to let Selena in. You let someone in, it made you vulnerable. You weren't in control anymore.

Selena looked up.

"There's a list of some ingredients for an elixir of immortality, like cinnabar and gold. And there's a map to someplace in Tibet."

"Cinnabar?"

"That's what you make mercury from. Mercury was in a lot of the Chinese immortality formulas. It probably killed most of the people who took them. It might even have killed the Emperor. But China has known high grade deposits of cinnabar. They wouldn't care about that."

He held a bore light in the chamber of the .45, looked down the barrel.

"There's a reference to 'burning silver rocks' in the formula that I don't understand," she said.

He ran a cleaning brush through the bore.

She turned another page, studied it. "Do you think the Chinese government is behind this?"

"No. I think it's Yang acting on his own. Maybe he's just nuts, looking for an elixir of life."

Selena brushed hair back from her forehead and frowned.

"There has to be a rational purpose behind all this. I'll feel a lot better when we know what it is."

Carter watched her studying the text. She had retreated onto familiar ground, the expert linguist.

He'd had his share of beds but he'd never been a woman chaser. Besides, the Corps was hard on relationships. Then he'd met Megan and knew she was the one. It was a miracle to him that she'd felt the same way. When she died it left a hole inside him, big enough to pull him in and cover him up if he let it.

He'd plugged it with war. He was good at war, it was pretty much all he knew how to do. But making love with Selena had changed something. The hole was coming unplugged. It made him nervous, the feeling. It wasn't something he was used to.

Chapter Twenty

Harker sent a Gulfstream GIVSP to pick them up at Beale. It was a government executive model, all leather and luxury and wood inside the cabin. Five hours later, the lights of Washington stretched away off the port wing.

They stepped off the plane at Andrews. The air was hot and humid and smelled of jet fuel and diesel, with a hint of ripe garbage and stagnant water.

Ronnie was waiting. He wore another shirt from his Hawaiian collection, this one a hallucinogenic riot of purple, red and orange featuring waving palm trees in green and dancing Hula girls.

His black Hummer was parked inside the security zone barriers. On the way in Nick looked over at Selena, leaning back with her eyes closed. Maybe they'd ended up in bed because they'd been under fire together. Maybe it was the mine. Maybe it was karma. Whatever it was, he knew he'd better be careful about her.

At the Project building Ronnie went with them to the apartment.

"The Director said tell you when you got in there isn't anything can't wait for morning, so the two of you should make yourselves at home. There are two bedrooms for privacy."

Ronnie's expression gave no indication of what he might be thinking, which told Carter everything he was thinking.

"We meet with Harker at 0700. I'll see you then."

"Thanks, Ronnie."

"Hey, no problem. See you tomorrow."

He closed the door.

The living area where they stood was furnished with a hide-a-bed couch, lamp, coffee table and two chairs. A self contained kitchen unit featured a sink, burners and small fridge. The overhead lighting was uninspired, the carpeting a faded blue government industrial. The bedrooms had twin beds.

Selena turned to him.

"I think he knows we slept together."

"You picked up on that. There's no law says we ought to hide it."

He looked at her and wanted her. He stiffened. She saw it.

"Nick." She was tense. "I can't do this right now. Have sex, I mean. Part of me wants to, but it's too much, everything is moving too fast."

He wanted to crush her against him but her words brought an odd sense of relief. Maybe he wanted more than casual sex with Selena. The thought unsettled him.

"It's okay. It's like you said. Sometimes people end up in bed after something happens."

The tension went out of her face.

"You mind if I use the bathroom first?"

"No, go for it."

She went into the bath and closed the door. He thought about tomorrow. Harker would have a plan. She always did.

Chapter Twenty-One

They ate a mediocre breakfast in the cafeteria and at seven were in the Director's office. Stephanie was there, sitting at a computer console set off from Harker's desk. Steph had a wide, pleasant face and dark hair cut in bangs. She wore a black and red combo that concealed a few extra pounds. Gold bracelets jangled on her wrist.

She looked like the sort of person you'd see standing at the edge of a soccer field cheering on her kids. Stephanie didn't have any kids. She had a Glock 40 millimeter in a speed draw holster tucked high on her waist. She had the Project.

Harker said, "There's a new twist on Yang." She pushed a piece of paper and her pen across her desk to Selena. "Before I get into it, I need you to sign this."

"What is it?"

"I'm upgrading your security clearance. You sign that and you go to jail if you repeat anything you hear in here. You can't talk about it with anyone except us."

Selena said nothing. She signed.

Harker put the paper in a drawer. She said, "Deng Bingwen defected. Langley's got him."

Carter was stunned. "He's been building bombs for them for years. Why would he come over now?"

"Yang wants a war and Deng wants no part of it. Or so he says. He says Yang heads up a group called the White Jade Society. According to him it's a cover for a conspiracy to seize power. Langley is listening to what he says about China's nukes, but they don't believe him about a coup. They don't think anyone could pull that off, or would even try. If he's telling the truth, the money Yang stole could help fund a takeover."

Selena said, "The White Jade Society? White jade symbolizes immortality in Chinese culture. Maybe that's why they wanted the book. But it's just an old formula. No one could take it seriously."

Carter tugged on his ear. "Who's in this group?"

"Colonel Wu is one, but he's small fry. It wasn't hard to get a list. They're heavy hitters. The head of their naval forces, two of the missile base commanders, the Minister of Railways and several senior generals from the PLA, including two armored division commanders. There are other government and military leaders."

She tapped her pen. "A coup would destabilize the entire region. Pakistan, India, Russia, Iran. All those countries over there ending in 'stan'."

"You call Afghanistan stable?"

"Don't be a pain in the ass, Nick. You know what I mean."

Harker was definitely in Director mode. He decided to keep quiet.

Her intercom buzzed.

"Special Agent Jordan is here."

"Bring him up."

Jordan wore a blue suit and blue silk tie with gray accents that matched the color in his close cropped hair. The collar of a crisp, white shirt cut a deep crease in his thick neck.

He reminded Carter of pictures of Leadbelly, the famous blues singer. Big, hard, with a life of being black in America written deep inside his face. Jordan was a serious man.

Harker settled back in her chair. She said, "We identified one of the men who came after you in California from prints on the wine bottle. He's Wu's gofer."

Stephanie tapped on her keyboard. A picture came up on the big monitor.

"That's him," Carter said, "the one who tossed the grenade. Ugly bastard, isn't he?"

Jordan cleared his throat and pointed at the screen. "His name is Choy Gang. He's a real piece of work. The night you were in that mine a CHP patrolman made a routine stop outside San Francisco. He wrote up a safety violation. When he gave it to the driver he noticed something and went for his gun. The driver blew him away, three shots, nine mil. The camera in the cruiser taped the whole thing."

On screen, the video played. An arm and part of a face came out of the driver's window. There were three flashes as the gun fired and the officer went down. The video was badly lit but the hard looking face behind the gun was Choy's.

Jordan continued. "We got lucky and found a print on an empty casing. They usually burn away, but we've got a new process that sometimes can bring them out. We matched it up with Choy. We sent people over to the Consulate yesterday.

"They were told Choy was no longer in the country and had left two days before for the People's Republic, so there had to be a mistake in the identification. The Consulate representative said several weapons used by the security guards had been stolen a week before, so perhaps that was why Choy's prints were found. He expressed his sincere condolences over the death of our police officer and offered any assistance he might be able to provide. Then he showed our agents the door."

Nick had to say something. "Can't you get a warrant?"

"Not for the Consulate. It's off-limits. We don't want any incidents here."

"Shooting a cop isn't an incident?"

"Not big enough."

"What about Wu and Connor?"

"There's no hard evidence. Anyway, Choy is gone and there's nothing we can do about it."

Jordan looked at Carter as if it were all his fault. "What I want to know is why the Chinese are throwing grenades at you and in general making a whole lot of trouble."

Harker said, "Tell him about the book, Nick."

"What book?" Jordan ran his finger under his tight collar.

"An ancient book that belonged to Selena's uncle," Nick said. "The Chinese were looking for it when they killed him. He hid it in California. We went there to retrieve it. Then Choy showed up and you know the story.

"They were after the book, because why else drive up there? We think the attack here in DC was an attempt to kidnap Selena and get the location of the book from her."

"What's in it that they want?"

"We don't know yet. We'll find out, now that we have it."

"Where is it?"

Selena held up the book. "Right here."

Two old pieces of wood with yellowed pages between. It had already cost at least eight lives and might cost more before they were done.

Jordan loosened his tie. "I've been authorized to brief you. My unit tracks Asian criminal or terrorist activity. Something's up involving the Chinese Triads and Wu is mixed up in it. We followed him to a meeting with the Triad bosses from San Francisco, Oakland, New York, and Houston. That's a big deal. They never get together like that."

Jordan looked around the room, then at the Director.

"Why is a senior officer from China's military intelligence ordering sanctions and meeting with Chinese criminals? You want to help me out with that?"

Harker tapped FDR's pen on her desk while she considered what Zeke had said. Carter watched her. He knew the look. The analyst in her was computing possibilities. Debating how much to say, whether to bring him in. She made up her mind.

"We've received some new intelligence but we haven't had time to analyze it. What I'm about to tell you is speculation. You need to bear that in mind."

Jordan nodded.

"It's possible there is a group plotting to take power in China. The meetings Wu had with the Triads could have something to do with that."

"A plot to overthrow the Chinese government?"

"Yes. Colonel Wu is part of the group we're concerned about. It's led by General Yang. Head of their MI."

Jordan frowned. "The Triads don't like Communists. They'd like to see a change in government over there."

"Could be where the money comes in," Ronnie said. "The money he stole from Selena's uncle. Pay them to do something."

Harker tapped on the desk. "How could the Triads help Yang? Maybe in China, but here in the States? Why would he need them for anything?"

Selena brushed hair back from her forehead. "How do you take over a country as big as China? If we knew that, we might get an idea of what Yang wants from them."

Jordan said, "How do you take over China?"

Carter said, "You take out the heads of the government, all at once. You make sure the military is on your side, especially the army."

Ronnie picked at a surfboarder on his shirt. "You need surprise," he said.

"That's a given." Carter tugged on his ear. "Let's assume a coup was in progress. Go back to our original question; what could the Triads do here to support Yang over there?"

Jordan loosened his tie a little more. "What does Yang need to pull it off besides surprise?"

"Well, he needs time," Carter said. "Once he sets things in motion, the clock starts ticking and he wins or he goes down. He needs time to consolidate control and get his hands on all the strings."

The Director tapped her pen. "What would upset his time schedules?"

"Communications breakdowns. A problem with the military units. Interference from nations outside China could do it. World reaction is a big factor. What would we do, for example?"

Zeke unbuttoned his collar, a major breach of FBI dress code. Carter imagined J. Edgar turning over in his grave.

Harker's pen was going full speed on the desk. She realized what she was doing and set it aside.

"China is a known factor, with a stable government. A right wing coup would be dangerous. We wouldn't want that to happen."

"You think there's the political will to intervene, Director?" Jordan settled into his chair.

"If the President thought national security was at stake. But the risk of war would be huge."

"How could you keep us from getting involved?" said Jordan.

"If we wanted to? You couldn't. Unless..." Carter stopped.

"Unless what?"

"Unless we were occupied with something else. Something that had our attention while Yang took over."

"It would have to be a damn big attention getter," Ronnie said. "It would have to be something national, something that drew a lot of resources."

"What about a terrorist attack?"

Everyone looked at Selena.

"Well," she said, "don't look at me like that. Isn't that what you do here? Go after terrorists?"

"Yes." Harker watched her.

"An attack would keep everyone busy. Yang could use the Triads to make trouble while he grabs power."

Ronnie raised an eyebrow. "That's really devious. Remind me not to play poker with you. But we'd find out it was him. We'd have to do something."

"What? Send in troops? Nuke China?"

The room was silent as each of them thought about that.

"How many in the Triads?" Harker picked up her pen again.

Jordan said, "Several thousand in the Bay Area, if you count the youth gangs. They're usually sent as enforcers. Thousands more spread out over the country, particularly Houston, L.A. and New York. We're not certain."

Stephanie said, "We need more data."

"How do we get that?" asked Jordan.

The Director tapped her pen. "For openers, there's the book. Why does Yang want it? Selena, I need you to get it translated. I assume computer time will help?"

"It will. I've identified points in common between what I can read and what I can't. I want to run a matrix comparison. It should give us an idea."

"Good. Stephanie, program it in for her. While Selena is working on the translation you can run probability scenarios. I want to see what the computers say about what we've been discussing."

"Yes, Director."

Harker said, "All we've got is speculation and Deng's story. We have pieces of intelligence but we don't have any proof. We may be wrong."

"You don't think that," Jordan said.

"It doesn't matter what I think. I can't go to the President and tell him someone's trying to take over China without hard facts."

Jordan looked at his watch. "Director, I can let my boss know what we've been talking about, but no one's going to do much based on speculation."

"I'll brief you as we develop this."

"I guess that will have to do."

When Jordan was gone Selena said, "I'd like to go back to my rooms at the Mayflower. No offense, but that apartment of yours is depressing. It's confining, hard to think in. I need room to pace around."

"That's not a good idea. There's no security at the hotel."

Carter said, "She could stay at my place. I've got a spare bedroom. It would be a lot more comfortable than downstairs. There's an empty unit next door to mine. Ronnie can set up in there and keep an eye on things."

Harker gave him a curious look. "You think it's safer than here?"

"No, but it's safe enough. There's a security desk, cameras. They have to think Selena and I are dead in that mine."

"Selena, are you comfortable with that?"

"I guess so." She gave Nick a thoughtful look. "There's no reason those people would know we're still alive."

"All right. Just make sure you take every precaution."

Harker stood. "Let's get going."

Chapter Twenty-Two

Selena, Nick and Stephanie went down to the computer room. Wide doors of thick glass separated the room from the hallway. Stephanie punched in numbers on a keypad and stood close to a facial recognition scanner mounted on the wall. A line of green light tracked back and forth across her face. The glass doors slid open with a quiet hiss.

The room was frigid with arctic air conditioning. Half a dozen towering Cray super computers finished in an irritating red lined both sides of a polished aisle stretching the length of the room.

Stephanie walked past them and stopped at a large, semi-circular console in front of another Cray. This one was gray-black. Mounted on a tall cooling unit, it loomed over them like something out of a sci-fi movie, a huge, dark block transported from an alien dimension. Hundreds of blinking LEDs signaled it was active.

"This is Freddie." Stephanie took a seat at the console. "He's a Cray XMT, tweaked and maxed out. Freddie uses a multithreaded platform with global shared memory and parallel processing. There are over eight thousand CPU's in these cabinets. We can run a million simultaneous threads right here."

"How much memory?" Selena asked.

"Sixty-four terabytes. It's perfect for your book. We're linked to NSA and the rest of the National Security Network. Freddie will access every database, match patterns and look for anomalies. There's a database for every known language, ancient and modern. We can develop probability scenarios relevant to the content of the book and any other factors we choose to put in. When I'm not programming Selena's information, I'll be running those."

Stephanie looked at the computer as if it were a lover.

"We have as much time on him as we need. We'll input the book. You create the matrix for me, I'll program it in. Then we let it run."

Selena took a notebook from her handbag.

"I've already started."

They sat down and got to work. Carter thought about the discussion upstairs. Everything came back to Yang and Wu, and through them, to the White Jade Society.

White jade, immortality and Chinese Triads. It was like something out of a 50s comic book, but it wasn't funny.

***

On the other side of the country, Colonel Wu's scrambled phone signaled a caller. Very few people had that number. He hoped it wasn't the General on the line.

"Wu."

"This is Juggler," a voice said in English.

Wu sat up in his chair. Juggler was the code name of one of his best informants, stationed in Washington.

"Yes, Juggler."

"The Connor woman is here in Washington. She is traveling with a man who works in one of the counter-terrorist units. Apparently there was an armed confrontation with your men? In any event, they arrived last night."

"You are certain it is the right woman?"

"Certain. There is concern here. Speculation is high as to reasons for events, but there is no firm analysis yet. You have been identified as involved and your meetings with certain individuals in San Francisco have been noted."

Wu smiled. Confirmation the FBI had trailed him, but he already knew that. It was part of the plan. His negotiations with the Triads were complete and it was almost time to return to China. But not yet. There was still a chance to get the book. The day had just gotten better.

"The woman is staying with the agent, a man named Carter. It is a non-secure building." Juggler gave him the address.

"Good, Juggler. There will be a deposit in the usual way. Inform me of any new developments."

"Yes." The call ended.

With an address and a name Wu had a man's life in his hands. Whoever Carter was, his secrets would soon be Wu's. He knew Carter had been in California, from the insurance slip Choy had recovered.

Carter was probably the man who had stopped the attempt to kidnap the niece. He'd killed two agents in California and stopped Choy. The direct approach had failed. It was time for something more subtle. Wu knew the perfect person for what he had in mind. He picked up his phone and dialed a number in Washington to make the arrangements.

Now he could contact the General and give him a positive update. Things were looking up.

Chapter Twenty-Three

In a corner office on the fourth floor of the Ministry of State Security in Beijing, Senior Investigator Yao Aiguo studied a folder of reports. It was a hot day. The windows were open to the humid, smog-filled air outside. A small black electric fan fluttered the papers on his desk.

A large portrait of a beaming Chairman Mao hung on one wall of the office, across from a picture of the current President and Party Chairman. The room was painted a dingy yellow. It was sparsely furnished with a few wooden chairs, the desk where Yao sat and some filing cabinets. A picture of Yao and his parents provided the only personal note in the room. A cheap print of the famous mountains on the Yangtze River, now submerged under the waters of the Three Gorges dam, rounded out the decorations.

Yao looked at the latest report from the West and picked his nose. He looked at the result and wiped it off under his chair.

The reports from San Francisco about Colonel Wu bothered him.

Yao looked out his window at the heavy traffic crawling along on the broad avenue below. Motorcycles and scooters wove like manic squirrels in and out through thick clouds of exhaust smoke spewing from the trucks and busses. The leaves of the trees lining the boulevard hung wilted and defeated in the stifling heat.

An agent reported a meeting in a restaurant between Wu and his sergeant, Choy. Wu had sent Choy after a book belonging to a capitalist banker. The banker was dead. Yao had a thick file on the man, Connor, a heavy investor in Chinese industry. According to the report, Wu was responsible for the death. Why had Wu killed the American and sent someone after the dead man's book?

Inquiries had been made at the Consulate regarding Choy and the death of an American police officer. Now Choy was on his way back to China. It was all spread out in the papers on his desk. The eyes and ears of the Te-Wu, the Chinese Secret Service, reached across the Pacific as easily as to the next room.

Wu was supposed to be in San Francisco to probe the Chinese community there about money being funneled from America to the independence movement in the Tibet Autonomous Region. But Wu walked in the shadow of General Yang.

Why would Yang concern himself with a rabble of monks and peasants who had no possibility of achieving their revisionist goals? That kind of intelligence wasn't important enough to send a high ranking officer to investigate. Something wasn't right.

Few people in China had the authority and resources Yao wielded as a Senior Investigator of the Secret Service. He never gave up on an investigation until it was finished. He lived by the words of Sun Tzu, and it had made him one of the most successful agents in the two thousand year history of the Service.

If one waits patiently by the banks of the river, the Master had said, *sooner or later the bodies of one's enemies will float by.*

When they did, Yao would be there to pluck them from the water and make sure they were dead.

For Yao, it was simple. Loyalty to the nation and the Communist Party formed the foundation of a stable society. Yao thought society was even more important than family, the bedrock of Chinese culture. The greater good of the nation was the standard that must be followed. Yao's given name meant Love of Country. He considered himself a patriot and guardian of the greater good.

He reached for another file, this one on General Yang. In the People's Republic, no one was above investigation. All top military leaders received periodic scrutiny. If there was nothing irregular, there was no need for concern. If there was, measures were taken to correct the situation.

Yang's file gave no indication he was anything but an outstanding example of the professionalism now infusing the People's Liberation Army.

The file noted that Yang had founded a social and cultural group called the White Jade Society. Membership consisted of high-ranking officers and senior government leaders. Such societies were common. Belonging to a group of powerful associates was expected for someone in Yang's high position. The General was a man of influence in today's China.

He studied the file. Yang was Chief of Military Intelligence, the most powerful position on the General Staff, important in the daily oversight of China's considerable military might. He was also a member of the Central Military Commission of the Communist Party Central Committee. Anything to do with the Commission was political at the highest level and therefore dangerous. Yao would have to pursue his inquiries with care.

Yao's success as an investigator was based on obsessive attention to detail and a highly developed ability to think like his quarry. Why did Yang want Connor's money? Connor had been wealthy beyond belief. Yao made a note to follow the money trail.

Wu would never kill such an important man without orders, so there had to be some direct benefit to Yang. Money had always been a corrupter of men. If money was behind this, Yao would root out and expose Yang's complicity, but somehow it didn't feel right. Yang would not be able to spend that kind of money without being discovered and punished.

If it wasn't money, what else would motivate Yang? Wu had sent his Sergeant to fetch a book. What was in it? Had he been successful? Yao would assign a team to Choy when he arrived home. General Yang was in Beijing and surveillance would begin immediately. Colonel Wu was in San Francisco, but that was no obstacle. Yao would contact his agent in the Consulate and give him instructions.

Yao looked out the window. He decided to elevate Yang and Wu to priority level. Until he found out what they were doing, they were under suspicion of being enemies of the State, distinguished careers or not. Yao trusted his instincts. He would find out what was going on, it was only a matter of time.

He put his hands behind his head, leaned back and looked out into the hazy air of Beijing. Yang was up to something treasonous, he could feel it. Yao breathed deeply of the smog and felt the exhilaration of the hunt beginning.

Chapter Twenty-Four

Selena made herself at home in the spare bedroom. She had a few things sent over from her rooms at the Mayflower.

Carter's apartment was minimal in terms of decoration. A good copy of a Paul Klee painting hung over the couch. The carpet was a neutral tan. There were Japanese woodcuts on one of the walls. The furniture was European Modern, clean and functional.

Ronnie sat on the couch, reading a magazine. He'd set up shop next door. The book was locked up back at the Project. Selena had scanned it onto her laptop and was working on the translation.

Carter was in the kitchen putting together a salad and pasta. He liked salad and pasta. It didn't challenge his culinary skills, which were minimal at best. Selena's cell phone rang. He heard her talking, voice excited and pleased.

She paused, covered the phone. "This is an old friend, Cathy Chen. We used to go out and have drinks, go dancing, that kind of thing. She's here in Washington and wants to get together. We're not supposed to be out on the town, but I thought she could come over here and we could talk. You don't mind, do you?"

"No, of course not."

Selena gave directions and hung up.

"I need to let security know downstairs. When is she coming?"

"She said it would take about half an hour."

"Then we'd better eat. Everything's ready."

"Best news I've heard today," said Ronnie from the couch.

Carter set the food on the table and cracked a bottle of Pinot. He called security and told the guard to expect Selena's friend. They sat down.

"How are you doing with the translation?"

"I've got the Sanskrit done and I'm making progress with the Linear A. It's all here on my laptop. You remember I told you one of the ingredients for the elixir was something called burning silver rocks?"

"Yes?"

"The text says the silver rock turns black. The directions say to crush the rocks and leach them with what is probably some kind of acid. That turns the rock gold, or at least yellow in color. I've never seen the particular word construction before. Then you powder the result and mix it with the other ingredients in a liquid infusion. Or maybe it's a solution."

"Sounds like Alchemy. The Alchemists were always trying to turn things into gold."

"This formula already contains gold. I have an idea about those rocks. I think they're uranium ore, extremely high grade. I asked Stephanie to program my translation into her scenarios to see what comes up. We'll know tomorrow."

"How do you figure uranium?"

"What kind of rocks 'burn'? There's nothing in the text about heating them. The only thing I could think of is something radioactive. I did some research. Uranium ore can be silver in color. It oxidizes and turns black."

"China has uranium deposits. Why would that interest Yang?"

"China's deposits are poor quality. It takes a lot of processing to get anything you can use."

"Like for bombs?" Ronnie asked.

"Yes. If those rocks are from a high grade deposit, Yang would want to know where it was. There's only one known deposit like that in the world, in Saskatchewan. The Canadians get as much as seventy-five percent useful refinement from their raw material. The regular stuff produces only one or two percent."

"That would give Yang something to speed up China's nukes program. It makes more sense than hunting for an elixir of life." Carter drank some wine.

Ronnie buttered a piece of sourdough bread and took a large bite. The crumbs dropped on the polyester surf scene he was wearing.

"What do you think, Nick? Is Yang planning an attack here? He's got to be crazy if he thinks we wouldn't retaliate."

"Crazy as a fox, maybe. Politics being what it is, he might pull it off by setting someone up as the fall guy, like a terrorist group or even the Triads. They're right here and a lot easier to go after than whoever is running things in Beijing."

"But the Triads would blow the whistle on him."

"Sure, but where's the proof? It would be their word against his, and he'd be sitting on the trigger of China's nukes. If you were a bunch of our politicians trying to calm everyone down, would you tell the truth? They'd spin it like crazy."

"You'd think Yang would be satisfied with all the power he's already got."

"Power is never enough," said Selena. "At least it seems those who have power always want more."

"You're a cynic." Ronnie said.

"It's true here at home. Why would it be any different in Communist China?"

Carter took a fork full of pasta.

The buzzer rang. He got up and went over to the intercom. "Yes."

"Mister Carter, your guest is here."

"Send her up." He looked at Selena. "Your friend is downstairs."

"You'll like her."

Ronnie wiped his plate with bread and downed the rest of his soda. He never drank alcohol. He'd seen families and friends destroyed by it on the Reservation. "I'll go next door. Let me know if you need me for something."

There was a light knock on the door as Ronnie reached it. He opened it and stepped aside.

Cathy Chen had long, jet black hair and classic Eurasian beauty. Her golden skin and good looks would fade in a few years, but for now she was in her prime, radiating vitality.

She wore a burgundy silk cheongsam, cut low and tight against her body. It showed off her slim figure to perfect advantage. It would have made some women look like a high priced hooker. On Cathy Chen it provided the touch of elegance and style it was meant to convey. A necklace of delicate white jade graced her throat. She carried a paper bag with a high end shop logo on it. The neck of a bottle stuck out.

"Cathy!"

"Hi, Selena."

They moved toward each other and embraced. Ronnie glanced at Nick, shrugged his shoulders, and closed the door behind him.

"Cathy, this is Nick."

She took his hand, her touch cool. Her eyes were bright. He thought he detected something there, but then it was gone.

"Nice to meet you, Nick. This is your place?"

"Yes."

"Great view." She turned to Selena. "Hey, girlfriend. What have you been up to, aside from Nick, here?"

"Oh, not too much. Nick and I have been hanging out some. I'm working on a translation and doing some consulting work."

"It's about time you hung out with someone. You haven't been seeing anyone since that jerk you tossed in Greece—what's his name…"

"Ted. But Nick and I are just friends."

"Oh sure." She gave him a look. "Well, it's great to see you."

"How about you, what are you doing?"

"I just started with a consulting firm here in Washington. They've got a client in China and they hired me as the token Asian."

"Oh, come on, Cathy, no one's going to take you on as a token. Where are you staying?"

They began talking away. After a few minutes Cathy broke out the bottle she'd brought with her.

"Let's open this. I know you appreciate wine and this one is supposed to be excellent. It's Australian. They're making some really good stuff now."

Nick got out an opener, some fresh glasses, and pulled the cork. Cathy poured. She held up her glass.

"Money, health, love and time to enjoy them. Here's to you."

They clinked glasses. The wine was good, full bodied and smooth, with an underlying taste Nick couldn't pin down. They moved into the living area and sat down, carrying the glasses.

Cathy glanced over at Selena's laptop, still open on the desk.

"Is that the translation you're working on? What's it about?"

"Yes. It's an old Sanskrit text on medicine. Nothing very earth shaking."

"You always were a whiz at that kind of thing. Working right from the source. I had enough trouble researching the information that was already translated."

Carter felt dizzy. The light was fluctuating. Cathy looked at him.

"I don't feel very well," Selena said.

"Can I get you anything?" said Cathy.

Selena's wine glass slipped out of her hand and dropped to the floor. The wine spread in a widening stain over the carpet. Nick tried to get up, but his legs turned to rubber and he crashed to the floor. His vision blurred. The last thing he heard was Cathy Chen telling Selena she was sorry.

Chapter Twenty-Five

"Nick. Nick." Ronnie's voice was urgent. "Nick! Wake up."

He opened his eyes. He had a hell of a headache. Ronnie bent over him.

"Where's Selena?"

"She's okay, she's awake, just not feeling so good. Jesus, Nick, I thought you were dead when I came in."

Suckered and drugged. He remembered the odd taste in the wine. He got to his feet and a blacksmith shop opened up inside his head.

Ronnie helped him to the couch where a white-faced Selena was sitting with her eyes closed.

"You all right?" Carter touched her arm.

"I think so. What happened?"

"We were drugged. Your friend slipped it into the wine."

"Nick, I'm sorry. I can't believe this."

He looked around. Selena's computer was gone. Nothing else seemed out of place The drugged bottle of "really good stuff" sat half empty on the coffee table..

"Not your fault, don't be sorry. How could you know she would do this?"

"Why would she drug us?"

"She took your computer. She must be an agent for Wu. Nobody else would know you were working on the book."

Selena looked stricken. "The whole book was on that computer. That means they have it, Yang's got what he wants."

"Then maybe now they'll leave us alone. Don't worry about it. We'll figure out what to do. I've got to call the Director."

"I'll do it." Ronnie placed the call. Harker wasn't going to be thrilled at the news. After a minute Ronnie hung up.

"The word's out on Chen. I gave her description and we've got security tapes we can pull from downstairs. We'll find her."

"How long were we out?"

"Not long. I checked back about half an hour after I went next door. When you didn't answer, I let myself in."

"That bitch." Selena was furious. "I thought she was my friend. She was my friend. I'd like to get my hands on her right now."

"We'll get her," Carter said. "I wonder how Wu knew we were in Washington? The last the Chinese saw of us, we were buried in that mine."

"That's something we're going to have to find out." Ronnie went to the kitchen and brought back two glasses of water.

"Drink up. Guaranteed, no drugs."

Carter woke in the middle of the night. The bedroom door was partly open. He heard muffled sobbing coming from the living room. Selena was sitting on the couch, her head in her hands. He was about to go to her when something stopped him. He knew about grief. Sometimes it needs to be a private thing.

He went back to bed, but it was a long time before he fell asleep.

He dreamed of Megan.

Megan was across the street, waiting for a bus. He waved, but she didn't seem to see him. Endless streams of cars roared by and he couldn't get across to her. He saw the bus coming and she still hadn't seen him. He called her name but no sound came out.

Then he was standing next to her. She looked at him, shook her head, a sad expression on her face.

"There's no point in waiting, Nick."

"Waiting for what?"

"For the bus. See?"

She pointed at the large, black bus bearing down on them. The destination sign said AIRPORT.

The driver was visible through the windshield. He was faceless and he had a grenade in his hand.

"Where are you going," Nick said.

"There's no point in waiting."

Then he was back in the village, feeling the rifle kick back against his shoulder, one, two, three times, watching the grenade come toward him, watching a child die.

He woke soaked in sweat, heart pounding, his mind filled with thoughts of loss.

Chapter Twenty-Six

Next morning Harker was dressed in her trademark black pantsuit. She wore gold and ruby hanging earrings, a wild variation for her.

"How are you feeling, Nick?"

"Like I've got a world class hangover."

"I'm wondering how they knew you were here, and how they found you."

"It would have been easy enough. They had my name. I just didn't believe they were after us. They had to think we were killed in the mine."

"I agree. So how did they make the jump back to Washington?"

"Someone must have told them Selena was here," Ronnie said. "They could have tracked her to Nick's."

The Director tapped FDR's pen on her desk, thinking things through.

"Not many people knew you were here. The people in this room. The FBI. No one else is in the loop at this point. It must be the FBI."

"A mole at the Bureau?"

"Has to be. Someone told Wu you were alive and here in Washington. Sending your friend was smart, Selena, you would never suspect her."

Carter rubbed his bandaged ear. "They have Selena's computer and that means they have the book. It's what they've been after all along."

"We can't do anything about that now. Selena, how far did you get?"

"I translated all of the Sanskrit and I have good assumptions about some of the Linear A. It's an unbelievable story."

"How so?"

"The first part is a treatise on the immune system and circulation of the blood and has part of a formula for creating an elixir of immortality. Nothing we didn't know. Some information needed to complete the formula is missing. There's a reference to a second book called 'The Silver Garuda' that has the rest of it.

"The formula isn't what's important. If the book is true, it changes history. It says the First Emperor isn't buried at Li Shan. It claims he was taken to Tibet, where an order of priests would give him the secret of immortality. The text says the secret is thousands of years old."

"You're kidding," Carter said.

"That's what it says. It has a map showing where the emperor was supposedly taken. It's near Mount Kailash in the Tibet Autonomous Region."

Harker was toying with her pen again. "How do you evaluate the historical material? Is there any truth in it?"

"I don't know, but if it's true the emperor isn't in Li Shan and someone found his real burial site, it would be a fantastic archeological and cultural discovery. Emperor Huang was obsessed with immortality. He would have done anything to obtain it. Maybe he built his tomb to throw his enemies off track.

"One of the ingredients of the elixir is the powder of 'burning silver rocks'. The computer confirmed that those rocks must be very high grade uranium ore. Ore like that would impact China's nuclear weapons production."

Harker's pen drummed away on her desk. "Yang might want the book to find out where those priests got their supplies. But how would he know that? We just translated it and no one read it before."

"If he has the companion book," Carter said, "he'd know your book would have what he's looking for. Did you find out where these rocks came from?"

Selena brushed a lock of hair from her forehead. "No. But directions can be found where the emperor was taken. That location is marked on the map."

"How accurate is the map?"

"The names of the landmarks are archaic and we'd need to find modern equivalents. Mount Kailash is unmistakable. It shouldn't be hard. That part of the Tibetan Plateau is fifteen thousand feet high and barren. There's not much there except yaks and a few villages."

"We can pin down landmarks with satellite imagery and GPS," said Harker. She made a note. "We'll get that today. In the meantime, how shall we handle the FBI? Nick, you know Jordan. Is he our mole?"

"I can't see that. He's dedicated. I don't think he's the one."

"Then we need to bring him up to speed. We have to inform the FBI we think there's a leak. Steph, how are you coming with those risk scenarios?"

"They'll be finished this morning."

"Good. We'll meet with Jordan this afternoon. Anything else?"

No one had anything to add.

Chapter Twenty-Seven

There was no sign of Cathy Chen. Selena, Ronnie, Stephanie and Nick were in the Director's office with Jordan. Harker told him about the theft of Selena's computer. She tossed out the conclusion there was a mole in the Bureau.

"I don't believe it."

"Do you have a better explanation? Someone passed the information to Wu. Your people and ours are the only ones who knew Nick and Selena survived. General Hood at NSA is in the loop now. It's not him and it's not one of us. It's got to be someone in the Bureau."

"Am I a suspect, then?" Jordan was getting angry.

"No."

"I don't like what you're saying."

"I don't like saying it. If I'm right, we have to find out who the informant is. If I'm wrong, I'll owe you an apology. What I want to know now is if I can count on you to help us sort this out."

Jordan took a deep breath. "All right, Director. But I think you're wrong."

"Then help us prove it."

"I'm not sure where to start."

"Communications," Carter said. "Our mole had to contact Wu. Run a trace on the phone numbers of people in your unit, cross reference Wu's numbers from our intercepts, see if there's a connection. NSA does this all the time."

"I wouldn't call Wu or his contact from my own phone if I were the mole."

"People get over-confident. They make mistakes. It's worth a try."

Jordan nodded. "Okay."

"Financial records." It was Ronnie. "We run checks on everyone in the Asian Criminal Enterprise Unit and see if someone's getting richer than they're supposed to be."

"I can get authority for that," said Jordan. "All right, I'll do it. But I want to keep this internal. If one of ours is bad, then we have to be the ones to take him down. Agreed?"

Harker nodded. "Agreed."

Carter felt sorry for him. Who needs to hear someone you're working with might be a traitor?

"Is there anything else, Director? I'm due back at headquarters."

"No. I know this isn't easy."

"No, it's not. I think you're wrong, but you're right about one thing, we have to know one way or the other." Jordan got up, annoyed.

Stephanie escorted him out. When she returned, the Director went on with the meeting.

"We will no longer involve the FBI in what we're doing, until we know who tipped off Wu. I didn't want Jordan to hear the next part of our discussion. Stephanie, what do the scenarios indicate?"

"As we thought. High probability of a conspiracy to take over control of China. The computer factored in the defector interviews, all the rest of the intelligence we've been getting from China in the last few months, the FBI's concern about the Triads, Wu's actions, everything.

"Selena was curious about a reference to burning rocks. The computer confirms it refers to high grade uranium ore, over ninety-seven percent probability. The process described in the book is the same as what we use today to produce yellowcake. That gets refined into uranium oxides. You put that through centrifuges to get the enriched uranium you need for bombs. You can get yellowcake from low grade ore but it's tedious. High quality ore yields a lot more for the same effort."

"That would explain the passage in the text about changing from silver to yellow or gold," Selena said.

The Director set her pen to the side. "What about the immortality elixir? What does the computer say about that?"

Stephanie adjusted the gold bracelets on her wrist. "The computer doesn't have the bias we do about the existence of an elixir of immortality. It projects the elixir may be discovered."

"What's the probability of success?"

"For finding the complete formula and the place where it was manufactured, eighty-six per cent. The same for finding the location of the uranium. Regarding the coup, that's more hopeful. At best, there's about a fifty-fifty chance Yang can pull it off."

"What happens if he doesn't find the elixir?"

"Still fifty-fifty. They're not related."

Carter said, "Does the computer back up our ideas about the Triads?"

Stephanie nodded. "Provide a distraction while Yang brings up the tanks. I was careful not to program in our conclusions. The computer was analyzing the same intel we have and its conclusions are similar. The scenario indicates high probability for West Coast targets in the Bay Area, but we could be looking at attacks on a national level. The emphasis is on disruption of basic infrastructure, including the Golden Gate and Bay bridges, the transportation system, water supply and especially power sources."

"What do you think will happen, if we're right?" Carter tugged at his ear.

Harker picked up her pen. "It could lead to war."

"Let me see if I've got this right, Steph," said Ronnie. "If there was a big terrorist attack here there'd be plenty of speculation and talk, right? World attention?"

"Yes."

"And that would keep the Chinese government and everyone else preoccupied?"

"Yes."

"So while the world is looking the other way, Yang makes his move and takes over."

Stephanie nodded agreement. "That's about it."

Harker tapped her upper lip with her pen. "The big question is when? It must be soon, or why move on Connor and grab his accounts? Nick, if you were doing this, when would you do it?"

"I'd pick a time when our guard was down, when people were thinking about something else. Like a holiday."

"The Fourth of July." It was Selena. "That's five days from now. It's the only holiday coming up anytime soon. Big crowds for fireworks, traffic jams, lots of confusion. If they're going to try something soon, I'd bet on that."

"That makes sense." Tap, tap, tap on her desk. "I'm going to have to give a heads up to Homeland Security. I can't go to the President yet."

"But how much can we tell them," Nick said. "Whatever we give them is bound to leak. Yang will find out we're on to him."

"I only have to tell them enough to get them to raise the security watch. I can do that without giving away the store. The main thing is to get them on it. This is going to get complicated."

Elizabeth dreaded the nightmare of Washington bureaucracy. If the various agencies started putting in their two cents they'd argue about what to do and how to do it and who would be in charge and form a joint task force. It would be next year before anything happened. There wasn't time for that.

She made up her mind. "It's Homeland Security's job to be on the lookout for an attack. We can alert them, but that's all we can do and all we have to do. We've got mobility the others don't and we need to take action. I want something to back up our analysis."

"How do we get that?" Carter reached under his jacket and adjusted his holster. He felt a headache start. He knew what was coming.

"Right from the start everything has centered on the book. Yang wanted what's in it and now he has that. He has the same directions and information we do. His best chance at finding out anything more is to look for the place where the emperor was taken. That's in Tibet. We need to get there before he does, document anything we find and block Yang from getting it."

"That area is pretty remote," Carter said. "We could get in with minimal risk of detection, but how long will it take to find this place? We don't even know for sure it exists."

"We'll run satellite images and cross reference with the map in the book. If we can get a good idea where, we'll go in."

"Who's going?"

"Don't worry, Ronnie, you're on the team."

"You need me along," Selena said.

"You don't know what you're asking," Carter said.

"You don't think a woman can do the tough stuff?"

"That's not what I mean."

"What do you mean?"

"We'll have to jump in. It's rugged terrain and high altitude. If the Chinese are there it could get bad, fast."

"I've been skydiving for years, I'm qualified. I have over seventy jumps. None of you speak the languages and you couldn't make sense of any writing you might come across. You need me."

"It's not a goddamned farmer's field. It's the Himalayas, for Christ's sake."

Selena just looked at him.

Harker said, "Anyone on that team has to be armed, Selena."

"Guns don't bother me."

"They're not guns, they're weapons. How do you feel about shooting someone? You think you could do that?"

Her heart started pounding. She took a deep breath. "If I had to."

"You have a point about the language barrier." Tap, tap.

There was silence. After a moment Carter said, "How would we go in?"

"I think a B-1B modified for Special Ops, out of Dyess. That plane is perfect for high altitude penetration. Chinese radar won't pick it up. With a small team we can give you a vehicle, supplies, everything you need. How many personnel do you want?"

"Fewer is better," said Ronnie. "If we run into opposition, more bodies won't get us out of trouble and we lose mobility with more. Keep it small."

"Nick?"

"I agree with Ronnie. One vehicle, weapons, a few days of supplies. In light and out as fast as we can. But I want to know exactly what we're getting into before we get on that plane."

"We'll get as much intel as we can." Harker's pen tapped, went still. "Selena, I'm willing to put you on the team but I want Nick to get you familiar with the weapons you'll have to carry."

"That's fine by me."

"Wait a minute," Nick said. "Selena's not combat trained."

"Then I guess you'd better get her up to speed. She goes. We don't have a lot of time. Yang and his people are going to get there as fast as they can. We have to beat them to it."

"You're putting us at risk."

"She goes." Harker's voice had an edge in it. Carter had heard it before. It was her don't-fuck-with-me voice.

He gave in. "When do we leave?"

"We have to set up transport and supplies and get a clear location. If it's a go, tomorrow night. That gives you time to work with Selena on the range. Ronnie, you get on logistics. Make sure nothing points back to us and that you've got plenty of whatever you need. Better add climbing gear. It'll be cold weather and thin air. Lay in oxygen."

"What about radiation equipment? If there's anything there, we need to know it."

"Good point. Take a counter and dosimeters for everyone."

"Are you going to tell the President?" Carter asked.

"No. Not yet. He needs to be able to deny it."

She didn't say what they were all thinking. If Rice had to deny it, something would have gone wrong. Big time wrong.

Like that, they were on their way to Tibet.

Chapter Twenty-Eight

Colonel Wu made the call on his encrypted satellite phone.

"Yang."

"Sir. I am pleased to report success. I have a complete copy of the book in my possession."

"You are sure it is the correct book."

"Yes, sir."

"Is it the original?"

"No, sir, it is a computer transcription with a complete scan of the original and translation. After this call I will transmit it to your private terminal."

"Where is the original?"

"As far as I can determine it is inaccessible."

"What is the status of your negotiations with the Triads?"

"Everything has been agreed to as you wished. They are ready to carry out Summer Wind on the American holiday. I offered four hundred million American dollars and full independence, with mutual security agreements, for Taiwan. As you predicted, the money by itself would not have been enough. Offering Taiwan was irresistible. The bosses are all what the Americans call high rollers. Gamblers. They could not refuse to gamble for stakes on the world's table."

"It is a gamble they will lose. Very good, Senior Colonel Wu. You will return home immediately."

Wu flushed with pride. Senior Colonel! The hard jump in the military hierarchy.

"Yes, sir. Thank you, sir."

"You've done well, Wu. When you arrive, report directly to me."

"Yes, sir. Do you have any other instructions?"

"None at the moment. Transmit the information." Yang ended the call.

A few key strokes on his computer and the information was on its way. Wu got out a suitcase and began packing. There was a plane leaving in four hours.

In Beijing, General Yang set the phone down and allowed himself a moment of satisfaction.

The Elixir of Immortality. The goal of thousands of years of Chinese tradition. It could be his. But it was probably just another old recipe that brought death, not life.

A raid in Tibet had turned up a Sanskrit text on the First Emperor, called "The Silver Garuda." It was known that Yang collected anything about the First Emperor and his search for immortality. The book had found its way to him.

The elixir of immortality was a defining element in the life of Emperor Huang. Yang thought of the Emperor as a kindred spirit, a model to be emulated and surpassed. Huang had taken a vast land ruled by feuding warlords and beset by barbarian enemies and forged it into an empire. He had started China on the path of greatness. Anything remotely related to him was of interest.

When Yang read the translation he'd seen the possibilities. It was clear the formula used potent radioactive materials. According to the text, directions to the source of those materials could be found in a second book, the one now residing on his computer.

The quality of China's uranium made refinement time-consuming and expensive. With the location of superior deposits he'd have what he needed to bring hundreds of the new warheads on line. Lighter, more deadly. The designs were in place.

That made him think of Deng, the treasonous little dog. It was annoying that Deng had defected. Sooner or later Deng would be eliminated. Meanwhile, others carried on his work.

It would take time to ready the missiles. Perhaps two years, but Yang was patient. As for the elixir, once he had the complete formula, he'd test it on prisoners. The book was found in Tibet. He'd use Tibetans for the trials. The corners of his frog like mouth turned upward in a smile.

He went to his computer and opened the message. Yang was shocked to learn the emperor was not at Li Shan, more so when he saw where he had been taken. The site was marked on the map in the book. When Colonel Wu returned, Yang would send him there.

His thoughts turned to the plan. The American holiday was close. It was time to activate Summer Wind, the operation that would change the destiny of China forever. A new Dynasty would be born.

Yang picked up his phone and began calling the others. Mixed in with inconsequential conversation was the same message each time. Spring has ended, summer is upon us. The planes would remain on the ground unless he released them. The tanks were ready. The submarines with their missiles would be his. So would the ICBMs targeted on the West. That would keep the Americans and other foreign dogs at bay. The railroads would shut down. Divisions commanded by members of the Society and trusted officers under them would occupy Beijing.

He'd arrest the entire Politburo Standing Committee of the Party and the President, cut off the head of the current leadership and replace it with himself. China would become the most powerful nation that had ever existed and step into her rightful place. Yang was certain the First Emperor would understand his ambition, if he were alive today.

For no reason at all he remembered the time he'd broken the big ceramic bowl his mother brought out for special occasions. It was the one painted with blue herons standing in the reeds, slim and handsome, like her. He'd been what, eight years old? He'd only wanted to fill it with water and sail his toy boat. It had slipped from his small hands and shattered into a thousand pieces on the tiles of the kitchen floor.

His mother had run into the room. When she'd seen what he had done, she'd begun shrieking and hitting him. She'd hit him again and again while he'd screamed, cursing and beating him with the heavy wooden paddle she used in the big cooking wok until it broke, until a neighbor had run in and pulled her away from him.

He'd never forgotten the feeling of powerlessness and shame. Well, it was different now. As to his mother, she had already paid for his humiliation. Yang had seen to that.

Yang opened a cabinet of carved teakwood on his desk. He pushed on a decorative dragon and watched the hidden compartment spring open. He took out a pipe, a lamp and a small ball of sticky opium. He went to the couch, lit the lamp and lay back on one arm. He lit the pipe and drew the blissful smoke deep into his lungs, drifting off into a pleasant dream of a vast, blue plain with endless rows of people kowtowing before him.

Emperor.

Chapter Twenty-Nine

Selena and Nick were in the basement range at the Project.

"What the hell was that about upstairs?" she said.

"You heard what I said. You haven't ever done anything like this, jumps or not. You sure as hell haven't jumped at high altitude."

"You don't think I can handle it."

He looked at her. "You want the truth? No, I don't. I don't want you to get killed. I think you could probably handle anything you're trained to do. You're not trained for this."

"I guess you'd better start training, then."

Carter saw it was a battle he couldn't win. First Harker, now her. Mules had nothing on women when it came to stubborn. Megan had been the same way, when she'd made up her mind about something.

"All right." He ran two man-sized silhouette targets down range.

"Let's start with our sidearm. What kinds of pistols are you familiar with?"

Her voice was neutral. Truce. "A .22 revolver when I was learning. Then I went to a .357 Colt Python. After I got used to the recoil, my instructor gave me a Glock. Either automatic or a revolver, I've shot both."

He laid two pistols on the table. He took one, ejected the empty magazine and pulled back the slide. "What's your first rule?"

"Mmm. Make sure it's not loaded. Or is."

"Right, and make sure it's not pointed somewhere it shouldn't be." He let the slide go forward.

"This pistol is a little heavy but it helps with the recoil. It was developed for US Special Operations Command, SOCOM. It's a Heckler-Koch like mine, chambered in .45 ACP. A lot of stopping power and made for close quarters, although it has good accuracy up to thirty yards or so with the laser pointer. That's this unit, under the barrel."

As he slipped into the routine of instructor he began to relax. He showed her how to turn the laser on. He pointed down range, centering the red dot on one of the targets.

"Where the dot is, that's where the bullet goes. Always aim for a center body shot, none of that stuff you see in the movies. We'll tweak the sights as we go along, so you'll be sure to hit whatever you're shooting at. This is the de-cocker lever. The safety is ambidextrous. You can carry this pistol cocked and locked."

"Maybe we won't have to shoot anything."

"Maybe. Show me your stance."

Selena took up her stance, a good hold, both hands, body crouched and turned to present a minimal target. Someone had taught her well. He made a minor adjustment to her elbow.

"Good stance. Let's load the magazines."

They filled four 15 round magazines and put on ear protection and goggles, niceties non-existent in the field.

"Lock and load." He inserted a magazine and Selena did the same, then they racked the slides.

"Aim for the center of the body, and fire when you're ready."

She fired, then again. She squeezed off the rest of the magazine. Carter followed suit. They laid the guns down on the bench and he pulled back the targets. Her target had a neat group of holes in the center.

They spent another hour with the H-K and he was satisfied. It was a relief. She'd said she could shoot, but he'd heard that from people who couldn't hit an elephant standing next to them.

"Now we have another toy. You don't have any experience with these."

He took out another H-K, the MP-5N submachine gun.

"This is our primary weapon. They only weigh around eight pounds and they've got a lot of firepower. This is an H-K too, developed for the Navy Seals. It has a safety just like the .45, so you can carry it ready to go. Ours will be chambered for .40 Smith, which gives us more bang for the buck than the regular nine millimeter. Thirty round magazine, snaps in here, charge like this." He showed her how.

"It has a folding retractable stock. You can carry it short or use it as an assault rifle." He pulled the stock out until it locked in place. "Let's try that first, it's easier to get used to."

They loaded up. He showed her how the selector switch worked and had her shoot in semi-auto, then moved her to full auto fire. She got the knack of getting off a three round burst with ease. Then they tried it without the stock extended. That was harder, but Selena picked up the trick of control.

He was impressed. She hit what she shot at. He hoped she wouldn't have to do it when someone was shooting back. That wasn't anything like this. When the adrenaline kicked in, all the fancy target shooting went out the window and you missed eight times out of ten. It wasn't the same.

He showed her how to clear a jam, but she didn't need to know how to field strip her piece. They were only going to be in Tibet for a short time. Ronnie and he would maintain the weapons.

"We'll also have these," he said, "but you won't be carrying them. Still, I thought you should know how they work." He opened a box of M-67 grenades.

"This is a fragmentation grenade. We're not going to practice with them here."

He smiled, but she didn't get the joke. The seriousness of what they were doing was sinking in. Pistols were one thing, machine guns and grenades, another.

"This is a safety clip. You have to remove that first. It keeps the lever down if the pin is accidentally pulled."

He mimicked removing the clip.

"Now the grenade is ready for use, but it's not armed until you pull the pin. It has a kill radius of 50 feet and does a lot of damage beyond that. To throw it, set your feet apart, hold this lever tight with your right hand and put your index finger of the other hand through the loop on the pin."

He showed her the arming position.

"Then you pull the pin. As long as the lever is held down it won't go off. You can reinsert the pin if you have to. Hold it next to your gut when you arm."

He demonstrated. "The way you pull the pin is to pull the grenade away from it, not the other way around. It requires a firm pull. Then you let fly and duck. You've got about 4 seconds before it blows. If you ever have to do this, just make sure it goes a long way away from you."

"You really expect me to throw grenades?"

"No. I just think you should know how it's done. Just in case."

"You have a knife for me, too?" There was something in her voice.

"Yes, you'll have a knife."

"Are you going to show me how to cut someone's throat? Or stab them in the kidney or something?"

"Selena…"

"Maybe I should have a flame thrower. Do you have a flame thrower for me, Nick?"

"Selena, what's the matter?"

"Nothing. I don't want to talk about it."

"How can you not want to talk about nothing?"

"Are we done, Nick?"

"Yes, but…"

Selena turned and walked out. The door to the range slammed behind her.

He tried to figure out why she was angry. She'd done fine with the pistol and the MP-5. She'd put fifteen rounds of .45 armor piercing right in the center of a man sized silhouette and never flinched. She'd picked up the tricks of the MP-5 in record time and had cheerfully chopped those silhouettes into confetti, so what was so different about grenades?

He thought about it. A grenade compromises our humanity. It's a symbol of all the forces that make us turn our backs on what Abe Lincoln called the better angels of our nature. All packed up in a nice, olive green package. Selena hadn't been trained to kill, as he'd been. She hadn't learned to set civilization and conscience aside because self-preservation and accomplishing the mission demanded it.

You threw a grenade, everything within a fifty foot radius was DOA. A grenade was indiscriminate. It wasn't like a pistol. With a pistol, there was an illusion of control, targeting a specific threat.

Carter thought about that kid in Afghanistan, who couldn't possibly understand what he was doing. What could be more evil then grenades in the hands of children? How could anyone think God wanted that?

The afternoon had turned into a black hole. He began stripping the weapons to clean them. Ronnie walked in.

"What's with Selena?"

"What do you mean?"

"She just went by without a word, looking pissed. You have an argument or something?"

"I wouldn't call it that."

"How did she do with the weapons?"

"She did well. If we get into something, I think she'd hit what she was shooting at. She didn't like grenades much."

"You think she should come along? It could get pretty hairy out there."

"You don't think she should go?"

"She's a woman and she's a civilian. She's not combat trained. She could get herself or us killed if we run into opposition."

"We need her. Without her we might not be able to figure out how to get into that complex. She's been under fire twice and she didn't lose it. Selena can take care of herself."

"Yeah, but she's never done anything like this. If we have any trouble she could be a real liability."

"I guess we'll have to make sure that doesn't happen."

"You going to be able to keep your feelings for her out of this?"

"Don't go there. You know me better than that."

Ronnie rolled his eyes at the ceiling, took a breath. They began cleaning the guns in silence.

After a while, Carter said, "How you coming on the logistics?"

"All set. I've got us a vehicle and everything we need. We'll transport to Dyess from Andrews, transfer over and be on our way as soon as Harker gives the word."

"Going to be an interesting trip."

"Roger that, buddy. I always wanted to see Tibet."

Carter found Selena upstairs. They walked out to the parking lot and got into her rented car. The ride back to the apartment was silent. One look at her told him he'd better not push it.

Chapter Thirty

Back in the apartment she disappeared into the bathroom. Carter heard her running a bath. He poured himself a double Jameson's and sat down. His land line rang.

"It's Shelley, Nick."

His sister only called when there was a problem or she wanted something.

"We need to talk about Mom."

"How's she doing?"

"She almost set the place on fire yesterday. I went over there and she'd left the soup on the stove and forgotten about it. The pan was burned through, the kitchen was full of smoke and she was sitting in the living room watching TV. She hadn't a clue."

"I thought those new drugs were helping."

"Those drugs are a rip off, that's what I think. Two hundred and fifty bucks a month and you get burned soup. George says it's a crime, you can't even deduct it."

"The soup or the drugs?"

"Oh, that's real funny, Nick. You're not the one who has to clean up after her."

She started in about his general anti-social tendencies and lack of family responsibility. Never mind the money he sent to help out. Never mind the times he'd flown out to be with his mother and see if there was something he could do. Never mind that he cared about his mother more than Shelley did, in spite of her self-righteous indignation. He'd heard it all before.

He cut her off. "What do you want, Shel?"

"Want?" She was getting angry, like most of the times they talked. "I want you to get her into a home, someplace where people will look out for her. I can't do this anymore. George says it's time you took a bigger role."

Her husband, the accountant. Carter thought he was a pompous ass.

"And what does George think that is?"

"You should take some time off from that stupid job of yours and come out here and find a place for her."

Shelley thought Nick was a paper pusher, working for some obscure government department doing meaningless, bureaucratic things she didn't want to understand. He let her believe what she wanted.

"What does Mom want?"

"It doesn't matter what she wants. She's not competent to decide what she wants. What she needs is for you to step up to the plate."

Now she was into sports clichés.

"I can't come to California right now. How about you and George look for a place?"

That set her off. Carter held the phone away from his bandaged ear while she shouted. He walked to the counter and poured another drink. He thought about telling her where George could put his ideas.

While his sister was busy yelling he thought about his mother. She was in the early stages of the disease, not far enough gone to forget she had a house or where she lived. Most of the time, she still knew who she was. She also knew she was losing it. It upset her, a lot. Living in her house was important to her, even if Shelley didn't think so. It wasn't time to move her out, yet.

"Shut up for a minute, will you?"

She stopped mid-yell. He heard a deep silence at the other end.

"She doesn't need to be moved out. Get someone to move in with her, a live in helper."

"We thought of that. George says it's just putting off the inevitable, why not get it over with? Her house will bring a nice price on the market. It would pay for her care."

Now he understood the urgency. Good old George, a solution for everything, with a nice, tidy sum to go in his bank account. The whiskey won out over family harmony.

"You tell George to go fuck himself, Shelley. You get someone to look after her, someone competent, and I'll help out with the cost. But don't even think about putting that place on the market and pushing her out of there. You and that asshole you call your husband try it and I'll make a lot of trouble."

"You can't talk to me that way!"

"I just did."

He slammed the phone down on the counter. He poured another drink. He sat down, thinking about his sister.

His father had never gone after Shelley when he was drunk. She still defended him. It was one of the reasons they didn't get along.

He'd calmed down by the time Selena came out of the bathroom, wrapped in a soft, white robe and toweling her hair.

"Who were you talking to?"

"My sister. She called about our mother."

"What did she say? You were shouting."

"Nothing. I don't want to talk about it right now."

"See?"

"See what?"

"How easy it is to not want to talk about nothing?"

She tossed the towel, sat down on the couch and began combing out tangles in her hair.

After a moment she said, "The grenade thing got to me. Nothing's normal anymore. Last week I was giving a guest lecture at UCLA. Now Uncle William is dead, my car is wrecked, someone tried to kill us at least twice and I was drugged and betrayed by one of my best friends. Then you show me how to throw grenades. What the hell's going on, Nick?"

"You've landed feet first in a big pile of shit. Now you have to deal with it."

She stopped combing and looked at him. "You have a way with words."

"Would it make any difference if I sugar coated it? It's different for me. I was trained to do whatever it takes to accomplish the mission. You haven't had that training. The fact is you're a key player. You've got to go along for the ride and hang on."

He took a drink. "It helps to know you have options, skills if you need them."

"Like what?"

"Like knowing your weapons and knowing you can use them."

Selena put the comb down in her lap.

"I didn't mean to jump on you back there at the range. I didn't like the idea I might have to blow someone up."

"Nobody in their right mind likes the idea."

He wanted to put his arm around her. He didn't do it. He didn't want to start something she wouldn't let him finish.

"Yang hasn't had time to get people in there. We'll get in and get out. We're not going unless we know where the formula or the emperor or whatever is hidden. We'll be gone before he knows we're there."

"You really believe that?"

"It's the only way to think about it."

"At the house when those men were shooting at us, I wasn't thinking about it, I was just running for the river." She picked up her comb. "It wasn't until later I realized I could have been shot."

She ran the comb through her hair. "I heard what you said in Harker's office. I'm afraid I'll screw something up and get someone killed."

She was going, whether he liked it or not. Now wasn't the time to voice his doubts.

"You already proved you can act without screwing up."

"What do you mean?"

"The car, when the Chinese were chasing us. California. If you'd had a gun then you could have shot back. It helps to know you can shoot back. If you couldn't handle this, you wouldn't be going, language skills or not. Harker knows it. So do I."

"I asked to go, didn't I?"

"Don't worry, you'll be fine. Not everybody gets to jump into the Himalayas."

"You sound like a tour guide."

He was keeping it light, but he knew it wasn't going to be a mountain vacation, whatever else happened.

She said, "Doesn't it bother you? The people you've killed?" As soon as she said it she wished she could take it back.

"What the hell kind of a question is that? I've learned to put it out of my mind. It doesn't do any good to second guess myself." A headache started behind his left eye. "The people I killed were trying to kill me. Shit happens. So I don't feel particularly bad about it."

Except for that kid. He got up and went into his bedroom and shut the door.

Selena sat on the couch and watched the door close behind him.

What had she gotten herself into? Harker had asked if she'd be able to shoot someone. She'd said yes, but could she? Would she have to?

If the Emperor was really in Tibet, if somehow the Minoans had anything to do with that, she wanted to be there. It was the adventure of a lifetime. No adventure worth a damn was without risk. Risk didn't bother her. Killing people might.

Stupid of her, to say what she did to Nick.

Nick was a different kind of risk. What was she afraid of?

Carter was still awake when his door opened. Selena came in, slipped out of her robe and crawled into bed with him. She was naked.

"I'm sorry, Nick."

He turned to face her. "I thought you said it was too much right now. Sex. All that."

"I changed my mind."

Suddenly they were clinging to each other, their hands moving over each other, trying to meld into each other. When he entered she clenched her hands on his buttocks and drew him in as far as she could and wrapped her legs around him.

"Jesus, Selena."

"Nick."

Sleep came later.

Chapter Thirty-One

The Project was Elizabeth's life. She spent more time here than in her Georgetown home. No one waited for her there. She'd given up on the idea anyone ever would.

It wasn't supposed to work out like that. She'd been married for a time, back when she was still young and idealistic, thinking she could juggle a career at Justice and a husband and family at the same time.

Wasn't that the new role model for an educated woman? Crack the glass power ceiling, make a lot of money, go to fabulous places in a Prada suit with a great guy who appreciated your mind along with your body, have a couple of kids and commute in a BMW?

The American myth of having it all. There wasn't anything wrong with the myth, if you could get it without selling your soul, but sometimes people and events didn't cooperate. She'd never had kids. He hadn't wanted them. Maybe children would have made a difference, but Elizabeth suspected it would have only made things worse. Her former husband had been with ATF. He was still with ATF. He was also still with the last woman he'd been cheating with before Elizabeth dumped him. Lately she'd heard that wasn't going so well. It was a small satisfaction, but the truth was she didn't really care.

She drove an Audi, not a BMW. She had power, she had the President's ear, she had money, she had a very nice home in the heart of elegant Georgetown. She even had a couple of Prada suits in her closet. None of that mattered much. What mattered to Elizabeth was making a difference, and she was doing that. The picture of the Twin Towers on her desk reminded her of why she did it.

Her life had turned into a study in black and white. She preferred the simplicity of dress black and white offered, but it was more than that. She could not understand people who thought compromise was always the solution. That negotiating with evil was possible. The irony of working in Washington with that attitude did not escape her.

Politically correct rationalizations about why terrorists had good reason for their tactics of fear and murder and how negotiation was the answer struck her as naïve and dangerous. The terrorist organizations were an enemy with philosophies of political and religious fanaticism leaving no room for compromise or peace. As far as Elizabeth was concerned, the world would be a better place if they were all destroyed. If her father were still alive he would have agreed.

Judge Harker had been well-liked in the small town where she'd grown up. Traditional values of hard work and honesty still flourished on the western slope of the Rockies. In her father's private world, a man's word was his bond, a handshake an agreement written in stone. On the bench, he was impartial and fair. Whatever doubts he might have had about the judgments the law required him to mete out, he left them in the courtroom.

When Elizabeth was growing up, the Judge would sit in his big green chair in his study, a glass of bourbon on the table beside him, and tell Elizabeth stories of a vanished America. Stories of the Revolution, the Founders, the Civil War. Stories of sacrifice, of heroism and wisdom and courage. She absorbed the history, and with it a love for her country. She still believed in the essential goodness of America, tarnished as it was. Maybe it was out of style, but it sustained her when the self-serving nature of Washington politics began to wear her down.

The Judge believed in hard facts, concrete evidence and fair play. He would not have liked the shadow world she lived in, but he would have been firm on the need to protect the country and proud of her for doing it. She wondered what he would think about this latest threat. A threat coming into view but not yet defined, potential trouble with a nation capable of annihilating a good part of America.

Nick and Ronnie came into the office, interrupting her thoughts. Time to brief them. A satellite photo of western Tibet filled the big screen behind her desk. When they were settled she used a laser pointer to indicate the landmarks.

"Following the clues in the book we focused on the area near Mount Kailash." She indicated the mountain with a red dot from the pointer.

"This is a coal mining village called Moincer."

The dot paused on a cluster of buildings west of the mountain, moved again.

"This is Kyunglung, a complex of caves used for religious rituals. The caves are shown on the map and are known as the 'Silver Palace of the Garuda'. At first I thought what we're looking for might be there, but it's just caves, nothing more. It was used for centuries by Bon magicians."

"Who are the Bon?" Nick's ear began itching.

"Bon was the religion practiced in Tibet before Buddhism. It's still practiced today, but with Buddhist elements."

Harker tapped her keyboard. The scene changed to show a satellite photo of a bleak hilltop covered with the ruins of a small city. The camera zoomed in on a whitewashed complex built into the side of the hill.

"The building is Gurugem, a Bon monastery. Those ruins above it looked promising, but they've been picked over for years. There's nothing there. However, I think I've found what we're looking for. Following a line north, about fifty kilometers, there's another set of ruins."

The satellite focus shifted to the remains of an ancient, square fortress on top of a hill. The outer walls were about the length of a football field on each side. Ruined buildings and rubble surrounded a square, open area with a large building set in the center.

"A deep sonar scan shows a cavern underneath those ruins, with something in it. My guess is that this is where the emperor was taken. It matches up with the map in the book. If anything is still left, that's where it will be. There isn't any military presence nearby. That's the good news. The bad news is the site is exposed and the terrain is rugged.

"You'll go in when it's dark to avoid being spotted from the monastery. You'll be in uniform and wear rank insignia, but no unit flashes or nametags. Nick, I'm making you a bird colonel for this.

"Your clearance will be Umbra. No one is going to question you. Your mission is to penetrate the area, find entrance to the underground complex, retrieve and document whatever information found there of value and bring it back."

"You forgot the bit about the tape self-destructing at the end."

"Excuse me?"

"Mission Impossible. Remember?"

"Very funny, Nick."

Ronnie ran his hand over his buzz cut. "Where's the drop zone?"

"It's too dangerous to drop right on the ruins. The mountains and air currents there make it high risk for you and for the aircraft."

Back to the broad shot, the laser dot moved west to a valley between the caves and the Bon monastery.

"We'll drop you here. It's flat, you won't have too far to travel and you can get in and under cover before anyone knows you're there. Once you're north of the monastery you shouldn't run into anyone."

"How are we going to get into that underground complex?"

"There's no way to tell until you get there. Selena and Stephanie are working on the translation right now, looking for anything that will help. Selena will have it with her. There has to be something in the book or on site that can show you how to get in, now that we know it's there."

"Any entrance might be buried under tons of rock. We could get there and wander around like tourists until Yang shows up. This isn't good, Director."

"Nobody said it was easy, Ronnie. You're wheels up tonight from Andrews for Dyess. I've got 24/7 watch on the surrounding area and I'll keep you informed if we see any military presence coming toward you. I will monitor the mission on live satellite and stay in voice contact."

"How do we get out when we're done?" Carter asked.

"Helicopter extraction from India. It's not far to the Indian border, but the route on foot is difficult, through the Lipu Lehk pass. It helps that you're going in summer, but the plateau is high, the air's thin and it's cold up there. It is the Himalayas, after all."

"And if we run into opposition?"

"Take care of it. No rules of engagement. We'll have the copters standing by across the border but you're on your own."

On your own, Carter thought. Meaning deniable.

"When you're ready, call for extraction. Get it done as fast as you can. Yang is bound to send someone down there when he figures it out."

"He must have by now," Carter said.

"So far we don't see any activity in the area, but that could change anytime."

"What are we looking for?"

"Anything to confirm the existence or location of a possible uranium deposit. If Selena's translation is correct there should be a map or records of some kind showing where all the ingredients for the elixir can be found. I don't think you're going to find the secret of immortality, but look for anything unusual. You won't know until you get there and see for yourself. Any other questions? Ronnie?"

He shook his head. "I don't have any."

"All right, then. Transport at 1800. Good luck."

Out in the hallway they waited for the elevator.

"What do you think, Nick?"

"About what?"

"About the whole deal."

"I think we're in for what our Chinese friends call an interesting time."

Chapter Thirty-Two

At 2300 hours they were airborne in a C-130J Super Hercules, an updated version of the Air Force workhorse. A Humvee with Pakistani army markings looked lost in the cavernous hold. The team sat on an orange strap bench along the side of the fuselage, listening to the drone of the Rolls-Royce engines. They were in battle dress, geared up for the cold weather waiting in the Himalayas. There wasn't going to be time to change later.

Nick went over the military GPS unit with Selena. It would guide her to the landing zone. She had skydiving experience but this was far different. They were jumping at high altitude and she'd never done that before. Wind and thermals could screw everything up. There was no room for error.

Their packs sat at their feet, loaded with rations, water, ammo, the MP-5N's, medical kits and assorted survival gear. Selena had a digital camera and video recorder to document anything they found. Aside from the H-Ks, the weight was down to around thirty pounds. At fifteen thousand feet and higher any weight would be a burden.

All three had pistols strapped to the left side of their chests and Ka-Bar knives on their right thighs. They had body armor that went far beyond the normal military specs. It was heavy, but it could deflect a .308 and keep you alive. They had helmets rigged for voice activated communications. They could pick up the team channel or the satellite uplink to Washington. The rest of their supplies were inside the vehicle. They'd get chutes and everything they needed for the jump at Dyess.

Ronnie pointed at the stripes insignia on his collar.

"I never thought I'd be wearing these again."

"Looks good on you, Gunny."

"You too, Nick. Like it used to be."

Dressed in camouflage battle gear and armed to the teeth, Carter thought Selena looked dangerous as hell. She had her laptop out, working on the Minoan text. Nick raised his voice over the noise of the engines.

"How are you coming?"

"I think I've got it. There are still parts I haven't translated but I think I know what to look for."

He waited.

"If I'm reading this right, we look for a labrys to mark the way."

"What's a labrys?" Ronnie leaned forward and looked past Nick at Selena.

"It's a double-headed axe. It was a symbol of power to the Minoans and later to the Greeks. It's ancient, no one knows when it first appeared. The labrys marked the entrance to the labyrinth."

"Where the Minotaur lived."

"Right, that's the myth. Once you entered the labyrinth, you never came out. There are some old mines and caves in Crete that might have been the original labyrinth. I've been there. They're spooky."

"What happened to the Minoans?"

"The current theory is that when the island of Santorini erupted it sent a tsunami over Crete and wiped everything out. That might have been the basis for the stories about Atlantis. Santorini was like an H-Bomb going off."

"I don't see how any Minoans got to Tibet." Carter bent over and adjusted his pack.

"According to the book there was a secret cult of priestesses in Knossos. They traced their teachings about immortality to India. Vedic Indian priests may have lived in Tibet and found their way to the Minoans. Or maybe someone changed the history to suit themselves."

"Women were the guardians of the elixir?"

"Yes. The cult believed humans could join the gods in immortal life if they performed sacrifices and took the right potions. A lot of cultures use potions or herbs to commune with gods or spirits. What's different here is the idea they could attain immortality in the physical body."

"You think that's what Yang is after?"

"Anyone who wants to take over China has an ego so big he'd think immortality was his right, if it existed. I'd bet on the uranium scenario."

"Did you find anything more about the formula? Ingredients, preparation, anything?"

"No. It's not complete. You'd have to be crazy to take it."

"Not if you tested it first," he said. "Researched it with modern techniques."

"Like on mice?"

"They already do that. There are mice that live a lot longer after scientists manipulate their genes."

"That's different. The mice aren't drinking gold and mercury, with a little radioactive pixie dust thrown in for good measure."

"You have a point," Carter conceded.

Selena went back to her computer.

He spent the rest of the flight to Texas thinking about the mission. It wasn't much different from when he was in Afghanistan. Like then, he was going into hostile territory with questionable intel.

Everything depended on penetrating Chinese airspace undetected and getting into that underground chamber. That assumed the sonar scan was accurate, that there was an underground chamber in the first place and that they could find the entrance if there was one. If they did manage to get in, they still didn't know what they'd find. He sensed a headache beginning.

Chapter Thirty-Three

Selena looked up from her computer. The decibel roar and vibration of the engines was something she couldn't tune out. She looked down the hold of the huge aircraft, all functional steel and aluminum, exposed struts, the orange strap benches, everything utilitarian and built for the purpose of war. It wasn't much like first class to Paris or Rome.

The others were used to it. The airmen were bored, that was easy to see, but this was a regular job for them. Ronnie was reading something, Nick had his eyes closed. His face looked strained and tired. He and Ronnie had probably been on hundreds of flights like this.

She was nervous and they hadn't even gotten to Texas yet. She was damned if she'd let the others see it.

She looked at the broken green and gray and black patterns on her uniform, touched the pistol strapped on her chest. The shape of her knife dug into her leg. The hard molded radio helmet was an unfamiliar intrusion on her head. She was encased in armor.

She felt like she'd fallen through the looking glass into the fantasy world of a video war game, but this wasn't a game. This was real.

Three weeks ago she'd been standing at a podium at Stanford, giving a lecture on Indo-European languages. Life was predictable and safe, if a little boring. Now she carried enough weapons to take out a small village. There was a reason for that, namely that she might have to use them, which meant someone might be using weapons against her. She wasn't at all sure she could handle it.

If that wasn't enough, she was about to jump into the Himalayas to look for a two thousand year old emperor and the elixir of immortality.

How did she end up here?

She looked over at Nick. She didn't know what to do about him. She wanted him, but she knew herself. She could fall for him. She knew enough about him to know he was wrapped in emotional armor a tank couldn't get through. She could try to break through it and the only thing that would happen was she'd hurt herself.

He was still in love with his dead fiancée. She'd be an ass to let herself love him. But damn it, she wanted him.

Chapter Thirty-Four

At Dyess Air Force Base an armed security escort met their plane. Brilliant lights lit the tarmac. A B-1B Lancer waited nearby.

Men transferred their gear under the watchful eye of a sergeant. The air smelled of rubber, jet fuel and Texas sage. The detail commander was a young lieutenant wearing pilot's wings on his fatigues. His name tag said Markham. He saluted.

"Welcome to the 7th Bomb Wing, Colonel. You'll be ready to go within the hour."

Carter returned the salute. "Thank you, Lieutenant. We're looking forward to the ride."

"Ever been in a B1 before?"

"No."

"It's a hell of an airplane, great avionics and defensive measures. Top speed is Mach 1.2, but we can come in at a hundred and twenty knots at low altitude and lay in precision targeting. You'll be flying in one modified for combat drops of personnel and equipment."

He looked around. "Where's the rest of your team?"

"You're looking at it. Just the three of us."

Carter saw him note the lack of insignia on their uniforms. They had no jump insignia, unit flashes or name tags, just rank markings, and Selena didn't even have those. Lieutenant Markham started to say something, thought better of it.

"Right, sir. Your jumpmaster is Senior Master Sergeant Johannsen. Once you're in the aircraft, he's your boss. He'll make sure you're checked out and everything is a go for the jump. You've jumped before?"

He glanced at Selena.

"We have. Is that Sergeant Johannsen I see coming?"

The man moving toward them was compact, about five nine and a hundred and sixty pounds. He was dressed in flight gear and wore a radio helmet. Johannsen moved with purpose, tight as a spring, with no wasted energy. He had eyes of pale blue ice and the look that comes from a lot of years in the service. Nick relaxed a little. They were in the hands of a pro. He saluted and gave them the once over. His eyes narrowed as he looked at Selena, but he said nothing.

Lieutenant Markham said, "They're all yours, Sergeant. Colonel, come back safe."

Markham saluted, got in his jeep and drove away. Sergeant Johannsen gestured at the bomber.

"Follow me, sir."

They walked to the plane and climbed in. It was hot in the Texas humidity but things would cool off soon enough.

The Humvee was lashed to a pallet near the converted bomb bay. The chute was being rigged by four airmen in flight gear. Johannsen took three chutes from a locker.

"I packed these myself, Colonel. You may not have used one before."

"It looks different."

"This is the High Altitude Precision Parachute System, HAPPS for short. This is the stealth model, no one will see you from the ground."

"It looks like a skydiving chute, but it's got more attachments on it." That was Selena.

Johannsen eyed the lack of jump insignia on her uniform. "You've jumped before?"

"Over seventy jumps. Seventy-two, to be exact. But maybe you could show me the ropes on this unit."

It was the right thing to say. Nick saw Johannsen relax a little. It was more than rare to see a woman on a special ops mission. Male chauvinism aside, everyone felt responsible for success, even when they didn't know what the mission was about. Johannsen would be lax in his duty if he weren't concerned. His job was to get everyone out of the plane safely. After that it was up to the three of them.

They put on the chutes under Johannsen's direction. He checked each one, pulling the harness tight. When it was Selena's turn, he paused.

"The harness is pretty tight. You might feel some pinching— umm—across your chest."

"Go for it."

He cinched it up and Selena gasped.

"This is your main cord. This is your reserve cord, here. The chute is fully steerable. You'll have oxygen, here."

He attached oxygen dispensers to the chutes. Then he brought three devices that looked like wristwatches out of a compartment.

"Put these on. This is the MA3-30 altimeter. It tells you everything you need to know. It's got a light switch and you adjust here and here."

Ronnie and Nick had used them before, but it was new for Selena.

"Set your altitude before you jump and we'll get you onto the drop zone with airspeed and timing. Your vehicle goes first, then you three. We're going to drop you from 23,000 feet. That gives you around 8,000 feet before you hit the ground, so you won't be up too long."

"Piece of cake."

"That's right, Gunny. Give it five after you go out and pull, and you'll be floating down softer than a balloon at a kid's birthday party. You'll be on the ground in no time. Let's get your packs on."

They strapped on the packs, low in front. When he was satisfied with the rigging, Johannsen reached down into the compartment again and came up with masks and insulated gloves. The pilot was warming up the engines. Johannsen held his hand to his helmet for a moment.

"Two minutes. Let's get you settled."

He led them toward the center of the aircraft. Strap benches lined the fuselage. The four airmen were already seated on the port side. The team took seats starboard and strapped in. Johannsen strapped in across from them and said something into his mike. The roar of the big GE turbofans increased and the plane began to move.

Party time.

Chapter Thirty-Five

Nick was dozing when Johannsen nudged him awake.

"One hour, Colonel. Pre-breathing in fifteen minutes."

Ronnie sat quietly. Selena had packed up her computer. Carter put his hand on her arm.

"You ready for this?"

"I guess so. I've never jumped from this high before."

"It's the same but the air's thinner, you weigh more with that pack and you'll come down faster. The tricky part is compensating for wind speed and direction. But you know how to do that. With the GPS you're not going to miss the landing zone. Even though we start high, we end high too. That makes it simpler. Just stay loose and you'll be okay."

She nodded.

"Free fall for five, then pull the cord. Remember to snap your chin to your chest once you're out and keep your hand on your reserve until your chute is deployed. Keep your legs tight together. The shock is pretty hard when the chute opens. Remember to land back from the balls of your feet."

Carter looked at his watch. "We'll begin pre-breathing soon."

"Pre-breathing?"

"This high, we have to get the nitrogen out of our blood. If we go out there without pre-breathing, our own CO_2 could knock us out and it's a long way down. Don't worry, this is standard drill. I've been through it before. Besides, the oxygen makes you feel good. When we change over to the bottles we use in the jump, be careful not to breathe any cabin air. Only pure oxygen. Okay?"

"Okay."

"Forty-five minutes." Johannsen's voice sounded in her helmet. "Begin pre-breathing."

They put on the masks. Johannsen hooked up the plane's oxygen supply and they began pre-breathing. Carter felt the old pre-jump feeling come over him. He was always wired before a big jump. He figured you could double that for jumping into the biggest, baddest, highest and coldest mountain range on the face of the earth. He saw the tension in Ronnie, but he'd been through this before. He knew Ronnie was silently repeating the Blessing Way to himself, one of the Navajo ritual traditions. Carter wasn't worried about him. He put his hand on Selena's shoulder and felt her relax, just a bit.

Another typical day in Special Ops, he thought, except now I'm a civilian, so what the hell am I doing here? He noted the mind chatter and shut it down. The oxygen was kicking in and he felt clear and strong.

Johannsen's voice crackled in his helmet. "Ten minutes. We're going to depressurize now. Change over to your personal oxygen."

Nick felt the change in the hold and his ears popped. The plane was slowing down and banking through what had to be mountains outside. His altimeter read twenty-one thousand feet. Most of the peaks in this part of the Himalayas were a lot higher than the plane. He knew the wingtips were only a small mistake away from disaster. He hoped like hell the pilot was enjoying flying between them.

"Five minutes. We'll open the doors at two minutes. Weather says very strong wind, watch yourselves. The vehicle goes first and then you three. What order?"

"I'll go first, then Selena, then the Gunny, here."

Johannsen gave a thumbs up. "Roger, that. Two second intervals."

The plane climbed. The doors swung open and a blast of frigid air sucked away the little warmth of the cargo bay. The airmen got ready to dump the Humvee. The wind buffeted the fuselage.

"I hope we land near that sucker." Ronnie's voice crackled in Nick's helmet.

"These guys are good. They'll put it right on the money."

"Set your altimeters at twenty-three thousand." Johannsen's voice came through the helmet.

They moved to the opening. The engine notes changed as the pilot throttled back and the big plane leveled and slowed again.

"Get ready," Johannsen said. A green light flashed and the pallet with the Humvee disappeared into the Himalayan night. Johannsen held up his arm for an instant, threw it forward. Carter leapt into nothingness, arms spread wide.

Chapter Thirty-Six

The chute opened clean and hard. He looked up and saw two chutes blossom above. The plane was a dark arrow turning against the night sky. They were on their own.

A three-quarter moon spilled pure, silver light off the sharp peaks of the Himalayas. The snow-covered mountains gleamed in a shifting tapestry of light and shadow that stretched beyond the horizon. In the distance, Everest and Annapurna grasped at a deep, black sky glowing with stars.

The wind was bad. Control was difficult. He veered off course, checked the GPS, made a correction. His altimeter read seventeen thousand feet. Carter looked for the Humvee and saw the chutes below, far to the right, almost down.

Sixteen thousand feet and the ground was coming up too fast. He worked the lines and headed for a flat area. A strong gust made him shear left. He overshot the spot he'd picked out and came down hard in an area littered with boulders. The shock ran up his bad leg and right into his spine like electric needles.

He lay for a moment as the chute tried to pull him across the rough ground. The pain was like a knife in his back. He wondered if he was going to be able to get up.

It wasn't a good start. He got to his feet and another bolt of pain stabbed his back and radiated down his leg. He struggled with his chute against the gusting wind.

The ghostly moonlight lit the uneven terrain in shades of gray and black. Pools of deep shadow lay among the rocks. He limped back toward the drop zone. Selena was pulling her chute in about a hundred yards away. When he got there, she took off her mask. She took a deep breath of the thin air.

"That was tricky, that wind...Nick, you're limping."

"It's nothing. You see Ronnie?"

"I think he came down over there."

She pointed at a low rise as Ronnie came trudging over it. They high-fived. Ronnie winced.

"You okay?" Nick asked.

"Just a shoulder bruise. I came down a little hard. It's no big deal."

Now they needed to find the vehicle.

"Anyone see where the Humvee landed?"

"It's that way." Ronnie gestured over his shoulder. "I saw it coming in. Maybe a quarter mile from here. That wind screwed things up."

It took twenty minutes of scrambling over rough stones to find it. Nick's back hurt like hell. The pallet had shattered and the Humvee was half off onto the rocks. It appeared undamaged. They undid the lashings. The engine coughed and started. Ronnie drove a few feet away. They dragged a camouflage net over the pallet and chutes, good enough for the short time they'd be there.

Carter spread a map on the hood of the idling Humvee and got out the GPS. His back throbbed with steady pain. He braced against the side of the hood to take the weight off his leg.

"We're here." He tapped the map. "About eighteen klicks west of the mining town. The road is down there on the other side of that rise. Here's the monastery that's our principle landmark and here are the ruins we're headed for."

"That pilot knew his stuff."

"Makes you feel good, doesn't it? I could do without the moonlight, but it'll be gone soon. We've got around seven hours until dawn. With luck we can reach the ruins before light and get under cover. I'm going to call in."

A coded burst to Harker let her know they were down safe and moving toward the objective.

"Ronnie, you drive."

He pointed to a spot on the map where a valley wound its way into the mountains, before the road reached the Gurugem monastery.

"We'll cut north before we get too close to the building and head straight for the ruins."

They put the packs in back and climbed in. They drove off the hillside and onto the road. It was in good condition, gray and flat in the moonlight. The Humvee vibrated as they drove.

Ronnie said, "Steering isn't real good. Something might have got bent when the sled came down."

"Not much we can do about it."

"Nah, we're still making good time. But I wouldn't want to push it."

Now all they had to do was get to the objective and find a way inside.

Chapter Thirty-Seven

In Washington, Elizabeth studied the live satellite transmission from nighttime Tibet. She'd gotten the DIA to task a geostationary satellite to her for the duration of the mission. In daylight, it could define the insignia on a uniform collar from a hundred and twenty thousand feet up. At night, the latest infra-red technology tracked any heat source down to the size of a cigarette.

Elizabeth watched the heat signature of the moving vehicle carrying her team. Nick's coded message confirmed what she could see with her own eyes. They were down safe and heading for the ruins.

She zoomed out and scanned the surrounding area for signs of Chinese activity. The town of Moincer showed up as a leprous green glow west of the moving Humvee. There was no sign of vehicles leaving the town and heading toward the team. So far, so good.

Elizabeth had no illusions about what would happen if something went wrong. Political retaliation would be swift and merciless. China was off limits for armed covert ops. It helped that the team was in a remote region and that it wasn't in Yang's interest to draw attention there if something happened.

It was a long way to Tibet, but Yang was after something important there. Whatever he was after, getting to it first would complicate his plans. Whatever complicated Yang's plans was good, so she'd ordered the team into action, politics be damned.

She wondered if the relationship between Nick and Selena would be a problem in the field. It didn't take a trained observer to see something was going on between them. Elizabeth thought they were probably sleeping together, but there was some unspoken tension between them. Her first reaction had been to say no when Selena asked to go on the mission. But she had skills needed to boost the probability of success. Elizabeth always decided based on increasing the possibility and measure of success.

So far Homeland Security had not raised the alert level. It was always a difficult problem. Raise the level and get everyone upset, without certainty of attack? Or wait for more intelligence and risk missing the window of opportunity to stop something?

Harker was glad she didn't have to make that decision. In her gut, she felt an attack was coming. She had sounded the alarm; now it was up to others. In the meantime, she was doing what she could to disrupt Yang's plans.

Earlier she'd called State to give them a heads up. After the typical shunting around, she had reached the Assistant Secretary of State for East Asian and Pacific Affairs, Cheryl Wilson.

"You're telling me a coup is being planned."

"That is what our best intelligence indicates."

"What is the source of this intelligence?"

"I'm afraid I can't tell you that, Ma'am."

"Are you saying I'm not cleared for this information?"

"That's correct."

There was an audible intake of breath at the other end of the line. It reminded Elizabeth of a snake hissing before the strike. There was frost in Wilson's voice when she spoke again.

"Everything about China indicates a strong grasp on power by the party leadership. I cannot conceive of an attempt to overthrow the current regime. Your intelligence must be faulty."

Wilson pronounced intelligence as if the word left a bad taste in her mouth.

"None the less, in our best judgment a coup is in the works." Harker kept the annoyance out of her voice.

"Well, Director, I appreciate your call but I believe you are barking up the wrong tree. There is no possible way the PRC will undergo a radical change of leadership. I suggest you re-evaluate your sources and stick to your domestic mandate. Now, I have a meeting to attend. Was there anything else?"

No, nothing else, you idiot, Elizabeth thought.

"No, Ma'am."

"Then I'll say goodbye." Wilson hung up.

Elizabeth resisted the urge to scream. The arrogance of some high-ranking political appointees never failed to amaze her. They weren't all like that, but with people like Wilson having a say in foreign policy it was a miracle the country got along with anyone at all.

On the monitor, the satellite images showed the Humvee carrying the team had stopped. Dim spots nearby showed low level activity. That must be the monastery of Gurugem, Harker thought, and the team is deciding the best way to avoid it. She looked at the series of clocks on the wall. With almost six hours until daylight on the other side of the world, there was still time to get to the ruins before dawn.

Chapter Thirty-Eight

In the idling Humvee, Carter scanned a landscape turned ghostly green by his night vision binoculars. The road they'd been following turned out of sight beyond the base of a large hill on its way to the monastery. To the left, a broad valley skirted the hill and headed north. A cold, hard wind gusted without stopping against the vehicle.

He put the binoculars down.

"This should take us close to where we want to go." He traced the valley floor on the map. "If we don't run into any obstacles, I think we can get there in four or five hours."

Selena said, "I have to pee."

Ronnie and Nick began laughing.

"What's so funny?" She felt her face reddening.

"Nothing," Carter said. "Just tension, that's all. Hell, I do too. Pick your restrooms, everyone."

A few minutes later Ronnie put the vehicle in gear and they turned up the valley.

The peaks on either side were bigger than the highest mountains in the United States. They were only foothills to the massive giants not far away. The slopes were bare of vegetation and covered with stony debris and boulders. Lifeless rock stretched away in every direction with cold indifference. It was like driving on an alien planet.

The moon was almost down. The stars blazed incandescent overhead. Nick had never seen so many stars. There were clouds of stars, bright enough to cast shadows on the valley floor. The deep black, star-studded sky seemed to hint at something mysterious just out of reach. Under that sky, with towering, snow-covered peaks gleaming in every direction, it was easy to understand why people living here believed these mountains were the home of gods.

"How are you doing, Selena?"

"I've got a headache, but aside from that, good. I'm glad I don't have to hike this right now."

"Take a hit of oxygen. We don't want to get sick up here. We aren't used to the altitude, but we won't be here very long."

"I wonder what we're going to find."

"We'll know soon enough," Ron said. "We're about four klicks from the ruins."

The Humvee jolted up and down across a rough patch of rocks. A loud crack of breaking metal came from the front. They slewed to the right in a sliding shower of loose rock and dropped down hard onto a low boulder before Ronnie could stop. He killed the engine.

"What was that?"

"I don't know," Ronnie said. "Didn't sound good. The steering went."

They got out. The Humvee was hung up on the rock, the right wheel jutting up in the air. Ronnie got out his flash and looked underneath.

"Can't see much with all that armor plating." He grasped the tire in his hand. The wheel swung easily back and forth. "It looks like we walk. I think a tie rod or a control arm must have broken."

"Right, let's get it under cover."

They pulled the packs out of the back and covered the vehicle with camouflage netting. The Humvee blended into the landscape. Nick's altimeter showed 16,400 feet.

They shouldered packs and began climbing. They followed a steep draw, detouring around gigantic boulders and falls of rock. The wind was relentless, a freezing, brittle wind. Loose stones rolled like uneven marbles underfoot. Carter kept slipping. His back was on fire. His pack felt like it was full of lead.

The sky showed signs of dawn. He looked at the others. Selena was sweating in the cold air. Ronnie looked grim.

"Let's take a break," he said.

They stopped. He had to do something about the pain. He got out the med kit, took out a couple of pain pills, thought about it and put one back. This wasn't a good place to risk mistakes in judgment.

Three hours after they'd left the Humvee, they topped the final rise. A cold sun bathed the mountains in brassy, ominous light that offered no comfort from the chill wind. The prospect before them was daunting.

The ruins covered the crest of the hill in a jumble of stone. The outer walls were twenty feet high, built of flat stones fitted together. They stretched for over a hundred yards in each direction to form an outer square. Tumbled gaps gaped in the walls where stones had fallen. A building topped by a tall, stepped, pyramid-shaped roof dominated the center of the compound.

Carter pictured attacking those walls on foot with spears and swords and bows and arrows. In its day, the fortress would have been impregnable.

The silence was immense. The only sound was the constant keening of wind through the ruins.

The mountain dropped away from where they stood in a sweeping vista of snow-capped mountains and valleys. A waterfall that must have been two thousand feet high dropped straight down to a river winding below along the valley floor. A herd of yaks grazed on the side of a mountain in the distance, thirty or forty tiny black dots. A lone, golden eagle glided past, a thousand feet below.

Carter had never seen space like that. It wasn't only that the mountains were big. It was the distance around them, the way they forced themselves up into the thin sky. The scale of nature was overwhelming. It made him feel the size of an ant.

He consulted his GPS and pointed at a spot on one of the satellite photos.

"We're here, at the southwest corner of the outer walls. These four lines look like streets between buildings. We'll go along this wall and follow one in."

"They all converge at the center," Selena said, "at the building and the square around it."

"Isn't the center a big deal in these parts?"

"Yes. Mt. Kailash, over that way, was supposed to be the center of the world. That building is the center of this complex and the cavern is under it."

Ronnie spoke up. "Then why don't we start there?"

Another pre-coded burst let Harker know they had arrived and were proceeding. Carter put the phone back in his pocket and they set out along the west wall. Halfway down, they came to what was left of a gateway. The gate was long gone. A broad uneven avenue of frost-heaved grayish stone led straight toward the building with the pyramid spire at the center.

They headed in. Standing walls of gray stone and piles of rubble lined the street. Selena pointed out a carving of a giant bird on a tall, weathered column of rock.

"That's a garuda, same as the book name."

"What were all these buildings for?"

"Shops, quarters, stables. This place is a small city."

The wind moaned through the deserted stones, lifting a thin, gritty dust into the air. Selena paused at a building on the edge of the square. The roof was still intact. She stepped inside, into the ruins of a broad atrium.

The floor of the atrium was about thirty feet square. Uneven colored tiles formed an elaborate picture on the floor. Lichen grew between the tiles and many of the pieces were missing, but the design was still clear enough.

At the corners, curled leopards stood guard. In the center, a woman reclined on a low couch with curved ends. She wore a blue robe. She had long, black, curling hair circled by a gold band. Three women in robes of white attended her. One played a flute, another bore a basket of fruit, a third poured wine from a jug. All three had black, curly hair bound with a headband and lifelike eyes made from black and gold tiles. Above the scene, two women rode in a chariot, blond hair streaming behind them. The chariot was pulled by two winged griffins. Above everything flew a large bird.

"This is Cretan," said Selena. "This is amazing. The one with the wine is pouring from an amphora. It's definitely Minoan. Paintings similar to this were found in a Minoan burial chamber in Northern Crete. The women in the chariot are probably goddesses, maybe escorts to guide the soul to the afterlife."

"Then the Minoans were here, after all."

"It looks like it. This style of mosaic art is unique to the Aegean. Either the Minoans or someone who had contact with them had to have done it. Finding this in Tibet is incredible." She took out her camera.

They came to the edge of the square. The walls of the building at the heart of the complex were eroded from the endless winds, the ancient stone dark and stained. Narrow openings were set along the lower walls and in the roof.

"This is an early style of Vedic temple architecture," said Selena. "The pyramid roof was typical. I'd guess around 1800 BCE. Maybe a little later."

"It was a temple?"

"It must have been. This entire complex is laid out like a mandala, with entrances to the center from the four directions."

"What's a mandala?" Ronnie rubbed his face with his glove.

"It's a tool, a picture to help focus your mind. By looking at the picture and meditating on it you develop the ability to enter a spiritual dimension."

"You believe that?" he said.

"It seems to work for the people who practice with it."

Carter looked around the broad square, thinking what it must have been like when there were people here.

"This place was a mandala for real?" He rubbed his ear.

"That would have been the idea. Everything constructed to remind people of their spiritual nature and the transience of life."

"Then why are we here looking for something to make you immortal?"

"Immortality is the payoff in a lot of religions. It just takes different forms for different people. In the East, you get enlightened. In effect you become immortal. In the West, you live forever in heaven."

"Or hell," he said.

"I don't believe that," said Selena.

For the most part, the square was free of debris. They walked toward the building, stopped and stared at the structure.

Two massive columns held up an arched entry. Above the arch, a great, fierce bird was hewn into the stone. Still visible on each column was the sign of the labrys, the double headed axe of ancient Crete.

Chapter Thirty-Nine

Senior Investigator Yao waited in the antechamber of the Minister of State Security. He was nervous. It wasn't a good sign to be kept waiting this long. Unsmiling guards in dress uniform, assault rifles carried at port arms, stood rigid sentry at the entrance to the Minister's office.

Yao reassured himself. His investigation of General Yang was thorough. You didn't make accusations against someone as powerful as Yang without good reason and better facts. It was a foregone conclusion his report would be difficult to receive and subject to the closest scrutiny. Yao had faith in the system, but this was explosive.

The Minister's secretary emerged from within. He beckoned Yao forward.

"The Minister will see you now."

Yao read nothing in the secretary's tone. Ah, well, the tile was cast. Soon he would know the Minister's thoughts.

Minister Deng sat behind his desk, writing. The secretary led Yao to the front of the desk and took a seat at a smaller table off to the side. Deng continued writing. Yao stood at attention and forced himself to remain calm. Finally the Minister of State Security for the People's Republic of China capped his pen, set it down and looked up.

He was not smiling.

"Senior Investigator Yao. I have read your report." Deng held up a folder on his desk. "You have made serious accusations against General Yang." He looked at Yao as if expecting him to admit this had all been a foolish error.

"Yes, Minister."

"General Yang is one of the bulwarks of our military. He has served the people well for many years. You are sure you do not wish to withdraw this report?"

Yao took a deep breath. "Yes, Minister."

"I have reviewed your record. You also have distinguished yourself in service to the Party and the people. Whom should I believe in this matter, you or General Yang, if I ask him?"

"Minister, you should believe me!"

Deng looked surprised at the boldness of the response. It wasn't often that anyone addressed one of the most powerful men in China with such directness.

Yao went on. "General Yang is corrupt. More, he is hatching a plot involving the Americans, with the assistance of the Black Societies there."

"So you say in your report."

Deng looked at Yao, considered him for a long moment. He gestured to the secretary.

"Bring Senior Investigator Yao a chair. Block all appointments for the next hour. And bring tea."

Yao breathed an inward sigh of relief. Until that moment he had not been sure how his report would be received. Now the power of the Ministry would focus on Yang until the truth was revealed. At a nod from the Minister he sat in the chair that had been provided.

"Tell me the facts of your case, Yao. I wish to hear what may not be found in this report. There is always something."

Yao relaxed a little more.

"I became suspicious when I received a report from one of our agents in America. He was observing Colonel Wu and overheard his conversation regarding the American, Connor."

"Your report says that several hundred million dollars stolen from Connor were transferred to Yang and back again to America."

"Yes, Minister, that is correct. The accounts in America are controlled by the Black Societies. That increased my concern."

"It has increased my concern as well. What is the current status of your investigation? What is being done?"

"General Yang is being observed at all times and his communications have been intercepted and recorded for several days. Wu has returned to Beijing and is under surveillance. Wu's sergeant arrived home yesterday and I have agents following him.

"We recorded calls from Yang to the officers and officials listed in my report. Each call contained a phrase I believe was code to alert these men in some way. Minister, this is more than a case of corruption. General Yang is hatching a plot against the Party and has enlisted the aid of the Triads in America to accomplish whatever he is planning."

Deng sipped his tea. "The Triads back the Nationalist revisionists. We tolerate them because they stick to their criminal activities and don't interfere in politics. If Yang is enlisting their aid, it must have subversive meaning."

"That was my thought, Minister."

"In your report you mention a book Yang wished to secure. Do you have any further knowledge of this?"

"No, Minister. But I am looking into it. The key to that riddle lies in America. My agents are seeking more information, but as yet I have nothing to report." He paused. "Sir, to the Americans all Chinese appear the same. Whatever the Triads do, it will reflect on all of us. We will lose face before the world if their actions are public."

Deng nodded. "You have been thorough, Comrade Yao. When I first saw your report, I was skeptical. I wanted to see you to get a feeling for the man who wrote it."

Minister Deng looked at Yao. What he saw there seemed to satisfy him. He made up his mind.

"You have convinced me Yang is a danger. What do you suggest? Should we arrest him, do you think?"

Yao was shocked and pleased that the Minister would ask his advice on such a delicate matter.

"That, of course, is your decision, Minister. Since you ask for my opinion, I suggest waiting a little longer, until we get a better picture of what Yang is planning. I have ordered surveillance on all members of the White Jade Society and the others Yang contacted. All of their communications are being monitored."

"These men are honored leaders of our military and some of our most critical government ministries."

"Yes, Minister. That is what concerns me."

"You think all these men are conspiring against the Party?"

Yao became flushed, thinking about traitors.

"Yes, Minister, I do. Reactionary elements are always seeking to undermine the good of our society. If they are men of high rank and standing, their betrayal is that much worse. They must be rooted out, no matter who they are."

Deng nodded his approval. "That is correct. You have full authority to pursue this investigation as you see best. You have so far been discreet. See that you continue to be so. Keep me informed."

The meeting was over. Yao stood. "Thank you for your confidence, Minister. Your trust is not misplaced."

Deng dismissed Yao with a wave of his hand and waited until he was out the door. Then he turned to his secretary.

"Establish surveillance on him. Sometimes it is necessary to watch the watcher. I want to know what he is doing."

"Yes, Minister."

Deng thought about the conversation. Then he picked up the phone and placed a call to the President and Chairman of the People's Republic.

Chapter Forty

"This is the same as you find in Crete."
Selena looked up at the symbol of the double axe carved on the
pillars outside the temple.
"This is what the book was talking about. I never thought I
would see it in this part of the world."
"It's a long way from the Aegean Sea."
The interior of the building was in gloom. There was something
large in the middle of the chamber, a shape Carter couldn't quite
make out.
"What more does the book say, Selena? Are there further
directions?"
"After the part about the labrys there's a warning. Don't go in
there, bad things will happen and only the initiated can pass. Pretty
standard stuff."
"That would be priests?"
"Priests or cult members. There may be traps to prevent
intruders from getting very far. The book warns that the pursuit of
life will lead to death. Very dramatic."
"Yeah, and not very helpful." Ronnie looked up at the steep
pyramid roof rising into the cold Tibetan sky.
"The text says only those who see the vision of the great bird
will be able to pass. That's pretty much it, from what I've been able
to translate."
Carter looked at the axes on the entrance columns and the
garuda carved over the entrance. "The vision of the great bird. Must
be referring to the garuda again. What does that mean?"
"It could be anything. The words could refer to spiritual vision.
Or not."
They stepped into the temple. The pyramid ceiling had gaps and
looked like it might be ready to fall at any moment. The floor was
set with smooth, dressed stone. It was quiet and freezing cold. They
clicked on their lights. Double-headed axes carved in stone lined the
walls all the way around the room, spaced about ten feet apart and
roughly the same height from the floor.

Dominating the center of the room was a towering statue of the garuda, standing almost thirty feet high. There were traces of color where it had been painted in red, yellow and silver. Radiating outward from the base were four deep channels cut into the floor. Carter thought they might mark the four directions. A quick glance at his GPS confirmed it. The head of the bird faced east, toward the direction of the rising sun.

The detail on the statue was carved with a master's skill. Every feather of the great wings looked ready to ripple in the wind. A huge serpent writhed in agony beneath its claws. The fearsome beak gaped open and the bird sat half back on its haunches, wings spread wide, head tilted back, ready to lift into the air. It looked alive. It looked dangerous.

Sun shone through an East facing opening in the roof, painting the feet of the statue in a narrow patch of light.

"I don't see anything except that statue." Nick set his pack down on the floor. The pain in his back had settled to a dull throbbing. He put it out of his mind.

"There has to be a hidden entrance into the cavern below." Selena shone her light around the dark interior. "We should look for some irregularity in the walls, or maybe the floor."

They began searching for something out of the ordinary. Nick inspected the base of the statue while Selena and Ronnie made a slow circuit of the walls. They covered the floor. Time passed. They didn't find anything. No hidden doors. No openings in the floor.

The sun worked its way up the statue, illuminating the ancient carving. Suddenly the eyes of the garuda glinted golden as the sun struck them.

"Why are the eyes shining like that?" Ronnie walked toward the statue and peered up at the bird's head. "It looks like they might be made of gold. I want a closer look." He climbed the back of the idol until he reached the level of the eyes.

"What do you see?"

"Pretty sure it's gold. Wait a minute. There's an opening here."

He placed his flashlight behind the bird's head. Two intense streams of light beamed out of the golden eyes and illuminated one of the carved axes circling the room.

"Look at that!" Nick said. "How did they get the light to focus like that?"

"The vision of the great bird," Selena said.

"You think it's that simple?"

"I don't know."

Ronnie climbed down and dusted himself off. They walked over to the wall and looked up at the labrys pinpointed by the eyes of the bird. It looked like all the others, one of many.

"How do we get up there?" she asked.

"I'll boost you up," Ronnie said. "See if there's anything unusual about that axe."

Selena stood on his shoulders, bracing herself against the wall as Ronnie straightened. She played her light over the carving. She reached up and felt around it.

"Nothing."

"Try pushing it." She leaned into it with both hands.

"I think it moved a little."

"Push harder."

She pushed. The carving slid into the wall, stone against stone. There was a harsh grinding sound. Something heavy moved and rumbled under the floor. The statue of the garuda turned in a ponderous half circle until it faced west. It hesitated, then moved forward along one of the channels, uncovering a dark opening in the center of the temple floor.

Carter walked over and looked down into the opening. A narrow flight of stone steps descended into blackness. A stale odor of ancient dust and decay drifted up from below.

"I'd say we just found the way in."

Selena shuddered. "It reminds me of a bad dream I had once."

"Do we have a choice about going down there?"

"No, I guess not. What if that statue moves back and seals the entrance?"

"If the entrance was closed they had to have some way to open it from below, or another exit."

"Yeah," Ron said, "but this stuff is old. What if it doesn't work anymore?"

"Then we'll blow it open." Nick patted his pack. He had enough C-4 to take out the entire temple.

They started down the stairs. The steps were steep and narrow. They descended to whatever waited below. Black, cold rock absorbed the light.

At the bottom they stepped onto a ledge hanging out over a bottomless abyss. To the left, a wide passage led into the mountain, cut straight and square and lined with white stone. Another labrys was carved over the opening. Wooden torches, long cold, jutted at intervals along the walls in heavy, dark brackets that might have been iron or blackened bronze. The business ends were tarred with a sticky, brown substance.

"We might be able to use these," Carter said. He took out matches and pulled a torch from the wall. "Save the batteries."

The torch lit easily. It burned bright and made little smoke. The light of the flames threw an eerie, flickering glow back from the white walls of the hallway. Nick handed it to Selena, took down two more. One for Ronnie, one for himself. He was about to start along the passage, but Selena stopped him.

"This would be a good place for a trap."

"Why?"

"It's too easy. Anyone who made it past the statue and down the stairs would think the hard part was over. That's a good time to spring something."

"What kind of trap?"

"Spear traps were popular in the ancient world. You step on the trigger and a mechanism throws spears or arrows at you. Before you know what's happening, you're dead. Sometimes there's a false floor. It drops away and you land in a pit full of poison spikes or some other nasty surprise. Another trap makes something big and heavy fall on you or roll over you or seal you in somewhere. The Egyptians liked those. We'd be squashed like a bug."

"What do you suggest?" He eyed the innocent looking corridor.

"The spear traps should be relatively easy to spot. There have to be openings in the walls or the ceiling or even the floor, although they might be concealed. It's the floor traps or ceiling drops that worry me. If we can see a trap, we can probably trigger it or find a way through it. If not, we'd better be damn careful. Look out for ramps where something might come rolling down, or anything different about the walls or ceiling or floor."

"You make it sound like walking through a 3D minefield."

"That's a good way to think about it."

They entered the passage. Puffs of white dust rose from their footsteps and Ronnie sneezed. It echoed down the ancient passage.

Carter was strung tight. There was a sour taste in his mouth. This was Afghanistan all over again, except the enemy had been gone for thousands of years and the technology was from another time. It was old, but it could kill you as fast and as dead as anything from today's whiz-bang arsenals.

They moved slowly, scanning the floor, ceiling and walls for signs of traps. Every fifty feet he lit a torch, trying to dispel the feeling he was walking in a dark dream.

The passage curved. "Think we have a trap?" Ronnie said.

Three skeletons lay on the floor ahead. Fragments of old cloth and leather hung from yellowed bones pierced by thin wooden spears. More spears lay scattered and splintered about. Those bones had been there a long time.

Selena pointed at the walls on one side. "You can see the openings where the spears came out. They're all at knee height or above."

"What set it off?" Ronnie got down on all fours and crawled closer. "If you look hard you can see a difference in the floor. There's a thin line in the mortar. I think they stepped on these stones and that did it."

He lay down, reached forward and pressed on the floor. The stone moved. A half dozen sharp wooden shafts whistled out of the walls and splintered against the sides of the passageway. A flat, clacking noise came from behind the walls.

Ronnie inched back. "Automatic feed and reload. Pretty slick."

"If these two found their way in, how come the statue was still covering the entrance?" Selena asked Nick.

"Maybe somebody put it back and left the bodies here as a warning. We'll worry about the statue later if we have to."

They crawled under the kill zone and past the trap. They turned a corner. Ahead was a black opening and the end of the passage.

"We're getting close." Nick gestured at the opening.

He took two more steps and the floor fell away under his feet.

Chapter Forty-One

Elizabeth waved Zeke Jordan to a chair.

"We've got Cathy Chen," he said. "She was booked out of LAX to Hong Kong."

"Excellent. Where is she now?"

"In Los Angeles. She doesn't deny she was at Nick's place. She says she came over to visit an old friend and that Nick and Doctor Connor were drunk and high on something. She claims Connor passed out on the couch and Nick made a grab at her, tripped over the coffee table and landed on the floor. She says she doesn't know anything about a computer and that she got out of there after Nick made the pass. She was going to Hong Kong on business. If she'd known we were looking for her she would have come in voluntarily."

"Sure she would. What a story. Maybe a few days in isolation will help her memory."

"That's the plan."

"Are you any closer to identifying a possible informer?"

Jordan looked unhappy. "We do have someone. We're watching him to see if he makes any contacts. He's put aside a lot of money in an offshore account. I hate to admit it, but you were right."

"When are you going to drop the hammer?"

"As soon as we can tie him to the Chinese. Until then we're monitoring everything he does." Jordan tugged at his collar. "Is there anything new on the book or why the Chinese want it so badly?"

"You're sure this person is the one who tipped off Wu?"

"Why do I get the feeling you haven't told me everything, Director? Yes, I'm sure. This is our guy."

"I didn't want to brief you until you found the mole. We think we know why Yang wants the book. It might have the location of a new source of raw materials for China's nukes program. We're working to stop him."

Elizabeth didn't think Jordan needed to know they were working on stopping him in Tibet. She twirled her pen.

"We're certain Yang is planning a coup and that he's going to use the Triads to initiate attacks here when he makes his move. We think it's set for the Fourth."

Jordan was shocked. "That's only two days away."

"I convinced Homeland Security something was up. I'm not getting any cooperation from State, so that part is going to have to take care of itself."

"Two days isn't much time."

"Our indicators point to something in the Bay Area. That's the best place to focus resources."

Jordan rubbed his nose. "I'm going to have a hard time getting the Bureau to believe the Triads are moving into terrorist activity instead of another criminal enterprise. It's not part of their pattern."

Harker tapped her pen on her desk, thinking. Jordan watched her.

"Maybe we should let Yang know we're on to him. What do you think? He might reconsider his options, give us more time to expose him. We could use your informer. He could learn we're on to the threat. Then he'd try to contact Wu or Yang. It would kill two birds with the same stone. Yang would know we're prepared and maybe call it off. You'd catch your mole in the act and take him down."

Jordan smiled. "I like it. Even if Yang goes ahead, it should rattle his cage. People make mistakes when they get rattled."

"Then we're agreed. You let your mole in on our suspicion of a domestic attack tied to a plot to take over China. He doesn't need to know where the information comes from. Let him pass it along and then bust him. That ought to give more weight to your argument with the Bureau for an all out focus on July Fourth."

"Three birds with one stone."

"We don't have a lot of time."

Jordan stood up. "Then I'd better get on it."

After Jordan left, she brought up the satellite over Tibet. Nick hadn't checked in. If they were underground there was no way to send a signal. She was more concerned about the Chinese.

When the image came up she knew her concerns were real. It was nighttime again on the Tibetan Plateau. Heading toward Moincer was a convoy of four vehicles. They were some distance away, but that many vehicles all at once meant Chinese military. She tried the comm link with no response from the team. She had no choice but to wait for things to play out.

Chapter Forty-Two

Carter felt the stones tremble under his feet and jumped forward with everything he had. He heard Selena shout his name behind him. Pain shot up his spine. The floor fell away into a gaping pit. He caught the far edge of the opening with one hand, grabbed hard with the other and hung on, feet dangling. A cloud of white dust rose around him. He looked down. Twenty feet below, rows of sharpened wooden spikes reached for him like a mouth full of hungry fangs.

The walls of the pit were smooth. He hung above the spikes until he could get his arms over the edge of the opening and pull out to lie on the floor. He lay on his back and took a few, deep breaths, waiting for the pain to subside.

"You all right, Nick?" It was Ronnie.

"Yeah." He got to his feet, heart pounding. His back was bad, but if he kept moving, maybe it wouldn't lock up. He popped another pain pill and hoped it had some kind of muscle relaxant in it.

"Throw me a rope."

Ronnie tossed a line over and Nick tied it off on one of the torch brackets. Ronnie did the same. Selena and Ronnie went hand over hand until they dropped down on the other side of the pit.

"That was a hell of a jump." Ronnie slapped him on the shoulder. Nick winced.

"I felt it move just before it went. I hope that's the last of these things."

Another fifty yards of creeping along and the passage opened into blackness. They stepped through. Something glittered in the light of their torches.

They were in a chamber hollowed out from the heart of the mountain. They stood on a floor of smooth stone squares fitted together by a master mason. A broad flight of steps led up to a flat, raised platform. The other end of the platform was invisible in the darkness.

The torches cast shadows from columns spaced along the steps and the sides of the platform. Each column was elaborately carved with entwined serpents and vines. On top of each was a large, golden bowl.

"We need more light. Let's set up on the platform."

They walked across the stone floor and started up the steps.

The bowls were just above eye level. On a hunch, Nick dipped his finger into one. It was filled with some kind of oil. With a touch of his torch a burst of light and flame pushed the dark away. They moved up the steps and along the side of the platform, lighting the bowls. On the far end of the platform more steps led up to the entrance of a low, square building cut into the side of the mountain.

They stopped and stared.

In the light from the blazing bowls a soaring, giant bird spread wings of gold above the building. Upon its back rode a frightening figure sculpted of red stone. His head was two-faced, cheeks dripping with gold like melted butter, his four eyes black and burning. Seven tongues of flame licked out between sharpened golden teeth. His expression was fierce, his hair long, black and tangled, as if by a wild wind. He had seven arms circled with gold bracelets and three legs banded with blue stones set in gold. A necklace of golden skulls circled his neck. Seven broad rays of gold streamed like lightning from his body.

Beneath the bird, a frieze of double-headed golden axes capped the entrance to the building below.

The gold shone in the flickering light.

"That's Agni," said Selena, "riding the garuda." Her voice was filled with awe.

"Who's Agni?" Carter asked.

"He's one of the two most important Vedic gods, before Hinduism, very old. He's the god of fire and immortality. Usually he's riding on the back of a ram or in a chariot. I've never seen him riding a garuda. This is a really early depiction."

"That's a lot of gold up there." Ronnie gazed at the figure.

"Is that a ruby in one of his hands? It's as big as a baseball." Carter couldn't take it all in at once. He'd never seen anything like it.

"I think so, and those blue stones are probably sapphires." She turned in a circle. "Look at the walls!"

The flames illuminated murals in brilliant color circling the room. Beneath the pictures, the walls were filled with writing and symbols. The murals looked as if they had been painted just days before.

Selena walked down the steps and over to a mural next to the entrance. Holding her torch close, she examined the writing.

"My God. This is Linear A. It's written in Minoan. And beneath it." She stopped dead in her tracks.

"Beneath it, what?"

"Beneath it are passages in Sanskrit."

Carter walked over to her. "Can you read it?"

"I can read the Sanskrit. If the Sanskrit is telling the same story as the Linear A, it's the greatest linguistic discovery since the Rosetta Stone."

"That's what led to the translation of Egyptian hieroglyphics."

"Yes. No one's been able to really understand Linear A. There are theories, but none of them work all the time. It's mostly guesswork. That's what I was doing."

"It looks like pitchforks and chicken tracks."

Selena ignored Ronnie's comment. "This is a dream for me. I've been studying dead languages for years. If this is what I think, it will make history."

She held her torch high and gazed at the mural above the writing. It showed a tranquil harbor scene, sunlit buildings against an azure sky, white clouds, ships with high, curved ends, people bustling near the docks. The details were vivid, lifelike. Nick could almost feel the trees swaying in an ocean breeze.

"I think this is ancient Crete." Her voice was reverent. "This must be the harbor at Knossos."

They moved along the wall. Men in orange robes gestured before a bearded man on a raised throne. To one side of the throne a group of women dressed in white stood watching. One woman wore blue.

"King Minos?"

"Possible. The Sanskrit says they are presenting a warning to the 'Great King.' This is probably the palace at Knossos. Do you know what this means in the world of archaeology? It's like finding photographs of 1600 B.C."

The King didn't look pleased. Whatever the priests were telling him, he wasn't happy about it.

The sequence of murals grew dark. While children played on the beaches, a malignant, towering green wave bore down on the island. A seething, foaming wall of water crashed over the city, smashing trees, boats, people and buildings against the hills. Then came a narrow band painted black, as if the artist could not bear to show the destruction.

The next panel showed three sailing ships with high curved ends, plowing across a churning, wave-tossed sea under a smoky red and black sky. Standing on the decks were more of the robed figures in orange and white.

The scenes continued along the wall. A landing site under a blood-red sun. A long, overland journey through desert and plain, bearers loaded down with boxes and burdens, climbing toward snowcapped mountains in the distance.

The bearers came to a bleak hilltop. In the following panels a pyramid roofed building and houses were constructed. It was the temple site above.

The style of painting changed, the work of a different artist. Figures dressed in garments of the early days of the Chinese empire surrounded a large golden palanquin with closed curtains, borne on the shoulders of straining, bare backed slaves. The procession was entering the temple complex on the hilltop.

In the next panel figures bent over a Chinese man dressed in elaborate robes, lying on a white table. Men in orange and women in white, one in blue, stood on a platform lined with blazing sconces, arms raised and faces uplifted in supplication. Behind them the great golden bird soared with its rider. The painting mirrored what Nick could see with his own eyes.

The last panel was a detailed map. Carter recognized India, China and Mongolia. It was marked with Minoan and Sanskrit writing.

The murals told the tale of the end of the Minoan civilization. They confirmed the story in the book about taking the First Emperor of China to a secret place.

This place.

"I need pictures." Selena took out her camera. Her hands trembled.

"See if the writing can tell us anything we need to know. We'll take a look at the building."

Two V-shaped channels lined with white stone paralleled the steps going up to the building, ending at square openings on each side of a rectangular white slab in the center of the platform.

Ronnie and Nick walked around the slab. They climbed the steps and entered a large, square room. Their footsteps sent a fine cloud of gray dust into the air. Ronnie sneezed. He wiped his nose on his sleeve.

Tables covered with metal caldrons, tools and glass containers lined the sides of the room. A fire pit with iron rods and grates positioned over it took up one corner. Against one wall was a large closed chest of dark metal. Hanging above the chest was a long pair of tongs. Except for the thick dust, everyone could have downed tools and left a few minutes before.

"This reminds me of my old high school science class. Beakers, bottles, fire. I was bored in that class. Once I unscrewed a Bunsen burner on the lab bench and lit it. The flame was three feet high."

Ronnie laughed. "How'd the teacher handle that?"

"I got three days detention. Messed up football practice, Coach was really mad."

"What do you think is in that chest?"

"What's it made of?"

"I'm not sure. Some kind of metal."

Ronnie pulled his Ka-Bar and scratched the surface. A dull sliver of gray peeled away, leaving a shiny line under the point of the knife.

"It's lead."

The lid was designed to slip down around the sides of the chest. There were no hinges.

"What have we got, Nick, Pandora's Box?"

"I've got an idea."

He took a counter from his pack. The readout showed higher than normal radiation, but not dangerous.

"Let's open it up and take a look."

The lid was heavy. They lifted it and Nick felt his back spasm. They set it askew across the box. The chest was half full of black rocks. The counter reading climbed toward the red and the alarm went off.

"Back on."

"Right."

They got the lid back on in a hurry. Nick checked his dosimeter. Still okay.

"I guess we found what Yang is looking for."

"How'd the priests keep themselves from getting cooked?"

"You've got me, Ronnie. How did they know lead would protect them from radiation, or that there was any radiation in the first place? How did they build this place?"

"Nick, look over here."

A man dressed in orange robes stood in a corner alcove, arm outstretched, holding something white in his hand.

Chapter Forty-Three

Wu was stiff and sore from jolting over the rough road. The convoy had been on the road since morning, headed for the village of Moincer. From there it was still hours to the objective. Sergeant Choy rode with him in the command car.

Thirty soldiers commandeered from the 53rd Mountain Battalion in Lhasa rode in the three trucks behind. They weren't elite troops but they were used to the terrain and the altitude. Wu wasn't sure what he would find at the ruins. He'd need manpower to remove anything of interest there. The trucks would transport it back.

The General's instructions had been concise. Yang had spread a composite satellite photo on the table and placed his finger on a spot in the west of Xizang, formerly Tibet.

"Senior Colonel Wu."

"Sir."

"This is the monastery of Gurugem. Fifty kilometers north is a cluster of ruins. The directions in the book you procured lead there."

Yang placed his finger on the photo. A blurred image of regular shapes and fallen walls indicated an ancient compound.

"The nearest town is here, where the coal mines are located. There is a road to the monastery. From there you will make your way up this valley to the ruins. There is no road. Be sure you have adequate transport."

"Sir."

"Take men with you. Bring back anything you find of value."

"Sir, what am I looking for?"

"Sonar scans show a chamber under the ruins. You will find a way into this chamber. Look for artifacts of any kind. There may be maps. Look for anything that refers to the First Emperor. If there are records, collect or photograph them and bring the information back to me. Take radiation detection equipment. There may be a stockpile of radioactive materials, especially ore. If you find it, bring back a sample. If it is there, look for anything that shows where it was mined."

"What if the Americans have discovered this site?"

Yang looked unconcerned. "If any foreigners are there, interrogate and eliminate them. Find out everything they know. Dispose of the bodies and any equipment they might have. That should be easy in this remote area."

"Yes, sir. I understand. May I ask a question?"

Yang looked at Wu from under hooded eyes and nodded. For an instant it reminded Wu of a cobra, but he put the thought from his mind.

"Sir, may I ask the status of Summer Wind?"

"You may. Summer Wind is on schedule. We begin in two days, as planned. The Americans will be angered by events carried out by the Triads. Their anger will confuse them. The Chairman and the Standing Committee will be in Beijing. While they argue about how to respond to the Americans I will neutralize them. Then I will placate the Americans, blame the Committee and provide the scapegoats the American president will need for his people. Dead scapegoats in Beijing. The Triads in America."

"Sir, your vision leads us back onto the true path of our destiny. I wish I could be in Beijing when it happens."

Yang dismissed the flattery with a quick gesture, but looked pleased. "Your mission is crucial for our future. Do not fail me."

"Never, sir. I will start at once."

"Very good. Keep me informed."

Wu had saluted, turned on his heel and marched from the room.

Now, grinding through the darkness of western Xizang, Wu felt a glow of pride remembering Yang's praise. His reverie was shattered by the gunshot sound of a tire blowing out. The driver wrestled the vehicle to a stop. The convoy halted behind.

"Quickly, Sergeant."

"Sir."

Choy was out cursing, yelling orders. Wu stood smoking by the side of the road while the soldiers worked, fuming at the delay. It took twenty minutes before the wheel was changed and they were moving again. Two hours later, the yellow lights of the village of Moincer appeared.

They drove past neat rows of low houses built of whitewashed earth and stone, roofed with red tile. A few strings of prayer flags blew in the never-ending wind. Large, painted Buddha eyes stared out from some of the older buildings. They passed the ugly cement block that was Party district headquarters.

Tea carts and shops were open and crowded, even at this early hour. Wu would have liked tea, but there was no time to stop. Besides, he thought the tea in this region inferior. They drove past a man herding goats toward the market. People looked away as the Chinese convoy drove past.

The road out of town was smooth and they made good time. The lights from the vehicles revealed a stark landscape of treeless hills and patches of snow lingering in dark places untouched by sun. They passed a herd of yaks, black shapes humped like basalt rocks in the night. The night was fading and the valley was filled with deep, cold shadows.

They passed the monastery, a multi-tiered, whitewashed structure built into the side of a hill. Wu consulted the map. "Turn here. Stop."

Wu got out. A broad valley led north into the mountains. Choy stood behind him.

"Look here, Sergeant. What do you see?" He pointed at faint impressions in the fragile earth.

"Tire tracks. A wide wheel base, maybe a truck. Someone went this way, not too long ago."

"The tracks are not deep enough for a truck. I think the Americans are here before us."

"How would they get here with a vehicle, without us detecting them?"

"Who knows? When we find them, we'll ask them. Put the troops on alert, lock and load weapons. If the Americans are here, they will be armed."

"Yes, sir."

Wu's satellite phone buzzed in his pocket.

"Wu."

"This is Juggler."

Damn. What was this going to be? Wu had enough to think about. He forced his mind to English.

"Go ahead, Juggler."

"The government here has learned something is planned for July Fourth. They know the Triads are involved and are raising the alert status."

"What else?" Wu waited for the satellite delay.

"There is speculation regarding a military takeover in your country. Are you planning a coup?"

Wu drew in a breath. How did they learn of this?

"No, nothing like that is being considered. Your government is paranoid."

"What is going to happen on the Fourth? Are you planning an attack? Because I don't want to be anywhere near here if you are."

"What possible advantage would that give us? Of course not." The lie came easily. "The Triads are being mobilized against the Dalai Llama and the Tibetan Revisionists, that's all. Large demonstrations will take place. They will be forceful but peaceful. We will achieve maximum exposure by protesting on your independence day. You should not be worried."

By the time Juggler realized Wu was lying it would be too late to make any difference, but Wu needed to pacify him. Juggler was nervous. Wu decided his usefulness was over. There would be no more payments, but Juggler didn't need to know that.

"Excellent, Juggler. There will be a bonus this time. Continue to keep me informed of any developments, but there should be no more confusion after the demonstrations take place."

"I have to go. Someone's coming."

Juggler ended the call.

Wu stood in the early morning mountain cold and thought about what to say to General Yang. He walked away from the vehicle. Choy made to follow and Wu waved him back. He called Yang.

"Yes."

"Sir, I have just received a call from an asset in America."

"Yes?"

"The Americans have learned we plan something using the Triads. They suspect the existence of Summer Wind."

Silence. Wu waited.

"What is the reliability of this asset?"

"Very high, sir. He is embedded in their Federal Bureau of Investigation."

"This changes nothing. We will continue as planned. What is your current status?"

"We are starting up to the objective. I estimate three or four hours until we arrive. We found tracks and I believe the Americans are here ahead of us."

"Meddlers. Find and eliminate them. You have your orders."

"Yes, sir."

"Report when you have more information." Yang ended the call.

Wu turned and walked back to where Choy waited.

"Let's go, Sergeant."

The convoy began the climb to the ruins. Wu checked his pistol, put it back in his holster. With luck he would take the Americans by surprise. There couldn't be many of them, there were only tracks for one vehicle. He rubbed his forehead, trying to ease the pounding headache that had started. Damn this thin air. He coughed and spit out a wad of phlegm. Maybe it was time to cut back on his smoking.

Chapter Forty-Four

"Selena, come look at this." Nick called her over.

The three of them stood in front of the mummified figure.

"What's holding him up?" Ronnie held his torch close. The skin was old and brown and pulled tight over the bones of the skull. The eyes were black hollows in the face.

"Must be propped up, under the robe."

"It's one of the priests, like in the paintings. That's a piece of white jade in his hand." She stepped closer. "It's a carved figure of the emperor."

Carter remembered his dream of a robed figure in darkness, holding something white out toward him. The hair stirred on the back of his neck..

"What do you think they were doing in here?" He held his torch up. The flame reflected off the glass containers on the tables.

"Caldrons, fire, glass—it's a laboratory. I think they were trying to make an elixir of immortality," said Selena.

"It's beginning to look like it. You have any luck with the writing on the walls?"

"It's the linguistic discovery of a lifetime. The writing is a narrative and each panel has something written underneath about the painting above."

"Sort of an illustrated book." Ronnie said.

"Yes. This priest with the jade was part of a cult of eternal life. You saw that mural at the end, where everyone is standing around and raising their hands to heaven? The writing says the body was prepared for eternal existence. Immortality to these people meant you came back after death, and you had to have a body to do it. No body, no immortality."

Nick sat on a stone bench, trying to take stress off his back. "Belief in eternal life has been around since the cavemen. Lots of cultures put personal things like food and dishes in the grave for the dead person to use after death."

"The Minoans did that," said Selena. "Archeologists have found personal objects in Minoan tombs. They might have picked up on the idea from the Egyptians."

Carter tugged on his ear. "If the Minoans were leaving things in the tombs, they must have thought the body needed those things after death."

"But the Minoans didn't preserve bodies." Selena brushed a wisp of hair away. "They buried the dead in collective tombs and kept using the tombs over and over, pushing everything into a corner until it got full. These murals present something radically different. First you die, the body's preserved, then you come back in the same body and live forever. That's a huge divergence from what we know about Minoan and early Vedic civilization. The Indians cremated their dead. They still do."

"What's the elixir for?" Ronnie asked.

"I think they wanted to create a real formula for staying alive forever."

"Why here in Tibet?"

"The story on the walls says the priests started from here, went to Crete and then returned. It doesn't say when or why or how they could have known about the Minoans. The part about the emperor is clear enough. Huang was brought to this spot, to receive the elixir. That would have been in 210 B.C.E."

"I wonder what they did with him? We haven't seen anything that looks like a tomb." His back was stiffening up. Time to get back to work.

Ronnie looked at the mummy. The priest grinned back. "What's next, Nick?"

"Selena gets videos of everything. You and I look for anything that might interest Yang. Selena, if you record all of the writing we can translate it later. Once you've got your pictures we'll get out and blow the entrance. I don't want Yang down here poking around."

"You want to blow up that statue?"

"We don't have a choice. We got in easily enough. Whoever Yang sends will have the same information we have. We'll just seal the top. In the future someone can re-open it, if that's the right thing."

She shook her head. "I never thought I'd be part of destroying the archeological find of the century. I'd better finish getting my pictures."

Carter reached out to take the piece of white jade from the mummy's hand. It didn't move. He tugged on it and the arm came up as the jade came free. As he turned to give it to Selena the floor shook under their feet.

Something was happening deep under the stones. The room started to shake. Bits of mortar and trails of dust fell from the ceiling. A glass bowl slipped from one of the tables and shattered.

Taking the jade figure of the emperor had triggered some ancient mechanism. They ran out of the room, down the steps and into the great outer chamber. A thick silver fluid gushed into the channels cut along the sides of the steps and flowed down into the openings by the white slab on the platform.

"That looks like mercury," Selena called above the rumble of moving stone.

It was mercury, a hell of a lot of it. They stood at the foot of the steps and watched a rectangular white block slowly rise in the center of the platform. After a minute the flow of mercury in the channels slowed to a trickle. The rumbling vibration died away.

They walked over to the block. It was chest high and illustrated with elaborate scenes of life in ancient China. Selena ran her hands over the carvings.

"This entire container is made of white jade. I think it's a crypt, or a sarcophagus."

Carter stood next to her. "What do you think is inside?"

"Not what, who. I think the First Emperor of China."

"Still alive, you think?"

"Smartass. You want to take a look?" She trained her video camera on the sarcophagus.

"Give me a hand, Ronnie." The lid was sealed with a sticky resin. They used their knives to dig it out.

They fumbled for a handhold and moved the lid away from one corner. Inside Nick saw a foot wearing an elaborate brocaded slipper. A foul smell seeped from the crypt.

"Phew." Ronnie turned his head away.

"No place for the stink to go after they sealed him up."

"Slide the lid further over, Nick."

"It can't weigh more than a couple of hundred pounds. Let's set it down."

They lifted the lid off and rested it against the crypt. Nick looked in. The First Emperor of China lay on his back, on a golden pillow, wrapped in robes of golden silk embroidered with thousands of pearls. He wore a tall headdress of jade. On his chest lay a heavy disk of white jade, hung on a thick gold chain and inset with a large golden dragon. A small box of white jade was placed at his feet. But it wasn't the box that caught Carter's eye. It was the emperor's face.

He looked as if he had died yesterday.

"Jesus," Ronnie leaned over the coffin. "My doctor doesn't look that good and he's a lot younger. He looks like he's sleeping."

The emperor's face was pear shaped and sallow. Thick black mustaches drooped down on either side of his mouth. His lips were full and his cheeks rounded. There was a hint of cruelty in his features.

"How did they do this?" Nick said. "It makes the Egyptians look like amateurs."

"It must be the formula." Selena laid a hand against the Emperor's neck. Soft. Cold as death. "The formula wasn't for living forever. It was for preserving the body. That fits with what I read on the walls."

Nick reached down and lifted the box from the emperor's feet. Inside was a stoppered bottle of glass, filled with a light green liquid. He held it up. Flecks of golden light danced within the fluid.

"Anyone want to take a shot at living forever?"

Chapter Forty-Five

Charlie Chan put the phone in his pocket. He shuffled papers on his desk and thought about the conversation he'd just had with Colonel Wu. His cubicle was small, in keeping with his status in the FBI's Asian Criminal Enterprise Unit. Mostly he did grunt work, interviewing Chinese speaking immigrants and shop owners, translating odd pieces of information. The last few days there'd been nothing but the most boring assignments. He couldn't see the relevance of what he was working on. Soon it wouldn't matter anymore.

He was rattled. What if Wu wasn't telling the truth? If there was going to be an attack, Charlie wanted to be far away when it hit. The FBI and everyone else would go into search and destroy mode, looking for any possible connection. He'd always been careful, but you never knew. It was time to get out.

There was plenty of money in his offshore account, enough to start over, maybe in Hong Kong, where the PRC had a tolerant capitalist policy. He would be back among his own people, where no one made fun of his name. For years he'd listened to jokes about the Chinese detective of black and white movie fame. Well, now the joke would be on them.

Charlie took the picture of his parents off his desk and put it in his briefcase. He closed the briefcase and stood up just as Zeke Jordan and two other agents came to his cubicle. They blocked the way out.

"Going somewhere, Charlie?"

Charlie put on his best number one son smile.

"Got to interview a shopkeeper in Chinatown. Someone's threatening to break his windows and worse if he doesn't pay up. You know how it is, Zeke. It's hard to get anyone in the Asian community to talk, but this one seems cooperative. I want to get a statement from him."

Zeke turned to the other agents standing with him. "Get a statement. Charlie's really on it, don't you think, guys?"

Charlie didn't like the way they were looking at him.

"Make any phone calls lately, Charlie?"

"What do you mean? I make calls all day."

"I meant long distance calls. You know, overseas, maybe even China?"

"I don't know what you're talking about. What's going on, Zeke?"

"How are you planning to spend all that money?"

Charlie felt his chest constrict. How did they know about the money?

"What money?"

"The two hundred and fifty thousand or so you've got down in the Caymans."

"You've got to be mistaken, Zeke. How would I get that much money?"

"Now that's a real good question, Charlie. Isn't it, boys?"

"Real good."

"Charles Chan, I'm taking you into custody under authority of the Patriot Act on suspicion of aiding and abetting a terrorist conspiracy. Hook him up."

The two agents moved in. One pulled Chan's arms behind his back and handcuffed him. He wasn't gentle about it. The other took Charlie's gun and badge.

"Hey, take it easy, that hurts. You got this all wrong. I want a lawyer. I've got rights."

"No lawyers, Charlie. As for rights, traitors still get a few, but I don't remember right now what they are."

Jordan reached into Charlie's jacket pocket and removed the phone.

"I wonder what we'll find here? Should be some interesting numbers. Take this scumbag downstairs and lock him up. Get him out of my sight."

All work on the floor stopped as the agents frog-marched Charlie away, struggling and protesting. After a moment the sounds of the office resumed. Jordan went back into the cubicle and sat down at Charlie's desk. He didn't think he'd find anything but he was going to look just the same. He took a few deep breaths.

Zeke loosened his tie, waiting for his blood pressure to return to normal. He forced himself to sit quietly. His doctor had him on meds but sometimes they didn't seem to have much effect. His wife was always trying to get him to eat salads and take vitamins and lay off the burgers and fries. Rabbit food, he called it, the stuff she served him. There was always McDonald's on the way to work.

After a few minutes he felt better. A rotten apple like Charlie tainted everything. It made him angry.

He called for a tech to take the computer and phone in for analysis. During the next hour he went through Charlie's files. He would give Chan a little more time to realize the full implication of his situation and then begin the interrogation. Zeke didn't think Charlie would be much of a challenge. They had him cold, his only hope was to tell what he knew and try to bargain for lighter punishment.

They were making progress. With Cathy Chen and Chan in custody they had hampered Wu's operations. Jordan knew Wu was back in China, so the big question was whether it would make any real difference.

He called Director Harker.

"We've got our mole in custody."

"Have you begun the interrogation yet?"

"Not yet. I'm letting him sweat a little. His phone and computer are in the lab now. We had his cubicle bugged and recorded him making a call to Wu. They've probably got the intercept at NSA."

"What was the number?"

Jordan gave her Charlie's cell phone number.

"We didn't hear Wu's end but Chan told him we knew about his plans, so by now Yang knows we're on to him. Should be interesting to see what happens."

"It might not change anything, but it's got to have Yang worried. Stress causes mistakes. I'm hoping he'll make a few."

"You get any help from State, yet?"

"No. As far as they're concerned I should mind my own business and stick to finding second rate terrorists, which is pretty much what they think we do over here. That mostly works to my advantage, but the tradeoff is sometimes people don't take us very seriously. It's State's problem, anyway."

"I'm beginning to see you do a lot more than analyze possibilities, Director."

"I'd appreciate your discretion about that. I keep a low profile."

"Working with you has turned this into the most interesting week I've had around here in years. Low profile works for me. Anything you need from me?"

"Not at the moment. Let me know what you learn from your mole."

"I will."

Jordan flipped the phone shut and put it in his shirt pocket. Time to go talk to Charlie.

Chapter Forty-Six

The contents of the bottle swirled and sparkled with dancing glints of gold in the light of the burning bowls. Selena brushed back a loose strand of hair.

The smell of decay from the sarcophagus was getting stronger. The fresh, life-like tone of the Emperor's face was taking on a bruised look, the color darkening.

Nick took the bottle and placed it back in the box. He put the jade box back at the emperor's feet.

"How about the pictures on the walls, Selena?"

"I've already got most of it. Just a few more."

"Make it quick. We're running out of time before someone shows up. Ronnie, let's look around one more time."

In the workshop they searched through the objects scattered about on the tables. They steered clear of the chest with the uranium ore.

Selena called out. "Hey, I'm done."

"All right, let's get out of here."

"What about the emperor?" said Selena.

"What about him?"

They glanced over at the emperor. He wasn't looking good. Pools of putrid fluid were forming in the crypt. When they'd unsealed the lid, the air had started a chemical reaction. Immortality wasn't what it was cracked up to be.

"Shouldn't we put the lid back on? It seems the right thing to do."

Ronnie and Nick looked at each other, shrugged, and went over to the crypt. The bones of the face were already showing through the rotting flesh. The stench was terrible. They wrestled the lid on.

They shouldered their packs.

They went back the way they'd come, climbing over the pit and past the spear trap to the ledge at the foot of the stairs. Torches still burned in the passage. At the top of the stairs the statue was where they'd left it. Carter took C-4 from his pack and began shaping charges. Ronnie stood guard at the entrance. Selena photographed the garuda.

He placed the charges to collapse the floor around the stairwell and demolish the main doorway into the temple. He thought about it and placed a few more. The roof might come down, but he wanted to make sure no one else would get in. At the least, the entrance to the chamber would be closed and the stairs filled with rubble. He inserted the detonators and hooked up the timers.

"All set. I'm giving it ten minutes." He activated the timers.

They left the torches burning on the floor and stepped out into the daylight. Nick called Harker. As she picked up he heard the noise of trucks grinding up the mountain.

"Director, we're ready to get out of here."

"Where are you?"

"We're just outside the entrance to the building in the center of the ruins. I hear vehicles."

"All right, I see you on satellite right now. There are four vehicles approaching, three trucks and a command car. You've got company."

Her voice was distorted, fading in and out. There was a lot of interference from atmospherics.

"I'm having trouble hearing you. Can you call in a strike?" He waited for the delay.

"Not without starting World War III. I'll call for extraction. I can see what's happening and let you know what the Chinese are doing, but you've got to handle this yourself."

In Washington, Elizabeth watched the three members of her team duck back inside the building. On the western edge of the complex, the Chinese convoy halted. Soldiers jumped from the trucks and began to deploy. An officer gestured and pointed. Elizabeth zoomed in. Rank insignia of a Senior Colonel. Wu, she thought.

"Nick, about thirty bodies plus an officer, I think Wu. They're deploying along the west of the ruins and to the south. They're cutting off access to the valley. Now they're beginning to move into the complex."

Ronnie and Selena could hear Harker in their headsets. They knew what was happening.

"Okay, Director. Keep talking. I won't be answering much."

He looked at his watch. Six minutes until the charges blew. From the archway where he stood he couldn't see any troops over the rubble beyond the courtyard. They still had a little time.

"We'll go out low and fast to the east," he said. "There's plenty of cover once we're out of the square. Selena, stick close to me, stay low. I'll take the point, Selena in the middle, Ronnie, you bring up the rear."

They dropped low.

"All right, let's move. Go!"

They ran across the open courtyard and behind some large standing stones without getting shot at. His earpiece crackled.

"Good move, Nick. They're across from you to the west and below to the south. Half of them are moving toward the center, you should see them soon, the others are working their way along the wall."

The transmission was clearing up.

A dozen soldiers scrambled over the rubble and ran toward the entrance to the temple. Ronnie tracked them with his weapon. Selena looked worried, but she had her MP-5 ready.

Quietly, Carter said, "Hold your fire." He laid his hand on her arm. "Remember, short bursts. Try to keep your breath easy." She nodded.

I can do this, she thought. I can do this.

More soldiers appeared in the square and fanned out along the perimeter of the courtyard.

Nick signaled. They moved away from the square, zigzagging between clumps of stone and half standing walls, working eastward. Harker's voice came loud and strong over the link.

"You are still clear to the east. Soldiers are entering the central building. Wu is on the edge of the square directing them in. There are ten hostiles moving toward your position."

Carter looked at his watch. Thirty seconds to detonation.

"Get ready," he said. "When it blows everyone's going to be busy for a few seconds. Make a run for it, over there." He pointed to a gap in the outer wall, thirty yards away.

Ten seconds. Five. The explosion was big. Maybe he'd used a little more C-4 than he needed. There was no time to look.

They ran full out. Rocks and chunks of stone from the explosion rained down around them. Ten yards short of the gap the distinctive chatter of Chinese QBZ-95 assault rifles sounded behind them. Chips of stone sprayed around the team as they dove through the opening.

Swirling black smoke and yellow dust rose high over the courtyard. The tall pyramid roof of the temple was gone. Ronnie was firing, shiny brass cases ratcheting from his H-K and bouncing off the stones. Selena looked stunned. Nick reached around the corner of the gap and fired blindly, risked a glance, fired at a soldier as he tried for cover and brought him down. Ronnie ejected a magazine, jammed another one in.

Harker's voice came through.

"Still three in front of you. More coming around from the south. They'll see you in a minute. Extraction team is in the air, ETA sixteen minutes."

Nick took out a grenade, pulled the clip and the pin, let go of the handle and threw it over the wall. He heard screams as it went off.

"Ronnie, go!" He pointed and Ronnie took off along the wall for the northeast corner.

He pulled Selena to her feet. "That way."

A Chinese soldier came over the wall and clubbed him with his rifle. Carter went down hard, his eyes blurring. Sound stopped. He struggled to move. He watched the Chinese raise his weapon, everything moving in silence and a strange light and slow, fluid motion, the soldier silhouetted against the cloudless sky.

He thought of Megan.

Red spots blossomed on the soldier's chest, stitching a neat pattern across his uniform. His eyes opened wide. Blood bright as fire gushed from his mouth and he fell sideways to the ground. Nick stumbled to his feet. Suddenly he could hear again.

Selena stood ten feet away, looking at the man she'd just killed, her MP-5 held close by her cheek. He watched her face register what she'd done.

Nick picked up his weapon and grabbed Selena's arm. They ran for the far corner. The ground along the wall was flat for twenty feet or so until it dropped away in a steep slope to the right. They ducked and dodged between piles of fallen stones from the broken walls. Bullets whined and ricocheted all around.

Ronnie was almost to the corner when a clatter of automatic fire came from behind and he went down. Nick turned and fired, Selena beside him. They brought down the shooter. When they reached Ronnie, they dragged him around the corner.

His leg was bloody. There were two holes on the back of his uniform, but his body armor had deflected the rounds and kept him alive.

"Shit," he grunted, face tight with pain.

"How bad?"

"Thigh shot. Probably broken ribs. God damn it!"

"Selena, cover us. Keep your head down, quick looks, reach around the corner and fire in their general direction."

She nodded, grim-faced, stuck her H-K around the corner, and began firing short bursts. Nick cut Ronnie's pants leg away. The bullet had gone all the way through, from the back to the front of his thigh. Nick bound him up with a strip of cloth torn from the pants.

"Looks like it missed the bone and artery, amigo. Think you can stand on one leg?"

"Yeah."

Ronnie was pale. Things had just gotten more difficult.

Harker's voice sounded in his ear.

"ETA for extraction, eleven minutes. I can see eight hostiles still moving around plus Wu and Choy."

"Tell them we've got wounded. Tell them to expect ground fire. I'm going to try to get to the northwest corner."

"Roger that."

The sky was a dirty yellow color, dust from the explosion drifting everywhere. He knelt by Selena.

"How's your ammo?"

"Getting low."

He gave her another magazine. "We have to get to the next corner. There's a chopper coming. We need to stay alive and knock down a few more of them."

"How's Ronnie?"

"We'll have to help him. You're doing great. You help Ronnie, you and he watch the front, I'll cover the rear. Up there." He pointed. "Go!"

She jumped up and helped Ronnie to his feet. They started toward the far corner, Ronnie hopping on one leg with his arm around Selena's shoulder. Nick risked a look around the wall, ducked back as flying chips cut into his face. He reached around, firing, and saw another enemy soldier collapse.

Selena and Ronnie had made it to the end of the wall. He caught up with them. They crouched behind a tumble of rock at the corner.

"ETA six minutes." The voice of the Director was distorted again by atmospherics. "Wu and four others are back at the trucks. Four coming toward you, around the corner."

"Coming this way." He pointed. "Let them get part way down the wall." They waited, weapons leveled. Four men appeared, running low and hard. Selena and Ronnie and Nick opened up at the same time. The storm of bullets ripped through the soldiers and turned their crisp uniforms into bloody rags. They crumpled and slid down the side of the hill.

"Just five left, now, down there." He gestured toward the Chinese trucks parked fifty yards away, visible in quick glances between the rocks giving them cover. "They have to come to us. Let's wait here."

"Suits me." Ronnie looked white and haggard. Blood stained the improvised bandage on his leg. Selena looked flushed. Carter's face was swelling where he'd taken the blow and his jaw hurt. His back felt like it was in a vise.

"ETA three minutes." Harker's voice echoed in his ear. "You should hear them any minute now. We sent you a Pave Hawk with Apache escort."

That made him smile, even though it hurt. The Pave Hawk only had a couple of fifties or 7.62's on it, but the Apache was a different animal altogether. Colonel Wu was about to get a big surprise.

"Tell them to take out those vehicles as soon as they can get a lock. Make sure they know where we are. I'll make smoke."

"Roger that."

He pulled a smoke marker from his pack. In the distance, he heard the choppers.

"ETA two minutes."

He pulled the pin and tossed the marker. A bright orange plume of smoke billowed upward. Chips flew off the rocks around them from a barrage of automatic fire that said Wu knew where they were. It wasn't going to do him much good now.

Three helicopters popped up over the next ridge, laboring hard in the thin air, two Apaches leading the way. A big man stood up by the Chinese trucks with a shoulder launcher. Carter recognized the man from the porch in California and locked him in the sights of his MP-5. He gave him a full magazine. Choy went over backwards as the launcher fired.

The missile snaked straight up into the air, stretching a white plume of smoke behind. It wandered uncertainly, then turned and headed straight for one of the Apaches. Carter held his breath.

A dark shape streaked out of the lead helicopter and met the missile in mid-air. The explosion slapped against their ears.

The Apaches launched rockets.

Nick hit the dirt. The blast rocked the ground. Stones tumbled off the wall, bouncing around them. When he looked again, two of the trucks were engulfed in flame. The gunners on the Apaches opened up with 30 millimeter chain guns and the burning trucks and remaining vehicles blew apart. The smoking remains of an engine sailed out of the sky and buried itself in the ground ten feet in front of him.

The Pave Hawk settled down hard on a flat area. Six troopers jumped from the hatch and fanned out to form a perimeter while the Apaches hovered overhead. Carter stood.

"Selena, you take one side, I'll take the other."

They carried Ronnie at a trot toward the helicopter. A medic came out to help and lifted him in. They climbed in after him.

"Good Morning, Gentlemen."

The voice belonged to a Captain wearing Army Rangers flashes on his uniform. His name tag said Riggins. He looked surprised when he saw Selena.

"And Lady. Strap yourselves in. We're leaving. Just the three of you?"

"Right. Nice to see you, Captain. The Gunny here took a hit in his leg.

"Saw that. We'll get to it right away, Colonel."

He didn't ask any questions. Captain Riggins said something into his radio. The troopers on the ground pulled in and boarded.

The Pave Hawk lifted and turned south toward India.

Carter looked out the open hatchway. The courtyard of the temple was littered with bodies. The temple was a jumbled pile of broken stone. Nothing moved but dust and smoke eddying in the chill wind. No one was going to visit the Emperor for a while.

Flames rose fifty feet into the air from the remains of the Chinese convoy. There was no movement on the ground, no weapons fire toward the chopper.

Safe.

He felt the tension start to drain away. His back was an agony of fire. He shifted on the hard seat and turned to Selena.

She was staring out through the open hatch, watching the Himalayas slide by as the helicopter descended into a long, wide valley toward India. Overhead, the steady beat of the blades drummed away.

She turned toward him. Nick had seen that look before, when someone came face to face with their own, violent death. When they began to understand the power of life and death they held over others.

In combat everyone was an instrument of death. The initiation wasn't easy. Some broke. Some got stronger. He could see Selena was one of the strong ones.

"You're all right."

She said nothing.

"People go through months of training to prepare for something like that and screw it up. You did everything right. You could have been a Marine."

She almost smiled. Then a distant look came into her eyes. After a few seconds she said, "Now I know what you meant."

"About what?"

"About shooting back. About defending yourself. I felt like a different person back there. I don't know who that person is."

"It takes time to make room for that, find a way to fit it in."

She took off her helmet, ran her fingers through her hair, her eyes reflecting some new thought, some undefined reality.

"You've been doing this for years."

"Yes."

"Does it get easier?"

"No. You have more familiarity with it, but it's never easy. It's just something that has to be done. You do it and think about it afterward."

His words would never replace what Selena had left back there with that dead soldier by the wall, the moment she pulled the trigger.

His earpiece sounded.

"Nick, you there?"

"Yes, Director."

"No sign of life at the complex. I think you got them all. You're minutes from Indian airspace and the Chinese won't follow you there. They scrambled fighters out of Chengdu, but they won't get to you in time."

"That's good news."

"You'll be landing in a restricted area on an Indian airbase. We have an understanding with the Indian government about using their facility. We don't want them to know what you were doing. A C-130 will be waiting. How's Ronnie?"

"He's good. A thigh wound and some cracked ribs. The medic gave him morphine and he's a happy guy right now."

"Selena?"

"She's fine, Director."

"What did you find?"

"What we went for and more. We've got our evidence, but I'll wait for the debriefing. Director, we made a mess down there. The Chinese aren't going to be happy about it."

"I'll worry about the Chinese. I'll see you tomorrow in Washington. I'm signing off for now."

He leaned back against the armored plate and closed his eyes. It had been a long, long day.

Chapter Forty-Seven

It was 10:02 in the evening on July Fourth in Washington. Elizabeth sat in the coolness of the VIP waiting room at Andrews Air Force base, waiting for the team to touch down. A driver and vehicle stood by outside. She was thinking about the possible fallout over the battle with the Chinese. Her phone signaled a call on the scrambled circuit.

"Harker."

"Director, this is General Hood. What is your current location?"

"At Andrews, waiting for the team."

"There's been a major incident in California. Someone blew up three electrical sub-stations. Oakland, San Francisco, the peninsula, Sacramento and the Central Valley are without power. A large portion of Northern and Central California is down. The cascade is threatening to take out the West Coast."

"How did they get through security?"

"We don't know. The attack was well coordinated. All stations went down at the same time. I'm on my way to the White House right now. The President has called a meeting at 2300 and you need to be there."

"On my way."

"You'll be escorted to the Situation Room when you arrive."

"Who will be in attendance?"

"The President, his Chief of Staff, the Director of Homeland Security, the Director of National Intelligence, the National Security Advisor, CIA, Westbrooke from the FBI and General Holden from the Joint Chiefs. That's as of this moment. There may be others."

"What is the alert status?"

"The President has ordered the military to DEFCON 4. There is as yet no indication of hostile intention from any national entity. Homeland Security is holding at Elevated Threat alert until we have more information."

"I understand. I'm leaving now." Harker stood and started for the door.

"Elizabeth."

Harker paused mid-stride. General Hood rarely used her first name.

"Does Rice know about your operation?"

Elizabeth had briefed Hood earlier. He was an ally. If word got out about Tibet, she'd need allies. She had decided it was best to protect the President, in case something went wrong.

"No. I felt it better to wait."

"Watch your step in there. Heads will roll over this."

"I appreciate the advice, General."

"See you there." The call ended.

She dialed Stephanie.

"Steph, there's a situation on the West Coast. I've been called to a meeting at the White House. I want you to pick up the team. Get them out of sight and back into civilian clothes."

"Yes, Director."

"I'll call in when I know more. I won't be available for awhile. Hold down the fort until I get back."

"Got it."

Harker ended the call. The Project was handled. A few minutes later her driver was breaking speed limits and weaving through late night D.C. traffic toward the White House.

Harker did a quick mental review of everything she knew about Yang and the operation. She might need to explain why she'd ordered a covert operation on Chinese sovereign territory. Some of the people who would be in that meeting had no idea the Project conducted black ops traditionally under the mandate of CIA or SOCOM. Her cherished low profile was about to evaporate into thin air.

She looked out the window. They turned onto Pennsylvania Avenue and neared the traffic barriers marking the outer security zone for the White House.

Her vehicle was passed through the security checkpoints. They stopped at a side entrance of the White House, away from the cameras watching the front for signs of newsworthy people or activities. She was met by two secret service agents wearing dark suits and earpieces. They had Glocks clipped to their waists in fast draw holsters.

"Director Harker?"

"Yes."

One of the agents handed her a badge to clip onto her lapel.

"Follow us, please."

This part of the White House was unfamiliar to her. She followed the agents down a long hall lined with period paintings of the nineteenth century. The walls were light beige. The lighting was subdued. The carpet was soft under her feet.

The Situation Room was located in the basement of the West Wing. A few turns and a short flight of steps down and she found herself at the entrance. A secret service agent stood by a lead lined cabinet at the door.

"May I have your phone, please, Director?"

Harker turned off her phone and handed it over. The agent placed it in the cabinet with several others. She wasn't the first to arrive.

"Do you have any other personal electronic devices with you?"

"No, that's it."

"If you need to make a call, please use one of the booths."

A row of wooden phone booths stood along the wall, modern echoes of the 1950s.

"Thank you."

Inside, a long conference table took up the center of the room. It was flanked by wide brown leather chairs. Blank television monitors covered the wall at the far end. Two tiers of computer terminals were set off to the side, manned by Air Force technicians.

The National Security Advisor was in animated conversation with General Holden, Chairman of the Joint Chiefs, and the Director of National Intelligence. Half way down the table General Hood was talking with the Acting Director of the CIA, Wendell Lodge. Harker knew Lodge well from previous encounters.

Lodge was old school. Yale, Skull and Bones, five foot ten and elegant in a gray Brooks Brothers suit and college tie. Career CIA, he was 60 years old. His hair was tailored white, with the look that came only with regular four hundred dollar haircuts. His face was rosy and flushed, lending him a kindly, avuncular air that had deceived many a politician or underling.

Harker knew Lodge was nobody's uncle, kindly or otherwise. He demanded absolute obedience from his subordinates and never forgot or forgave a personal slight or a professional mistake. His boss was in Bethesda Hospital on life support. Lodge was about to step into the DCI slot unless the political process blindsided him with someone from outside the Agency.

General Hood beckoned her over.

"You know Director Harker, Wendell."

"Elizabeth," Lodge said, "nice to see you again. I hear you've been up to something with our Chinese friends. Was your operation successful?"

He smiled, but Harker wasn't fooled. She remembered Hood's warning that someone's head would roll. Lodge would be one of the executioners manning the guillotine if it came to that.

"It's good to see you, too, Wendell."

"We were just talking about your theory a coup in the PRC is tied to what's happening in California. We haven't picked up any indications of a takeover scenario at Langley."

By using the word theory Lodge was letting her know he was not convinced a coup was in progress or relevant to the current situation. It didn't matter that he had to know of Deng's warning about General Yang.

It was CYA time, and Lodge was a master of the game. Elizabeth wasn't surprised. No one wanted responsibility for being caught unawares by a terrorist attack of this magnitude.

"I suspect that will come up today," Harker said. "Whether or not a coup is actually being planned, I believe the Chinese are behind whatever is happening in California."

"I hope you can back that up, Elizabeth. That is a serious allegation."

Harker decided to feed him a little information.

"You are familiar with General Yang Siyu?"

"The head of Chinese MI?" Lodge gave her a look of interested attention.

As if he doesn't know exactly who I mean, she thought.

"The same. In cooperation with the FBI, we have established that General Yang has been plotting with the Chinese Triads on the West Coast. We tracked payments amounting to four hundred million dollars from Yang to the Triads. The money was stolen from an American investor."

"Are you talking about William Connor?"

"Yes. We identified and detained two of Yang's agents, one of whom was embedded in the FBI. He was caught red handed talking with Yang's principle aide. He passed along the information that we suspected a coup and expressed concern for his personal safety because of unspecified events planned to take place today."

Lodge raised an eyebrow. "Why wasn't Langley informed, Director?"

"I believe that was the responsibility of the FBI. They handled the discovery and detention of Yang's people. Perhaps they were embarrassed to find out one of their own is a traitor."

Harker knew that her political survival, even the survival of the Project, might depend on how this man read the situation. If he decided to oppose her, she was in trouble. There was no harm in letting the FBI take some of the heat. Besides, what she said was mostly true.

As if on cue, FBI Director Gordon Westbrooke entered the room, followed by the Director of Homeland Security, Joseph Wiseman. Harker watched Lodge's eyes narrow as he observed Westbrooke. Behind Lodge's back General Hood gave her a look of approval.

"I look forward to hearing more about this, Elizabeth. Let's get together soon. Perhaps lunch next week? I like to talk with you about something, but this isn't the place. If you'll excuse me, I think I'll go have a little chat with Gordon." He nodded at Hood and moved with purpose toward Westbrooke.

"You're on your toes today, Director," said Hood. "That was neatly done."

Harker glanced at her watch. It was almost 11:00 P.M. Kevin Hogan, President Rice's Chief of Staff came in.

"The President will be here momentarily," he said. "Please find your seats."

Chapter Forty-Eight

President Rice entered the room.

"Good evening, everyone. Please be seated." Rice took his place at the head of the table and the others sat.

President James Rice was in the third year of his first term and deep in the quicksand of presidential politics. Descended from early American colonists, he was named after an ancestor who'd fought in the American Revolution. He'd served with distinction as a young Marine officer in Vietnam. At sixty-seven he looked ten years younger. His face was strong and comforting, with hazel eyes that seemed to speak directly to you alone. He was popular, charismatic when he chose and possessed of a streak of integrity that defied the conventions of the political world. Harker liked him.

"Let's get started. Joseph, what is our current situation?"

The Director of Homeland Security cleared his throat.

"Mister President, power is out throughout Northern and Central California, Oregon, Southern Washington and Western Nevada. The effect is spreading as other stations in the grid try to take up the load. The electrical utilities have gone to rolling brownout in an effort to head off more failures.

"The Governor of California has called out the Guard. All civilian emergency forces have been activated. Emergency power is up and running at all medical facilities. We are currently at Elevated Alert."

"Are we certain these explosions were not accidental?"

"Yes, Mister President. They occurred at exactly the same time and appear to have been selected to create maximum disruption in the grid."

"Any communication from terrorist groups?"

"We have received a statement claiming responsibility from a group calling itself the Beijing Great Nation Brigade."

"Is this a known group?"

"No, Mister President."

At that moment an aide entered and handed President Rice a note. Everyone watched as he read it. Rice looked up at them. He was grim.

"There have been explosions in San Francisco with heavy civilian casualties. Turn on the monitors."

Heads swiveled toward the end of the room. The monitors came alive. There was no sound, but the visuals were enough. All the major networks were showing scenes in the Bay Area.

A live helicopter shot zoomed in on bodies lying in the Ferry Building Plaza. A bomb had detonated under the restaurant at the end of the Ferry Building Pier. The restaurant was gone. The pier was mostly gone. Under the restaurant a reinforced concrete shaft had fed air into the BART tunnel running below the bay. It was gone. Where it had been, the waters of the Bay churned in a seething whirlpool, pouring into a black hole.

The networks were pooling shots. Injured and frightened people wandered aimlessly about. CBS switched to an interview with a panicked mother sitting outside what was left of the Ferry Building, clutching her child and sobbing.

CNN was running a banner saying the country was under terrorist attack. Fox had a right wing talking head sounding off. Behind him was a background shot of the Twin Towers burning.

Chapter Forty-Nine

"My God." It was Hansen, the National Security Advisor.

"Mister President." General Holden spoke from the end of the table. "I recommend we go to DEFCON 3. We don't know who's behind this. This may be a set up for a larger attack."

"Mister President, may I interrupt?" It was Lodge. "Before we take further action I believe we should hear from Director Harker."

Here it comes, Harker thought. Lodge was anticipating political fallout and diverting thoughts of an intelligence blunder away from CIA and over to her.

"Director?"

Everyone looked at her. She forced herself to keep her hands resting quietly on the table before her. A memory surfaced of her father, sitting in his big wingback chair in the den.

"Never let them see what you're really thinking."

Her father reached for a glass of bourbon on the side table by his big, green chair.

"When it's important, when the chips are down, you've got to conceal your thoughts and control your feelings. It's like poker; you can't let the other fellow know what you're up to"

Her father often seemed to confuse her with the son he'd never had.

"Yes, Daddy"

"Stand up for what you believe in. Don't lie, but you don't always have to say everything that's on your mind. You're smart and you're going to go far. It's certain there will be times in your life when you have to know when to hold 'em and when to fold 'em."

She decided to reveal the Tibetan operation, before Lodge sandbagged her. It was time to hold 'em.

Lodge was watching to see how she would handle it. To hell with him.

"Yes, Mister President. Ten days ago we discovered a ranking officer of Chinese Military Intelligence was responsible for the murder of William Connor, the noted investment banker. This officer reports directly to General Yang Siyu, head of Chinese MI.

"Large sums of money were taken from Connor's accounts and transferred to the control of General Yang. That money was again transferred to accounts here in America controlled by the Chinese Triads.

"General Yang heads a group in China called the White Jade Society, composed of senior military and government officials. Analysis of intelligence indicates that this group is plotting a coup to install General Yang as the new leader of China. His man met several times with leaders of the Triads. I believe Yang is using the American Triads to create a diversion here while he seizes power in China."

Rice interrupted her.

"Director, you believe a coup is underway in China and that these terrorist events are related to it?"

"Yes, Mister President."

"That is a very broad supposition."

"Yes, sir. May I continue?"

"Go ahead."

"Thank you, sir. William Connor was murdered for money, but also for an old book in his possession. General Yang went to great lengths to obtain this book, which Connor had hidden. An attempt was made here in Washington to kidnap Connor's niece in an effort to learn where it was. Five Chinese agents were killed by one of my team during that attempt."

There was a murmur around the table. She had their attention.

"We retrieved the book. Again, Chinese agents attempted to intervene. Two were killed, as well as a California police officer. We asked ourselves why this text was so important to General Yang. Translation revealed clues to the location of a deposit of high grade uranium ore somewhere in modern China.

"We believed Yang wanted to find that deposit to enhance China's nuclear weapons program. The book pointed to a specific location in the Tibet Autonomous Region where directions to the deposit could be found.

"The translation of the book was stolen by one of Yang's agents. That agent is in custody, as is another, deep cover agent we discovered embedded in the FBI. That informer contacted Yang's man and expressed concern about a possible attack here today."

All eyes turned to Westbrooke. He gave Elizabeth a hard look. I have made an enemy there, she thought.

"Based on our analysis, I ordered a team into the field. We needed to know if a uranium deposit exists, since this would impact China's nuclear programs. We needed more intelligence to inform us about Yang and his plans. The only way to get it was to go to the source revealed in the book."

"You sent a team into Tibet."

"Yes, Mister President."

"How were they inserted?"

"B-1B and high altitude jump."

"Armed?"

"Yes, sir."

"And?"

"The team reached their objective and confirmed the existence of a previously unknown high grade uranium deposit, located in the Inner Mongolia Autonomous Region."

"Any complications?"

"There was a confrontation with Chinese military personnel as the team prepared to leave. More than thirty Chinese were killed. The team was then safely extracted to India. They are arriving at Andrews as we speak."

The table was silent, all eyes on Elizabeth and the President.

The President looked at Holden. "Were you aware of this operation, General?"

"No, sir."

"How about you, Wendell?"

"We were informed of the operation after it had been executed."

"Not aware, then. General Hood, you knew the details of this mission?"

"I did, sir. The data was solid. We had to know if the ore deposit existed."

Rice turned to Elizabeth. "Why was I not informed, Director?" He was getting angry.

"Sir, the decision was not taken lightly. I felt deniability was a factor, as we were going into Chinese sovereign territory. Therefore you were not informed. It was my intention to brief you as soon as our information was complete.

"I want to point out, sir, that I alerted Homeland Security to a potential terrorist threat. I also attempted to inform State regarding a possible coup in China, but was rebuffed."

"Who was contacted at State?"

"The Assistant Secretary for Asian and Pacific Affairs. She was quite adamant there was no possibility of a takeover in China, or even an attempt at one."

Rice turned to his Chief of Staff.

"Set up a meeting with State for tomorrow, and have him bring the Assistant Secretary with him."

"Yes, sir."

"General Holden and Director Lodge. Focus your intelligence gathering resources on China. Look for indications a coup may be underway. General Holden, to address your request, I am ordering you to go to DEFCON 3. Director Westbrooke. Find out who is responsible for these terrorist acts. I want them identified. I want that now."

"Yes, Mister President."

"Joseph, stay at Elevated nationwide and go to Imminent on the West Coast. Follow our existing scenarios for terrorist attack. They should be adequate or we've all wasted a lot of time since nine eleven."

"Yes, Mister President."

The presidential aide came in and whispered in the President's ear. Rice nodded and a uniformed army Colonel came into the room. He went to General Holden, said something in a low voice and remained standing behind him.

Holden said, "Mister President, our satellites show unusual military movements in and near Beijing, in the central provinces and off the coast of the Chinese mainland."

"What kind of movements, General?"

"I can bring them up on the monitors, sir."

Holden went to the computer banks and spoke to a technician. In seconds the pictures of chaos in the Bay Area were replaced with a series of live satellite photos. It was full day in China. The images were clear. General Holden stood by the monitors and indicated one of the feeds.

"This is China's principle ICBM base, located in Luoyang, in the Eastern Central region. It's manned by the 80304 Unit of the Second Artillery Corps. We estimate they have 15 DF-5 and 25 DF-31 ICBM's targeted on the US and Europe. Average yield is around 3 to 5 kilotons per missile. The DF-5s are in silos. The DF-31s are on mobile launchers. They keep them in tunnels."

He indicated part of the picture. "Notice the movement of equipment outside the base. This is heavy troop transport and tank movement. The vehicles have blocked access to the facility and appear to be making a flanking or circling maneuver."

"Who commands that base?"

"General Lu Cheng, sir. He is known to be a xenophobic hard liner."

Elizabeth sat up straighter in her chair. Lu Cheng was a member of the White Jade Society.

"Have the silos been activated?" Rice asked.

"Not as of this moment, sir. We'll know if they do."

Holden turned his attention to another live shot, this time of a large city.

"This is Beijing. Again, you see extensive movement of tanks and troops. They're moving into Tiananmen Square and along all main arteries."

He signaled the Colonel and the image changed again.

"This is Hainan Island, off the Southern Coast. The Chinese have constructed a state of the art underground submarine base here, at Sanya. It is home to their most advanced nuclear ballistic submarine, the Type 0-94. Those subs carry twelve JL-2 missiles with two point five megaton warheads. Perhaps by coincidence, their top naval officer, Admiral Zhang Lian, arrived in Sanya yesterday."

Admiral Zhang was another member of White Jade.

"You can see a lot of activity, here, right where the pens are located, and two of their subs. It looks to me like they're readying for sea. Tanks and troop transports are moving toward the base. They're cutting off access to the rest of the island."

"What is your interpretation, General?"

"Sir, this appears to be an effort to isolate the missile and sub bases by troops. In Beijing, I'd say forces are securing the city. But it's not possible to say who is controlling those forces."

The room watched as four J-11 fighters, Chinese variants of the Russian SU-27 SK, passed over the submarine base.

Lodge spoke up. "Mister President, if Director Harker's assessment is correct, we could be looking at a coup in progress. This may be an effort by the current government to stop it, or those troops may be under command of the conspirators."

"Sir, those bases are controlled by members of Yang's White Jade Society." Harker wanted to make sure Rice knew. "General Lu is particularly dangerous, in my opinion. He could start a war with those missiles."

"Mister President," Holden said, "It's possible this is the beginning of a confrontation with the Chinese. I now recommend we escalate to DEFCON2. Sir, you should remove yourself to the secure bunker."

"General. Under no circumstances am I leaving the White House at this time. The last thing the country needs is a President who runs for cover when something happens." Rice raised his hand to stop further protest. "That's final, General."

"Yes, sir."

"What offensive naval assets do we have near China?"

"The Ronald Reagan and her accompanying AEGIS class escorts are two hundred and fifty miles off North Korea. There are two of our Ohio class boomers in the general area, the George Washington Carver and the Tennessee."

"General, order those ships to assume DEFCON2, but we will not raise the national level just yet. We have not gone to DEFCON2 since the Cuban crisis. I am not convinced we should do so now. We will wait. If those silos go hot I will reconsider. In the meantime, institute DEFCON3 for the rest of our forces."

"Yes, sir."

"We have to deal with these attacks in California. You all have something to do. Get going on it. General, monitor the situation in China and bring me your analysis in one hour. Call a meeting of the Joint Chiefs here for that time.

"I want no mention of this supposed group claiming responsibility. Until I have considered the implications of Director Harker's actions and until we have better intelligence from China I don't want anything made public. This meeting is concluded. Everyone make sure you are immediately available if I need you. Director Harker, Kevin, remain here."

Rice stood and the room emptied. When all had gone, Rice sat down again.

"Director, you may have started a fire over there, and I'm going to have to put it out. You'd better be right in your analysis. Now tell me the rest of it."

"Mister President?"

"Director, don't bullshit an old bullshitter. Your brief was to the point, but it's clear you are leaving something out. I want to know what it is."

"Sir, I felt the rest of it, as you put it, was irrelevant to the events on the coast."

"I'll be the judge of that."

"Yes, sir."

Harker told him what had been left out.

Rice turned to his Chief of Staff.

"Kevin, you are to forget what Director Harker just told us. Am I clear? None of this must get out."

"Yes, sir."

"Have the Director's team brought to me. I want to hear about this action in Tibet from them."

"Sir, Langley would be better for debriefing…"

"No. I'll see them tomorrow morning. Make room on my schedule."

"Yes, sir."

"Director Harker. Where is your team now?"

"They were due at Andrews an hour ago, sir. They were to be met and taken out of sight."

"Get them here in the morning. Coordinate with Kevin."

"Yes, Mister President."

"One more thing."

"Sir?"

"If word of what you have just told me ever becomes public it will create widespread difficulties. Make sure it does not."

"Yes, Mister President."

"We're done for now. There will be a meeting tomorrow with State. I want to hear State's assessment and I want you there as well. Kevin will let you know when. Now I have to prepare a statement to the nation. The American people will expect it."

Rice rose and was gone, escorted by his secret service agents, before Harker could say anything else. Not that there was anything else to say.

Hogan said, "Dead emperors?"

"Yes."

"Your people killed thirty Chinese?"

"They didn't have much choice."

"What was left behind? Anything pointing to us?"

"We were careful to use equipment that cannot be directly traced to the US. The vehicle had Pakistani markings. Supplies were non-specific to us. The Chinese will certainly figure it out but they will have a tough time proving it. I think we're in the clear there."

"You'd better hope so, Director. They're going to be pissed. For all our sakes I hope it turns out to be worth it. Let's set up the meeting with your people."

Harker called Stephanie and gave her instructions. Now it was up to the President.

Chapter Fifty

Stephanie met the team at Andrews and drove them back to the Project.

Carter felt like a sack of cement. Jet lag was on him like a wrecking crew on a Vegas casino. Pain killers had his back down to a dull ache. Ronnie came hobbling out of the bathroom. No showers for him. He had bandages around his damaged ribs, cracked by the Chinese rounds. His leg wound was tightly wrapped.

"Coffee, guys," Stephanie said. They each took a cup.

Steph's cell went off.

"Yes, Director." She listened. "They're fine. All right, I'll tell them."

She hung up. "Guess what?"

"What? Let me guess. We're getting on a plane again."

"No, Nick. The President wants to see all of you."

"The President? You're kidding."

"He's sending a car for you tomorrow morning."

"I know the President." Selena sipped her coffee. "He's a good man."

"How do you know him?" Nick said.

"He and my uncle were friends. We had dinner with him at the White House about six months ago."

"What's he like?"

"Straight forward. He has no patience with people who dodge the issues. He hides his thoughts well when he wants to, and he's not someone you want to cross. I'd say he's a genius when it comes to politics. He takes his job seriously. It determines everything he does."

"Why do you think he wants to see us?"

"I imagine he wants a first hand account."

"The Director said to turn on the TV." Stephanie set the coffee pot down.

"Why would she say that?" Nick reached over and turned it on.

"Holy shit," said Ronnie. "Isn't that San Francisco? The Bay Bridge in the background?"

"That's the Ferry Building. But what happened to the pier and the Plaza?" Selena's voice was strained.

"Turn up the sound."

In a few minutes they had the picture. The death toll was rising. Public services were compromised. Hospitals all over the Bay Area were overwhelmed.

Homeland Security had gone to Imminent in the West. People were ordered to remain in their homes. All public transportation was under military control. All government facilities were shut down or under heavy guard. In San Francisco the BART tunnels were flooded all along the Embarcadero and across the Bay to Oakland. Power was still out over most of California and the West.

The President was scheduled to address the nation in the morning.

"Yang," Carter said.

"Has to be," said Ronnie. "It's too much of a coincidence."

"I wonder what's happening in China? Yang must be making his move."

"I hope they shoot that son of a bitch." Ronnie said.

"They will, unless he shoots them first."

"You think he'll use those missiles?"

"Not unless he's completely crazy. He might threaten to use them. That would be a big mistake." Carter set his cup down.

"This could be Cuba all over again. That was too close for comfort." Ronnie drained his cup.

"At least Kennedy had a line to Khrushchev. I don't think anyone's got a line to Yang right now. We'd better hope the PRC is up for this."

"I never thought I'd be rooting for the ChiComs."

"Yeah, well, it's a strange world, Ronnie. In this case, the PRC is on the side of the angels. I just hope they move fast enough to stop Yang before he does something stupid."

"Like launch a missile?" Selena brushed a strand of hair from her forehead.

"Like that."

"God, I'm tired," she said. "I can't think about this anymore."

Stephanie stood up. "Come on, Ronnie, I've got a place for you down the hall. Get some sleep before you see the President."

The door closed behind them. Carter lay down and the next thing he knew, Stephanie was knocking on the door and saying coffee was up and they had an hour before heading for the White House.

Chapter Fifty-One

The nine men who ruled China were meeting at Party Chairman and President Zhang Jei's official residence in Beijing. No one ruled in China without the backing of the People's Liberation Army. The committee made decisions, but it was the PLA that enforced them. Several ranking PLA officers had been invited to the meeting.

General Zhou was Chairman of the Military Commission and Commander of the Beijing Military Region. He sat between Minister Deng from State Security and the Commander of the Guangzhou Military region in Southern China, General Liu. General Yang Siyu was at one end of the long oval table, next to Zhang.

Across from him sat General Hong, Commander of the Second Artillery Battalion, China's nuclear and ballistic missile force. Two chairs down Chen Tian, Minister of Railways, toyed with a notepad and pencil on the table before him. The rest of the Politburo Standing Committee filled out the seats at the table.

Problems of ethnic unrest in the Tibet Autonomous Region and China's western Xinjiang region were first on the agenda. The men were discussing strategies for suppressing the native protests when a messenger entered the room and went directly to the President. Zhang listened carefully, then turned to his colleagues.

"There have been several explosions on the West Coast of America, causing extensive damage. Their military has raised the national defense alert level and there are civilian casualties in large numbers. It is being treated as a major terrorist attack by the American government. We must decide on an appropriate response."

"We should raise our defense posture also." It was General Hong. "Russia, Pakistan and India are bound to do the same, and that will bring in Europe and NATO."

"NATO is a toothless tiger."

"Yes, but when the Americans act as if war is threatening, the ripples are always worldwide."

"What is the alert level of their forces?" asked General Zhou.

Zhang said, "They have moved to their Defense Condition Three. That is considered a high level of readiness, but short of anticipation of imminent attack. Their planes will be ready, some bombers sent aloft and all forces alerted, but no active missions will be launched. They have one of their nuclear carrier groups northeast of Korea in easy striking distance. There may be submarines we don't know about."

Zhang instructed an aide to bring in a monitor. In moments they were watching the events taking place on the West Coast of America.

President Zhang turned to Yang. "General, have you any information regarding these attacks on the Golden Mountain?"

He used the old Chinese term for California and the United States.

Yang felt a heady rush of anticipation. The explosions in the US were timed to coordinate with his presence in this room. Once these men were removed, nothing would block his rise to power.

Admiral Zhang Lian had control of the missile submarines at Sanya. Lu Cheng had locked down the base and secured the missiles at Luoyang. Armored divisions loyal to Yang were at this moment rolling through the streets of Beijing and other major cities. Rail traffic moved only to transport his troops. The air force was on the ground, where it would stay unless he released it. Outside, a cadre of Special Forces troops waited for his signal, which he now triggered from a transmitter in his pocket.

"Well, General? You seem preoccupied."

"I launched these attacks, Zhang." He used the rude form of address.

The President of China looked mildly surprised. "Ah. And why would you do such a thing?"

Yang was taken aback. This was not the response he had anticipated. The others in the room were still, watching the two men. For an instant he wondered if he had misread Zhang. No. He dismissed the thought.

"We have played whore to the West long enough!" Yang slammed his hand down on the table. "It is time to claim our proper place. We have everything we need to bring them to their knees. Your policies have diluted the true measure of our greatness."

Chairman Zhang studied his fingernails, looked at Yang. "You seek to change those policies?"

"They are changed. As of right now."

The door burst open. Soldiers of the elite Special Forces took up station along the walls and around the table where the men were sitting. Each was armed with the latest assault rifle, the QB-97. Resistance to such a force was futile. Some of the Standing Committee looked nervously at the soldiers surrounding them. Zhang appeared unconcerned.

Yang spoke again. "The missiles at Luoyang are under my control, as are our submarines at Sanya. All of our long range missiles are mine. In the future, if anyone tries to make things difficult for us, we will not hesitate to show them our strength."

The President of China turned to the others in the room. "General Liu. You command the region including the submarine base on Hainan. What do you say to this?"

"I am afraid General Yang has miscalculated. By now the base at Sanya will be completely surrounded on land. At sea, units have been ordered in force to the area to prevent any unauthorized, ah, adventures, on the part of our submarines. We have also established air surveillance."

"That is a lie," said Yang. "I spoke with Admiral Zhang before I entered this room. He assured me the submarines are under my command."

"Oh, that's right, you couldn't know. I regret to inform you that just after you spoke with him, Admiral Zhang had an unfortunate accident," said General Liu. "So sad. He slipped and fell overboard during an inspection and drowned. A state funeral and public services will be planned in Beijing for our revered naval leader."

"I have Luoyang."

"Ah, I am so sorry, General," said General Hong. "Luoyang is surrounded. General Lu continues to hold the base. However, you may find communication with him difficult. Should he indicate readiness to launch, countermeasures will be taken. If necessary, the missiles will be destroyed."

"You can't do that! That is our main deterrent to the Americans."

"You are a fool, Yang," said the President. "The Americans can annihilate us if they choose. That is why we have taken only a defensive nuclear posture over all these years."

Yang looked at the stone faced men sitting with him at the table and knew he was close to losing control. First Wu had failed him. His dream of a new dawn for China's nuclear missile forces had been buried under the rubble of those ruins. Wu's death was only just reward for his failure. Now his plan for ruling China stood in jeopardy. But General Lu still controlled the missiles. Yang's tanks were rumbling through the streets. And the elite forces were here with him in this room.

"You're the fool, Zhang. My tanks are in position outside. The people will follow me. Major!" He addressed the commander of the soldiers surrounding the table. "Seize these men. Take them outside. If they cause trouble, shoot them."

It was when the major drew his pistol and pointed it at him instead of Zhang that Yang knew he had lost. Behind the Minister of Railways, two soldiers moved forward and roughly grasped his arms, lifting him from his chair. He started to protest. One look at Zhang silenced him.

"It is you who goes outside, Yang, and that traitor as well."

All pretense of mild unconcern vanished as Zhang stood. He ripped the rank boards with their three stars and wreaths from Yang's shoulders and threw them against the wall. Zhang's face was flushed with anger. He turned to the major.

"Take them to the military prison. Place them in isolation. If Yang struggles, render him unconscious but do not kill him. Post a 24 hour watch. We have use for him."

"Yes, Chairman!" The major saluted, gestured with his pistol at Yang.

"The tanks," Yang said.

"The tanks are under my command. Take him."

They watched the men being led away. The door closed behind them.

President Zhang addressed the others.

"If the Americans believe we are to blame for these attacks, we face a serious threat of war. Raise our defensive posture, but be careful not to indicate aggressive intentions. This idiot has brought us to the edge of disaster. We must find a way to avoid it."

General Zhou left the room.

"We should call their President." It was the vice-chairman of the Standing Committee. "They will soon know what happened. We must talk to them. Tell them the truth."

"We would lose face!"

"Better to lose face than to lose Beijing or Chengdu. We can give them Yang, execute him, make diplomatic reparations, whatever is needed to show Yang acted on his own. Privately they may know, but it must not become public. It is not in their interest that it becomes public. They need us to keep their economy going. Perhaps we can mislead them with the extremist elements."

The meeting turned into a general discussion of damage control and how to spin the certain fallout of Yang's actions.

Outside the vine-covered walls of the President's villa it was another smog-filled day in Beijing. If the summer crowds noticed the large presence of military vehicles and personnel, they marked it off to another training maneuver. Life was good in Beijing. One shouldn't complain just because the rumble of tanks disturbed one's harmony.

Chapter Fifty-Two

The command center of the Second Artillery Battalion at Luoyang took up the entire top floor of Base Headquarters. From his corner office, General Lu Cheng could see the main gate to the west and the concrete abutments surrounding the silos and tunnels to the north. Government tanks had been in position outside the gates since morning.

Waiting.

It was now early evening. Yang had failed. Beijing was still trying to convince him to surrender the base, but Lu could tell they were growing impatient.

The sharp lines of Lu's face were bleak. It had all come down to this. A lifetime of service to China, brought to nothing by the timid minds of the Party leadership. Fools who could not grasp destiny. The choice would have to be forced upon them.

The base had been sealed. A security lockdown was in place. He'd told his troops that reactionary elements within the army had mutinied. Live ammunition had been issued. In the elite missile battalions there was little respect for the ground forces. His officers had no trouble believing him. They'd been told to resist with deadly force if anyone attempted to enter.

In the distance Lu saw a rolling cloud of dust beyond the gates. There was only one thing that made that much dust. More tanks, and trucks with assault forces. Time was running out.

Lu made his decision. He picked up his phone.

"Send Colonel Hing to me, immediately."

Hing was Lu's XO. It took two to do what Lu had decided. Lu went back to his desk and sat down. He looked at a picture of his father, taken just before he'd left for Vietnam. In 1968 his father had been an advisor to the NVLA during the opening days of the great Tet offensive. Lu had idolized his father. He had never forgiven the Americans for killing him.

There was a significant flaw in the security of China's nuclear arsenal. Beijing feared losing the ability to retaliate during a nuclear attack. Under certain circumstances, the commanders of the missile bases could launch on their own. It was felt that careful screening of the commanders, periodic investigation by the Secret Service and the need for two independent officers to initiate launch were sufficient safeguards. As an added precaution, coded radio signals could disable and destroy an errant missile. Those commands could be sent from Beijing if necessary.

That was true, except Lu had reprogrammed the missiles. Beijing's codes were no longer effective. Under the protocols Lu had put in place for a security lockdown, the missile crews were isolated. Once the launch codes were sent, no countermanding order would be followed.

Lu was proud of his doomsday machine. It had taken months to set up.

A knock. Colonel Hing entered. Lu wondered how he would react.

"Government forces are getting ready to storm the base." He gestured at the dust clouds drawing closer to the base, visible through the windows. "It's only a question of time before they're through our defenses."

Hing's face turned a sallow, sick color. "Then we have lost."

"Yes. But I do not intend to let them win."

"What will you do?" Hing looked at his superior. It dawned on him. "You want to launch!"

"Yes."

"But the Americans will retaliate."

"Our defenses are adequate. A few of their missiles will get through, but not all. If we strike first, their military will be severely crippled. We will be humiliated by them no more. Beijing will be forced to follow our lead or face defeat. They will be forced to take up our destiny."

Lu unlocked a steel drawer in his desk and took out a black metal case about the size of a briefcase. He set it on the desk, opened it and turned on the power. A screen lit up.

Ready.

To the right of the screen was an alpha-numeric key pad. Lu entered a series of numbers and letters. A message appeared on the screen.

Confirm.

The sequence required the palm print scans of the authorized commanders.

"Your hand, Colonel."

Hing stood where he was.

"I will not do this. The Americans will destroy us."

Lu walked over to the door and locked it. He took out his pistol. "You will do it," he said. He shot Hing in the chest, then again. The bullets drove him back against the desk and he fell to the floor.

Lu grabbed Hing's arm and pulled the body over to the launching device. He pressed Hing's dying hand onto the screen. The machine beeped. Lu watched a red light scan back and forth. The machine beeped again. A new message appeared.

Secondary Confirmation.

Someone was pounding on the door. Lu placed his hand on the screen. A beep, the red light, another beep.

Enter Launch Sequence Code.

Lu entered the sequence of numbers and letters that would tell the missile crews to launch.

Ready.

Lu looked up as the door burst open. Two of his men stood there, trying to make sense of what they saw. Lu flipped back a safety switch and pressed a red button.

Launch Initiated.

Klaxons all over the base began blaring at three second intervals. Now no one except himself could call the missiles back.

"Sir! What has happened here?"

Lu smiled. He placed the muzzle of his pistol in his mouth and pulled the trigger.

Chapter Fifty-Three

On the way to the White House, the team watched the President's address in the back of a black Lincoln stretch limousine. Rice appeared grave, angry and reassuring. He confirmed there had been a terrorist attack. He cautioned the nation against jumping to conclusions about who was to blame. He promised swift retaliation once the identity of the bombers became known.

He talked of nine eleven and Pearl Harbor. He expressed certainty America would rise to the challenge again and closed with a prayer for the victims and their families and for the nation as a whole. It was a masterful performance.

People were angry. There had been a leak. The news media were already speculating on Chinese involvement.

The team entered the White House through a back entrance. They were ushered to a room next to the Oval Office, where Rice was meeting with the Secretary of State and General Holden. Director Harker, General Hood and Rice's Chief of Staff were waiting there. Hogan was clearly on edge.

"When the President is ready he'll call us in. He'll set the conversation. Be ready to tell him about your mission. Keep it brief."

Carter decided he didn't like Hogan. He also decided to keep his mouth shut before it got him into trouble. He was tired. When he was tired he had no patience for things that annoyed him.

Harker said, "You put on quite a show over there."

"We almost made it out without trouble. Wu showed up at just the wrong time. What's happening in China?"

The three stars on Hood's shoulders glinted under the ceiling lights.

"Nobody's quite sure. It looks like Yang made his move and it didn't come off. There's been a lot of military movement, all internal. Heavy air and sea cover earlier at Sanya, but that seems to have lightened up. Now we're watching the missile base at Luoyang. Troops have surrounded the base. That's one of the reasons we think Yang failed. But those missiles aren't under government control. If Lu activates the silos we'll know it and things could get real hot. Holden convinced Rice to go to DEFCON 2."

That was bad. Nick shifted to ease the pain in his back.

"Any communication from the PRC?"

"Not yet. I don't know what the President is thinking, but if I were him I'd play a little cat and mouse. See if I could get them to call first. Meanwhile, Langley and everyone else is running around trying to figure out who set off those bombs."

"We know who set them off," Selena said. "The Triads."

Harker broke in. "We can't start arresting everyone in the Triads. We need proof, hard evidence. Some people aren't convinced a coup is behind the bombings. Some aren't convinced there's a coup attempt at all. They think China is initiating some large scale military adventure and they're worried. There are enough nukes at Luoyang to wipe out millions of our people and several of our cities. Sanya houses SSBN's. If they move to deep water, we could be in trouble."

The door to the Oval Office opened and an aide beckoned them in.

Rice was sitting behind his desk, in front of the tall windows fronting the Rose Garden. A large, round rug bearing the Presidential Seal filled the center of the room. A cluster of elegant, upholstered chairs were grouped in front of the desk. Sitting there were General Holden, the Secretary of State and Cheryl Wilson, the Assistant Secretary for Asian Affairs. The President rose and took Selena's hand.

"Selena. I was surprised to learn you were part of this. It's good to see you again. I was very sorry when William was taken from us. Everyone, please sit down."

"Thank you, Mister President," she said. They sat.

"Director Harker has told me about your mission. What I wanted was to look you in the eye and hear about it directly from you."

"It was an experience, Mr. President."

Rice glanced at his notes.

"Gunnery Sergeant Peete. You were wounded."

"It's nothing, sir." Ronnie sat ramrod straight in his chair in a suit and tie, holding the cane he'd been given at a perfect 90 degree angle. It was quite a change from his usual Hawaiian riot. He might as well have been on parade.

"At ease, Gunny. Give your leg a rest, you deserve it. " Ronnie relaxed by about a millimeter.

Rice looked at Nick. "Major Carter. You led the team."

Nick's service jacket lay on the desk. Sitting a few feet away from the President, he felt the aura of power that went with the office. He had no doubt he was in the presence of the most powerful man in the world.

"Yes, sir. Sir, I am no longer in the service."

"I know that, Major. However, you never resigned your commission, so that is not quite accurate. What were your instructions?"

"To penetrate an ancient temple complex in Tibet."

"For what purpose?"

"General Yang had gone to extremes to obtain the location of this complex. We weren't sure what he wanted. We only knew it was important to him. We felt it was in the national interest to get there first and confound any plans he might have for whatever was found. We were operating on the theory that what was bad for Yang would be good for us."

"You found evidence of a high yield uranium deposit?"

"Yes, Mister President. In the Inner Mongolia Autonomous Region."

Rice gave him a careful look.

"I understand you have video of the underground chamber."

"Yes, sir."

"I would like all copies of this video delivered to me personally. Is that clear?"

"Very clear, sir."

"Good." Rice sat for a few seconds, said, "How did the firefight begin?"

Carter told him the story. He smiled.

"Outstanding. Well done, Major. What is your assessment of the fallout from your mission?"

"Sir?"

"Fallout. Political, military. Consequences, if you like."

The President of the United States was asking for his opinion. It was a first.

"Well, sir, I don't think there are going to be any consequences to speak of."

Wilson made a sound of disgust. "Mister Carter, you illegally entered Chinese sovereign territory and attacked and killed over thirty of their troops. How can you possibly say there won't be any consequences?"

Rice's eyes flicked toward her, but he said nothing.

Carter felt his temper rising.

"First of all, they attacked us, not the other way around. Those troops were under the command of Colonel Wu, Yang's man. If I were running the PRC, I wouldn't want to make a big deal about it. It's a deniable incident in a remote region, the result of actions taken by a madman trying to take over China."

"You insist there is a coup being planned."

Carter looked at her.

"Are you as stupid as you seem?"

Wilson's face tightened into a puckered scowl.

Carter said, "Yes, I do insist. From our satellite intel, I would say it has already happened and succeeded or not. If it did succeed, we've got a problem that has nothing to do with Tibet. If it didn't, there aren't going to be any consequences from my mission."

Wilson's face pinched itself together and she was about to say something when an aide came in, whispered in Hogan's ear, and left the room.

"Mister President, President Zhang is calling."

"About time. Put him on the speaker."

Chapter Fifty-Four

"Sir..." Hogan was looking at Nick and the others.

"Just put him on the speaker, Kevin."

"Yes, sir."

"Mister President." The voice quality was good. Zhang spoke in Chinese, with simultaneous translation on his end. Rice gestured to Selena, pointed to an earpiece lying by a pen and pad on the end of his desk and indicated she should pick it up. He flipped a switch on his desk. China could not hear him.

"Selena, you speak the language. Listen and tell me if the translation is correct. Listen for anything that might help me understand this man."

She picked up the earpiece. Rice activated the phone.

"President Zhang. What can I do for you?"

"Mister President, there have been some events here. We do not wish to have these events, ah, misunderstood. I am calling to let you know our situation."

"Our satellites show unusual military movements. Some of my advisors are quite disturbed. Tell me, Mister President, should I feel disturbed?"

"No, no, not at all. We are merely conducting exercises. There is no cause for you to be alarmed. We have had a problem with one of our senior commanders, but it has been resolved."

Selena was scribbling on a piece of paper. Nick took it and handed it to the President.

Stressed, she had written. *Used idiom associated with desire to placate without admitting wrong-doing.*

"What was the nature of the problem?"

"It is unimportant, now."

"Mister President, there has been an attack on our country. We believe one of your ranking officers is responsible. If this proves to be true, there will be serious consequences for our nations."

"This cannot be true! Who is suspected?"

"Your General Yang."

There was a pause. Everyone watched Rice.

"Mister President." The voice on the speaker phone was flat, metallic. "Coincidentally, General Yang is the senior officer I mentioned earlier. He has been removed from command for promoting reactionary policies. If he has initiated attacks against your country it was without our knowledge or compliance."

"All that is well and good, Mister President, but it will not be enough." Rice allowed anger to creep into his voice. "Perhaps you can persuade General Yang to reveal how he accomplished his vicious and unprovoked actions. Our people are upset and angry. I assure you, President Zhang, if your government had anything to do with these events, consequences will be severe. Do I make myself clear?"

There was a rapid burst of Chinese in the background, several people talking at once. Selena scribbled.

Great concern. Someone arguing for a full war alert. Zhang is nervous. Someone saying he should tell you the truth.

After a moment the President of China came back on the line.

"President Rice. I will be candid. General Yang has been arrested for attempting to install himself as the new leader of our country. He admitted initiating attacks against you. We were unaware of these plans. We deeply regret that harm has come to your people. We have not yet had time to question him to determine more."

Scribble, scribble. *Sounds like telling the truth.*

"A coup?"

"Yes. We uncovered his plot to take power and were prepared for it. Yang did not succeed in taking control of our military installations."

Wilson gasped, a sound like she was choking on her own bile.

Rice tapped his fingers on his leg. "What about Luoyang?"

"Ah, Luoyang is being resolved as we speak. Should preparations for a launch be detected, we will prevent it. Mister President, we will not allow missiles to be launched under any circumstances. Please believe me. The missiles are equipped with a self-destruct system. We are prepared to destroy them if necessary."

General Holden reached for his pager. With an apologetic nod toward Rice, he stood and walked to the side of the room and took out his phone. Nick watched him go rigid.

"That is satisfactory, Mister President. We will monitor Luoyang quite closely. If we detect preparations to launch we will be forced to take appropriate counter measures. I sincerely hope it does not come to that."

"Mister President, any aggressive action toward our country would be very badly received here and met with strong response. I assure you, we have no hostile intentions."

"President Zhang, I appreciate your..."

General Holden interrupted. He still held his phone.

"Sir, the silos at Luoyang have been activated and the mobile platforms are emerging from the tunnels. They're getting ready to launch."

Rice looked at him. "You are certain."

"Yes, sir. Their launch sequence has begun."

"General, go to DEFCON1, but hold at Fail Safe."

Holden spoke again into his phone. Rice paused. He said, "President Zhang. I have just been informed that your missiles are being readied. We are now at the edge. You must take action, immediately."

Carter held his breath. Over the speaker, there was a confusing sound of many people speaking at once in Beijing and an angry command. The noise stopped. The voices of Zhang and his translator came through the speaker.

"Mister President. Our forces are entering the base at Luoyang as we speak. We can deactivate the missiles with codes sent from here. Please wait a moment."

Selena wrote. Zhang telling someone to send deactivation codes. They are raising their defense level. They may be panicking.

Zhang continued. "It will take seconds, Mister President. Please, let us not make a mistake."

Rice said, "If missiles are launched, we will be forced to retaliate, President Zhang. I am being deliberately blunt. You must stop this."

There was more excited conversation in the background. Selena wrote. Radio codes ineffective. They can't shut the missiles down from there. He's ordering an air strike on the base.

"President Rice." Zhang's voice was strained. "We are unable to disable the missiles by radio. We are taking other measures. Our planes will be in the air. If needed, we will launch our ABMs to intercept. I repeat, we have no hostile intention. Please do not misinterpret these actions. This is not an attack. We do not wish for war."

Everyone waited for Rice's response. He stood and everyone rose with him.

"President Zhang. I am now moving to my command center, where I will monitor your activities. I will call." He hung up the phone.

"Sir," General Holden said. "Marine One is standing by. You should remove yourself to Weather Mountain." Weather Mountain was an underground command center and fallout shelter for high civilian officials, near the town of Bluemont in West Virginia. It was forty-five minutes away.

Rice looked at him. "No, General. Even if we got there, you know as well as I do that it may not be adequate. We're going to KNEECAP. Send the Vice-President and the Cabinet to West Virginia."

"Yes, sir." KNEECAP was designation for Air Force One as an airborne command center in the event of war. Rice could stay up for three days, if needed, with refueling. Then the engines would fail. He'd have to set down before that, if there was any place left to land.

Rice said, "How much time until launch, General?"

"They're starting cold, sir. The DF-5s need to be fueled. Perhaps an hour or a little longer. Once they lift off, then another twenty minutes or more to impact on the West Coast, thirty minutes here, unless we can intercept. The DF-31s are a different matter. Once the mobile launchers are in place, a matter of minutes to fire."

"Can we intercept?"

"Not all of them. The AEGIS system around the Ronald Reagan can get some of them. Some of the Alaska ground based missiles will probably be effective. Sir..." He looked at his watch.

"Yes, General, I know." He turned to Harker. "You're welcome to remain here in the White House shelter, if you wish."

What he didn't say was that it wouldn't make much difference where they were if war began.

"Thank you, Mister President."

Rice strode from the room. Hogan and General Holden followed, with the Secretary of State and Wilson.

The team stood in the Oval Office and looked at each other. Ronnie looked down at the Presidential Seal on the rug.

"Might as well have a picture of Ground Zero on it. The White House doesn't seem like a real good bet at the moment," Ronnie said. "I wish I was back on the Rez."

"Let's go back to the Project," Harker said. "It's as good a place as any to watch the end of the world."

Chapter Fifty-Five

They sat in Harker's office. There didn't seem much else to do. War would begin or it wouldn't. No one had any illusions they were safe. Nothing would be safe within a hundred miles of Washington if the DF-5s made it out of the silos.

Maybe it was a good sign there had been enough time to get back to Project HQ. Stephanie was there. Elizabeth brought up a live shot of Luoyang on the monitor. It was a war zone. The main buildings were heavily damaged, shell pocked and surrounded by tanks. Troops scrambled toward the silos, but Elizabeth knew they were almost impenetrable from above.

"They've taken out the mobile launchers," Carter said. Smoking craters and twisted debris marked where the missiles had been positioned. "Zhang means it. He doesn't want a war."

Elizabeth picked up her pen. "He sent an air strike. That stops the quick threat. It looks like they bombed the silos."

"Will that stop them?" Selena said.

"Maybe. Maybe not. Those silos are hardened against conventional weapons."

"They could still launch."

"Yes."

"I hope they..." Carter didn't finish the thought.

From a dozen silos, missiles rose on pillars of fire. Three other silos erupted in huge balls of flame. The soldiers near the silos were obliterated. The images on the monitor disappeared under clouds of exhaust and smoke.

"Launch failure in three," Elizabeth said. "Those DF-5s are liquid fueled. The fuel must have exploded. It still leaves twelve."

"How long till they get here?" Ronnie asked.

"About thirty minutes. Unless we knock them down. Maybe Zhang will get some of them. The Chinese have ABMs around Beijing and Chengdu."

She moved the satellite shot over Beijing. "Yes, he's launching his ABMs. I hope they're good."

She opened the bottom drawer of her desk and took out a bottle of Cognac. She poured silently and handed glasses around. Even Ronnie took one.

They raised to each other and drank. They waited.

* * *

Off the shores of Kodiak Island in the Aleutians, Burt Rasmussen was operating a large winch hauling in the net with the day's catch. The sky was overcast and gray. This was the last run before the Sally B. headed back to port. A pretty good day.

He swung the net over the ice packing the open hold, where four of the crew waited, and lowered it down. Suddenly two bright bursts of light like newborn suns appeared far above in the gloom.

"What the hell was that," one of the men said. They stared upward. As Burt watched, a third sun blossomed.

"UFOs. Must be UFOs."

"Yeah, right."

"Maybe some kind of exercise. You know, military."

"Ought to be worth a beer at the Shack when we get in."

"Wonder what it means?"

It meant Burt would live to fish another day.

Chapter Fifty-Six

It was two days later. There were strands of gray in Harker's hair Carter hadn't noticed before.

She said, "That was too damn close."

No one said anything.

"The PRC got six of the missiles with their ABMs. The AEGIS group around the Ronald Reagan got three more. The last three were intercepted over the Bering Sea from Alaska. Without warning it wouldn't have worked out so well. If those last missiles had gotten past our intercepts, Rice was going to turn China into a radioactive wasteland. Checkmate for the human race."

"He had some balls to wait that long, " Ronnie said.

"What happens now?" Carter asked.

"There's a summit being set up with all the nuclear powers. It's a real wake up call. Maybe we'll end up with some kind of rational progress on nukes for a change."

"Sure," Carter said. "I'll believe that when I see it. What about Yang?"

"The PRC sent a video of his interrogation and execution to the White House. He gave it all up. The FBI is taking the Triads apart at the seams. The whole country is pissed at China. It's not a good time to be Chinese here."

There had been no way to keep the lid on. There had been a lot of incidents. Chinese businesses were vandalized, people beaten. There was a nationwide, grass roots boycott of everything and anything Chinese. The economy was poised to slip into deep recession. Congress was in an uproar. Rice was being attacked or praised in equal measure, but his approval rating with the public had skyrocketed. There was still an America to come home to.

Harker said, "There's a purge going on in China. Zhang has arrested the key figures and the Officer Corps is in disarray. They're hunting everyone down. There hasn't been anything like it since Mao."

She reached into her desk drawer and brought out the Cognac and glasses.

"Cheryl Wilson resigned from the State Department. She's going to teach at Princeton."

"I'd hate to be in one of her classes," said Nick.

Harker poured. Coke for Ronnie.

After a moment Selena said, "I wonder if the Chinese will excavate the site in Tibet?"

Harker said, "My guess is no. It would be a huge culture shock to find out the emperor isn't buried in Li Shan. I don't think the PRC wants any more shocks."

She sipped. "You three made a pretty good team out there. Selena, I've been thinking. Why don't we make it official?"

"What?" She was startled. "You want me to come work for you?"

"Not me. For the President. For your country."

"But I don't know how to be...a spy, or whatever."

"We can train you in the things you need to know. It's not spying, we leave that up to Langley. You have skills we need. The mission would have failed without you."

"I don't know what to say."

"Then don't say anything. Just think about it."

There was a pause. Stephanie changed the subject. "I can't imagine what it's like to sit in the oval office. You can't win. Half the people hate you and the other half think you're supposed to save the world, or at least their part of it."

Carter said, "What about everyone who thinks the US is to blame for everything wrong in their lives? Remind me not to run next election."

Selena smiled. "I'll vote for you if you run."

"Awwww. Me, too, Nicky," said Ronnie.

Harker laughed.

Carter raised his glass. "Good liquor."-

Chapter Fifty-Seven

Carter stood with Selena outside Grace Cathedral in the coolness of a San Francisco afternoon. The funeral service for her uncle was over. Sunlight sparkled off the waters of the Bay.

"It was a good service," he said.

She looked at him. "What are you going to do now?"

"Go up to my cabin until Harker comes up with something new."

She cleared her throat and brushed hair from her forehead. "It's getting late and it's a long drive. Stay in town tonight. We could get dinner somewhere or just eat in."

He looked at her, the depth of those violet eyes. "You're on," he said.

Her loft took up the entire top floor of her building. Two rows of painted columns ran the length of the main room, rising to a high, floral-patterned tin ceiling. Tall French windows let streams of light pour into each end of the space. Skylights cast rectangles of light on a polished wooden floor of light cherry. Large oriental rugs covered the floor at spaced intervals.

The kitchen gleamed with top of the line appliances, stainless steel and granite countertops. A wet bar and wine rack sat to one side.

The walls were painted in subtle earth tones and whites and showed off a mix of paintings and antique pieces of sculpture and art. Along one wall of the living area were six framed pages of some ancient writing. Track lighting lit everything with exact attention.

It was carefully arranged, but it was a place you could be comfortable in.

"This is beautiful."

"Thank you. I love this place. How about some wine?"

She pulled a bottle from the rack, opened it, and poured.

They sat down on a long leather couch under a painting. Carter eyed it.

"That's a Paul Klee!"

"Yes. I picked it up a few years ago. I saw the Klee copy you had in your apartment. I like his work."

He'd forgotten how rich she was. He was looking at a painting worth hundreds of thousands of dollars. Maybe even a million. Maybe more.

"You're not worried about someone breaking in here?"

She laughed. "Oh, no, you wouldn't believe the security. Uncle William owned the building and knew someone who worked in the CIA. He set it up. Besides, everything's insured." Her face changed for an instant when she mentioned her uncle. "I guess I own the building, now."

She set her glass down. "Nick...Oh, hell. I'm going to say what I think. What's going to happen if we keep sleeping together?"

The elephant in the room. She wasn't just talking about hopping in the sack.

He took a breath. "I don't know." He paused. "I know one thing, though. I want you," he said. "It's more than sex. I want you."

It was true. He hadn't admitted it to himself until now.

She raised her hand, touched his face, put her hand on his shoulder. He leaned toward her. Their kiss was light, gentle.

Selena led him into the bedroom. They undressed. He ran his hands over the smooth curves and hollows of her body. They lay down on the bed. Her hair smelled of lavender, her breath was sweet under the wine. He lost track of anything but the feel of their bodies moving together. After what seemed a long, long time he let himself go, a shuddering climax that burst over him in waves.

After a while he lifted away. He kissed her and looked into her eyes.

Selena saw something in the look on his face. She went suddenly still. She put her finger on his lips.

"Don't say it."

"Selena..."

"Don't say it unless you mean it."

He thought of the dream of his dead lover. "There's no point in waiting, Nick."

He felt a headache starting. He wanted to say it. He couldn't say it. Not yet.

Selena looked away.

Chapter Fifty-Eight

The night was warm and pleasant. Carter left the windows and screen door of the cabin open to let the breeze blow through. He was sound asleep when something woke him.

His mind tried to figure out what it was. Then he didn't have to think about it. A hammer being cocked makes a distinctive sound. The feel of cold metal against his head was just icing on the cake.

"Do as I say or die. Wake her."

"Who..." The barrel pressed harder into his skull.

"Wake her."

"Selena," he said. "Selena, wake up." He shook her by the shoulder. He felt her breath quicken, but she kept her eyes closed. She was awake.

"Selena, wake up. Someone's here."

She mumbled and rolled away.

"She is awake. If she does not open her eyes, you die. I will count three. One. Two."

Selena opened her eyes. The gun moved away and the figure stepped back from the bed. He was silhouetted against the window, his head skull-like, an angel of death.

"Who are you? What do you want?"

"You, Mister Carter. I want you. And that whore you are sleeping with. The esteemed Miss Connor."

"You haven't told us who you are."

"You don't recognize me? We have met before, so to speak. I knew your uncle, Miss Connor. He was not very strong, was he? He would have saved us all a lot of trouble if he had lived longer."

"Wu!"

"That is correct, Mister Carter. Former Colonel Wu. Senior Colonel, as a matter of fact. Things were going well until you interfered."

"How did you get here? I thought we were done with you in Tibet."

"Yes, that was difficult. I was unconscious for a long time. Once my patron's plans were discovered, I found it necessary to leave the country. But enough. Get up. Both of you."

He gestured with the gun.

They got out of bed, naked. Carter wished he had his pants on. He pushed the thought aside. Clothes wouldn't make a damn bit of difference to a bullet. Naked or clothed, it was all the same. He knew they didn't have much time.

"I was going to be a powerful man in the new China," Wu said. "You destroyed that. You must pay. There is nothing left for me in China. If I am to be destroyed, you must be also."

"What do you intend to do?" Wu's face was burned along one side, the wound still raw and ugly. From the corner of his eye Carter saw Selena's muscles tense, ready for whatever was about to happen.

"Do? I'm going to kill you. Then I am going to enjoy the charms of Miss Connor. Get on your knees. Now."

Not a good idea. Wu was a little out of reach, but it was now or never. Carter watched the gun. Then he heard the cat through the open screen door.

"UUURRRRPPP!"

Wu glanced toward that human sound and Nick launched for him. Selena leapt over the bed. He crashed into Wu and felt the hot burn of the gun going off by his face. He drove Wu back into the wall.

Wu was quick and he was strong. He twisted and got his arm around Nick's throat. He brought the gun up and then he screamed. Selena had a nerve lock on him.

Wu let go and drove his elbow into Selena's stomach. She went down gasping. Nick chopped at his wrist. The gun fired into the floor and went flying. Wu brought his hand down hard and Nick's left arm went numb. Wu deflected a kick to the groin and tried for a kidney strike but Nick slipped past and slammed the palm of his right hand up under Wu's nose and drove the cartilage into his brain. Wu went down hard on his back, blood pouring from the front of his face. His feet drummed on the floor.

Nick went to Selena, down on one knee, sucking in air.

"You all right?"

"Yes."

He checked the body for life signs. When he was sure Wu was dead, he went to Selena and held her naked body against his.

Then he called the Director.

Chapter Fifty-Nine

Harker had a cleanup team at the cabin before dawn. They took the body. There was a long, splintered gouge in the floor from Wu's bullet.

Carter poured a double Irish into his coffee and went out on the deck. The sun was creeping over the ridge in back of the cabin. Rivers of light streamed like white fire through the branches of the trees. Smoke-like wisps of moisture rose from the ground. The smell of pine needles and damp earth mixed with the steaming aroma of the coffee and whiskey.

Selena came out and sat down beside him, holding a cup. The air was cool and fresh. Nick sipped his coffee. Selena brushed a wisp of hair away from her forehead with her left hand and drank from her cup.

"This is a beautiful spot. It's so quiet." He sensed something behind her words. He waited.

"You know, I've studied martial arts for years, but I never thought I'd have to use them."

"The way you came over that bed after Wu, I thought you were flying. If you hadn't put that hold on him..."

He waited.

"I don't know who I am anymore," she said. "I mean, I do, but it's different. I keep thinking about Tibet and shooting that soldier. I killed people. I keep thinking I should be upset or guilty or something. But I don't feel guilty. I don't feel bad about Wu. I don't feel I did the wrong thing in Tibet. How can that be?"

A big question, with no clear answer.

"How did you feel in Tibet, in the middle of that firefight?"

"Frightened. Alive."

"More alive than ever before, right? You feel confused about that?"

She looked at him. "Yes." She paused. "No."

"What would have happened if you hadn't shot that soldier, pulled the trigger?"

"You'd be dead. Maybe I would be, too. Maybe Ronnie."

"Right. You made the only right choice. You didn't do it because you wanted to go out and kill someone. You did it because you had to. When you tell me you don't feel guilty, I'd say that's a damn good adjustment. When you say you're worried about why you don't feel guilty, it tells me you're a good person."

"You sound like you have it all figured out."

He laughed. "Sure, that's why they pay me the big bucks. I've got it all figured out. Enjoy the lack of guilt while you've got it and hope it stays that way."

"The whole thing didn't change much, did it?"

"What do you mean?"

"We didn't stop Yang. All those people are dead, and what we did didn't make a damn bit of difference."

"It wasn't our job to stop him. Our job was to find out what he wanted in that book. We did that. In the long run, maybe it makes a difference, maybe not. It's a crap shoot, what we do for Harker."

He blew on the coffee. "What do you think about what she said? About making it official? You could always just go back to giving lectures."

"You don't think that we—I mean us...that it might get in the way?"

"It won't if we don't let it."

"I'm thinking about it."

"Good enough."

After a moment she said, "I never thought I'd hook up with someone like you."

"Someone like me?"

"A man who wasn't intimidated by me or afraid I knew more than he did or who could put up with my bitchiness."

"You're bitchy? I hadn't noticed."

She gave him a look that said smartass. "I thought I'd find some nice, stable guy, some professional type. Then I meet you. Someone who blows things up for a living and wouldn't know stability from an eggplant. What are the odds on that?"

"We don't need to worry about odds."

"That's easy for you to say. What were the odds we'd get out of that mine, or out of Tibet once the Chinese showed up?"

"I don't believe in odds. If it looks like things are stacked against you, you roll the dice and tell yourself you can do it."

Looking over at Selena, he wondered where it would end up. For now, he was willing to let it be what it was. A roll of the dice. A beginning.

About the Author

I've been writing since I was twelve. I've done a lot of traveling and been in a lot of strange situations. I was in the Marines and spent years on the road as a professional folk singer. You could say that I bring a varied life experience to my writing. I live in Northern California in the foothills of the Sierra Mountains. I like riding old, fast motorcycles and playing guitar, usually not at the same time. Please visit my website at

http://www.alexlukeman.com.

I love hearing from readers and I promise I will respond to your comments. You can email me directly at:

alex@alexlukeman.com

Thanks for reading my book.

New Releases...

Be among the first to know when I have a new book coming out by subscribing to my newsletter. No spam or busy emails, only a brief announcement now and then. Just click on the link below. You can unsubscribe at any time...

http://alexlukeman.com/contact.html#newsletter

The Project Series

White Jade
The Lance
The Seventh Pillar
Black Harvest
The Tesla Secret
The Nostradamus File
The Ajax Protocol
Black Rose
The Eye of Shiva
The Solomon Scroll
The Russian Deception
The Atlantis Stone

Reviews by readers are welcome!

Notes

I did a lot of research for White Jade. The comments about modern weapons, Chinese arms and capabilities, the White House, etc. etc. are all as accurate as I can make them. If there are mistakes, they're all mine.

The history of the First Emperor is well documented, as is his quest for an elixir of immortality. His tomb at Li Shan has not been excavated. It's a very large building. The floor is said to be made of solid gold, laid out as a map of the Empire, with lakes and rivers of mercury. The ceiling is said to be studded with precious gems and pearls.

Of course, he might not be in there.

Recently a large deposit of quality uranium ore was discovered in the Inner Mongolian region of China, vastly increasing China's reserves.

"Connorsville" is based upon a real gold rush town not far from where I live. There is a mine, it is dangerous. The Chinese did dig secret tunnels under Marysville and Sacramento. The wealth of the gold rush was often brought to light by the hard sweat of the Chinese who came to the "Golden Mountain" to build a better life for themselves and their families.

Acknowledgements

My wife, Gayle, who read early drafts and made really good comments and who has to listen to me, again and again; Frank Macchi, formerly of the SFPD, who told me about the BART airshaft at the end of the Ferry Building pier and some cool stuff about the Chinese Triads in the Bay Area; Greg Skein, former Army Ranger; Glenn Frazier, a Vietnam Vet and neighbor, who keeps asking for the next book.

Emma Sweeney in New York took a lot of her valuable time to look at the book and made excellent comments that helped me become a better writer.

There are others. Thank you, all of you.

July, 2011

Keep reading for a preview of THE LANCE, Book Two in the series featuring the Project, Nick and Selena.

Preview: Book Two in the PROJECT Series

THE LANCE

CHAPTER ONE

Nicholas Carter looked at Elizabeth Harker and thought if there were any elves in the world, they probably looked like her. She was small boned and slim. She had milk white skin and small ears tucked under raven black hair. She had wide, green eyes. She was dressed in a black pantsuit and white blouse with a Mao collar. In two years working for her he'd never seen her wear anything but black and white.

Harker ran the Project, the Presidential Official Joint Exercise in Counter Terrorism. She was Nick's boss. Her boss was the President.

On Harker's desk were a silver pen, a picture of the Twin Towers burning and a manila folder. The pen had belonged to FDR. The picture was a reminder. The folder was likely going to shape his day. Working for Harker meant he never knew if the day might leave him hanging out on the edge and wondering if he could pull himself back in.

He heard Harker say, "Someone's thinking about making trouble in the Middle East."

"Someone's always thinking about making trouble in the Middle East. What's different now?"

He fumbled in his pocket, found a crumbly antacid tablet and popped it in his mouth. Carter felt the tremor of a headache starting. Harker picked up her silver pen and began tapping it on the polished surface of her desk. Each tap vibrated inside his skull.

"The President is speaking in Jerusalem on Thursday. We have a source who says there's going to be trouble. He wants a face to face meet."

Carter tugged on the mutilated lobe of his left ear, where a Chinese bullet had taken off the lobe a few months ago. The bandage was off. It had looked better with it on.

It was the same ear that itched whenever things were about to get dicey. It itched now. A gift or a curse he'd inherited from his Irish Grandmother, along with dreams he didn't want to have.

"Have you passed this to Langley? What do they say?"

"I'm supposed to back off and leave things up to the 'professionals'." There was an edge to her voice. "Lodge says there's no need for concern."

Wendell Lodge, Acting Director CIA.

"He says he and his Israeli counterparts have everything under control."

"Mossad?"

"And Shin Bet."

"What's Shin Bet?" said Selena.

Selena Connor sat next to Carter on Harker's leather couch. The ceiling lights caught the reddish blond color of her hair and turned her eyes violet. She wore a tan silk outfit and a pale blouse that went with her eyes. She was the first woman Nick had let get close since Megan died. He didn't know where it was going. Or if he wanted it to go anywhere. She was new to the team, which meant she had a lot to learn, which worried the hell out of him.

Selena brushed a stray wisp of hair from her forehead.

Harker said, "Shin Bet is Israel's version of the FBI, on steroids. They handle internal security and counter-terrorism. Mossad is foreign intelligence and ops, like MI6 or CIA."

Carter looked down at his hands and picked at a broken fingernail. "Lodge is a devious bastard and a narcissist."

"Whatever he is, he's not going to brush us off. You're going to Israel. You find something that threatens Rice's security, give it to Shin Bet and the Secret Service. They've got the manpower, let them handle it. You leave today."

"I always wanted to see Jerusalem. Maybe I'll get a little sightseeing in."

She set the pen down and folded her hands. "It's not a vacation, Nick. You're booked into the same hotel as the President as part of his party, right outside the Old City. The Israelis may not let you keep your weapon. They're sensitive about guns and you're not Secret Service."

"Who's the source over there?"

"His name is Arshak Arslanian. He has a shop in the Armenian Quarter." She slid the manila folder across her desk. "His photo and info is in there."

Harker turned to Selena. "Selena, you continue with Ronnie this afternoon."

Ronnie was the third member of Nick's team. He was just back from visiting his family on the Navajo Reservation in Arizona. He'd been coaching Selena. Physical training, weapons, codes, the tricks of personal survival. All the things that might give her a chance to make it through the next year.

Harker tapped her pen and looked at Nick. "You'll need a lot of time to clear security. You'd better get going."

CHAPTER TWO

The sweet scent of Jasmine vines wafted through the open window of a crumbling tenement in the Old City of Damascus. A man bent over a wooden table with a soldering iron. He wiped sweat away from his forehead with the frayed sleeve of his shirt and concentrated on his task.

Another man watched from a sagging couch pushed against one of the stained yellow walls. He wore a dark suit of European cut. His crisp, white shirt was open at the collar.

The man on the couch had a face that was blank, forgettable. His features were smooth and calm, as if life had never quite reached the surface. It was hot in the apartment, but the man was not sweating. His eyebrows were unnoticeable above his colorless eyes. His nose seemed to disappear into the vagueness of his features. His lips were a thin, invisible line.

The man at the table was called Ibrahim. The man on the couch was called the Visitor, but Ibrahim didn't know that. It was better that way.

The bomb was almost finished. It was a very fine bomb, perhaps the best Ibrahim had ever made, and he had made many. He was well known throughout the terrorist network. If you wanted something unusual, reliable and easily concealed, with the most destructive result, you sought out the Syrian.

Anyone with a simple knowledge of electronics could build a suicide vest or a roadside device, but few could do what Ibrahim did. The truth of his skill was easy to see. He still owned almost all of his fingers and both eyes, no mean feat for an old bomb maker.

He soldered the final connection. He set the iron down and allowed himself to relax.

"It is ready?"

The man in the suit spoke in Arabic, his voice quiet, pleasant. He got off the couch, looked over the bomb maker's shoulder. Ibrahim tried to place the accent. German, perhaps.

Ibrahim took an unfiltered cigarette from a crumpled yellow pack, held it in nicotine stained fingers and lit it. The harsh tobacco smoke formed a blue cloud as he exhaled. The man in the suit concealed his disapproval.

"Yes, ready. When you place the charge, set and activate the timer. There is a twenty-four hour window."

Ibrahim showed his guest the arming device, small like a woman's wrist watch. A red arrow was etched on the bezel surrounding the dial. The face was marked for twenty four hours. A second, smaller ring within the first was divided into twelve five minute increments.

"Set the hour by rotating the outer ring clockwise. Then, set the inner ring counter clockwise for fine adjustment. You can reset until you press this button. After that, no. The timer will run until your mark is reached. The bomb is safe until the time chosen. Then, boom."

The Visitor nodded.

"Give me the pack."

The Visitor handed Ibrahim a backpack. Bright yellow letters over a yellow and green ram's head imprint spelled out Colorado State University on the flap. Inside were socks, two tee shirts, a teaspoon or two of beach sand, a pair of hiking shorts, postcards, dirty underwear, a pair of Dockers, a package of condoms, sandals and a water bottle.

There were also two books. One was a popular paperback listing hostels and restaurants in Israel. The other was a hardbound travel guide to the holy sites of Jerusalem.

Ibrahim opened the guide to a hollowed out space where the bomb would be concealed. The new compound his guest had provided was a marvel of technology, fifty times more powerful than conventional Semtex or C-4. It had a color like sand or old, yellowed limestone and could be molded and shaped as needed. It seemed small, but the explosive force it yielded was devastating. It was also undetectable by current methods. Even the dogs would never sense it.

The book was well thumbed, innocent in appearance. The pages concealed shielding that blocked detection by the most sophisticated electronic equipment. Of course there was always a chance of discovery. The Jews and the Americans were good at counter terrorism. Ibrahim assumed the bomb was meant for one or the other.

Success was not Ibrahim's concern, nor was he concerned about where or how the bomb would be used. He knew it was good. His work was done. He placed the bomb in the book. He locked the pages in place that would keep a casual observer from noticing anything. He closed the cover and put the book back in the pack.

The haunting sound of the call to prayer echoed through the ancient city from speakers atop the Umayyad Mosque. Ibrahim would go to the mosque and refresh his relationship with God. The other could do as he pleased.

"You have done well, my brother." His client's voice was quiet, toneless. "Allah will reward you in the afterlife."

"There is still this life, no? You have brought payment?"

"Of course. I have it here."

The Visitor reached under his jacket and took out a silenced .22 Ruger automatic pistol and shot Ibrahim in the forehead. The bomb maker's mouth formed a soft oh. His eyes opened wide and rolled upward. The Visitor fired another round into the Syrian's left ear, a whisper soft as a baby's breath. The body toppled sideways from the chair to the floor. A trickle of blood ran out onto the worn, scarred linoleum.

The Visitor bent down and wiped a few spatters of blood from the end of one of his shiny black shoes. He took the backpack and placed it in a cloth shopping bag. He turned on a small radio set on the table. The rhythmic notes of an oud and drums filled the room with sounds of life. Ibrahim's neighbors would not notice anything amiss for some time.

The Syrian had been a good asset, but all possible trails to what was going to happen, any loose ends, must be eliminated. Ibrahim had been a loose end.

The so-called nation of Israel would soon cease to exist. All it would take to start the process was this one, small bomb. The Visitor closed the apartment door behind him and walked down the stairs to the cobbled alley below, whistling to himself.

CHAPTER THREE

Carter sat with his back against the wall at a café in the New City, drinking espresso, watching the crowd. The night was warm. The pedestrian mall where King George and Ben-Yahuda streets and the Jaffa Road came together in Jerusalem was packed with people.

For the Jewish people, Jerusalem was the center of the world. It was where the Messiah would some day appear. It was the place where God had commanded the building of His Temple, where every stone, pebble and grain of dust on the Temple Mount was sacred ground. Devout Jews all over the world recited prayers each day for the restoration of the Temple, destroyed by the Romans in 70 CE.

The most important shrines of Christianity were here. The tomb of Christ, the room of the last supper, the Garden of Gethsemane where Christ received the Judas kiss. The place where Pontius Pilate passed sentence. The place of crucifixion. Every Christian denomination in the world had a church or shrine somewhere in the Old City.

For Muslims, the al-Aqsa Mosque on the Temple Mount was one of the holiest sites in Islam. The Mosque faced the Dome of the Rock, where they believed Muhammad had ascended to heaven on a winged horse to receive instruction from God. The Muslims had lost Jerusalem to the Israelis in the 1967 war. They wanted it back.

Armies had fought over Jerusalem for three thousand years. The narrow streets of the Old City had run ankle deep in blood more than once. Unless someone found a path to peace in the region, Carter figured the streets would run with blood again.

He'd thought he was done with all that, with the blood, when he left the Marines. Now he worked for the Project. Even though he was a civilian, he was still waking up in war zones. He did his best not to think about it. Best thing, focus on the mission. It was why he was in Jerusalem on a perfect October evening. Someone had to do it.

Carter drank his coffee and watched the crowd, tracking, reading expressions, looking for anything unusual. His eyes never stayed still. It was an old habit and it was why he was still alive. He never assumed he was safe. He never trusted appearances.

A young woman in a red dress played an accordion nearby. She had long, dark tresses and she laughed while she played. A small group of smiling people stood in front of her, tapping their feet in time to the music. Children ran through the throng. Carter smiled.

The night disappeared in violent white light.

The blast sent Nick backward into the wall and down to the pavement. Pain shot up his spine.

Everything went white. He was back in Afghanistan. He could smell the dust, hear the AKs firing, the explosions all around him. Then the white faded. The flashback faded. He could still hear the echoes of the AKs and smell the dry dust of the street. For a moment he didn't know where he was. A pall of black smoke hung over torn bodies spread in a red smear across the plaza. A flat, dead silence filled his ears. Then the screaming started.

A heavy café table lay on top of him. He pushed it to the side and got to his feet. The woman in the red dress lay crumpled and torn nearby, her accordion shattered and silent.

Broken glass and smashed furniture littered the plaza. There was blood on him, but it wasn't his. Carter took a step and tripped. He looked down at a child's foot in a blue shoe. It was just a small foot. A piece of white bone stuck out of a pink sock.

He bent over and threw up the espresso in a yellow brown stream. The acrid, coppery stench of blood poisoned the clean night air. He straightened up and wiped his lips. Something caught his eye across the way.

A man stood off to the side of the plaza. He was of medium height, with close set dark eyes, black hair, a thin black mustache and neat beard. He wore a shapeless brown jacket, baggy brown pants and a dirty yellow shirt. He was talking on a cell phone.

He was smiling.

The smile vanished when he saw Carter looking at him. He turned and walked away, holding the phone to his ear.

Who smiles at a slaughterhouse? Carter started after him.

Brown Jacket picked up his pace. He glanced back and turned into a wide alley between two buildings. Nick wished he had his .45. The Israelis had refused to let him carry it. He began running. Shouts sounded behind him as he sprinted into the alley.

The alley crossed between the buildings to the next street over. Brown Jacket and two others stood halfway down. At the far end of the passage a white Volvo waited, motor running, one man inside. Brown Jacket said something to the two men and walked toward the car. The others started toward Nick.

The larger man wore a loose blue jacket over a dingy white shirt and jeans. His head was bullet shaped and shaven. His face was dissolute, with ridges of old scar tissue over eyes that looked dead. His ears were crumpled cauliflowers and his hands were broad clubs, scarred with swollen and broken knuckles. A street fighter, a boxer.

The other man was the leader. He was small, mean looking and dark, with shiny, squinty eyes, a scruffy beard and a nasty smile that showed gaps in his teeth. The two separated, a few feet apart, Squinty to Nick's right, Boxer to his left. A flash of steel appeared in each man's hand.

Knives. He hated knives.

Words from one of his instructors echoed inside his head.

You've got two choices in an alley fight. Run or attack. If you attack, if there's more than one man, go for the leader. Always take out the leader first.

He walked straight at them. Not what they expected. Then he sprinted at Squinty and shouted from deep in his gut, a harsh, primal scream that vibrated off the alley walls. It froze both men, just long enough.

Squinty lunged forward, the knife held straight out and low, coming up for a classic strike under the rib cage to rip the diaphragm and the aorta. Carter grasped his wrist and reached over with his left hand, levered up and out and broke Squinty's elbow, using momentum to fling him to the side. He side kicked and took out Boxer's knee.

The knee folded sideways at an impossible angle. It crunched and broke, an unmistakable sound of terrible injury and unbearable pain. Boxer screamed and slashed out as he went down. A cut cold as ice opened along Nick's thigh.

Boxer tried to sit up. Carter kicked him in the throat. He clutched his neck and fell back choking. His eyes opened wide in terror as he tried to breathe. At the other end of the alley, Brown Jacket got into the Volvo. As the car drove off, he threw Nick a look of venomous hatred.

Squinty reached for his knife with his left hand. Nick kicked him hard in the head, a kick that could have got him into the NFL. Back at the entrance of the alley two cops appeared, guns drawn, shouting. Carter raised his hands, fingers spread wide.

He guessed he was about to find out what the inside of an Israeli police station looked like.

Printed in Great Britain
by Amazon

67186318R00142